ALL THE LITTLE THINGS

LINDA SHANTZ

eBook edition ISBN: 978-1-7773003-2-6

Paperback ISBN: 978-1-990436-03-1

IngramSpark Paperback ISBN 978-1-990436-03-1

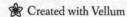 Created with Vellum

For my Woodbine circle, Theresa, Lorna and Nathalie; and my Saratoga circle, Juliet, Kim, Sharon, Jen and Alecia. Miss you all. One day we'll visit Mrs London's again!

CHAPTER ONE

EVERYONE SHOULD SET themselves on fire at least once in their life.

For Faye, that one time was Nate Miller. Oh, it had been exhilarating at first, dancing through the flames, assuming it wouldn't consume her – because she did not get attached. That was her rule. But somewhere along the way, something had gone wrong, and in the end, she'd been burnt. Crispy and black around the edges, with no one to blame but herself. Though she blamed Nate anyway, because hating him felt better than loathing herself.

And now, someone's hands covered her eyes from behind like blinker cups, to shield her from the scene on the shedrow.

Nate. Liv. A bottle of champagne, and...

"We're supposed to be dancing." Emilie, Liv's younger sister and perhaps, now, Faye's best friend, steered Faye away, and towards the band.

Faye's appearance was required at the Queen's Plate party. A whisker was the difference between that party being here, at Barn Five, home of Triple Stripe Racing Stables, instead of

1

Barn Twelve where her brother's trainees were stalled. *A whisker.* But while she could hate Nate for being the cause of her pain, she couldn't hate Liv for her horse having the victorious whisker. Okay, she did want to hate Liv, just a little, but not for that. And Nate was on the horse with that whisker, so...

"I called it, didn't I?" She hated being right about them, and couldn't help but look over her shoulder like the witness to a train wreck as Em dragged her away. Except it wasn't going to be a train wreck. It would be sweet, Liv, like one of her beloved horses, some combo of curiosity and self-preservation as she so cautiously moved closer to him; Nate holding out his hand like he was asking her to dance, all handsome and chivalrous. If she'd been watching a Hallmark romance instead of her best friend and her ex, it wouldn't be stinging like the wasps that hid out in the galvanized gates at the farm, coming from nowhere to pierce you when you disturbed them.

Em gave her another tug, but not before sweet got a little bit closer to steamy. There was some repressed stuff in her friend Liv, apparently.

"Maybe so," Em concurred. "You also told Liv not to use you as an excuse."

She had. Otherwise, Liv would have suffered in silence, continued to deny her feelings for the one guy even Faye had to admit was perfect for her.

"And I saw you eyeballing his friend," Em continued.

"Hmmm, yes. Time to get back on the horse, right?" Had she really just used a horse-based cliché? *This is worse than I thought.*

What she really wanted to do was to keep drinking the free-flowing cheap champagne, to wash away the image of Liv and Nate looking so...inevitable. But, to give Nate just a tiny bit of credit, getting his buddies to come play at the party had been a brilliant idea.

Nate's buddy from Calgary was a nice surprise. Not her type; he was tall, and Faye didn't know why, but she'd always gone for short men. Probably because they were accessible. Maybe she liked to take on their big egos. She'd grown up in a horse racing family, and spent plenty of time on the Woodbine backstretch in her formative years. Her six-foot brother was a giant back here. Nate, at five-six, was tall for a jock. He also lacked some of that ego. That probably should have been a warning sign for Faye.

She and Em elbowed to the front of the group collecting as the music started. She had a good view of the friend here. Will, wasn't it? Time to work with that. Em started dancing, and Faye joined in, because bouncing to the beat was as good a way as any to get her mind off the scene on the shed.

Will, as it turned out, was proving to be an excellent distraction. His voice was a bit rough, the timbre of it making things in her hum. The rakish angle of the guitar, the broad shoulders, and the beautiful long fingers that moved smoothly over the frets amplified the effect.

She leaned into Em, mouth by her ear, and hissed, "I bet he'd sizzle if I kissed him. I bet I'd burn my tongue."

Em laughed. "That's more like it."

Faye knew now she was Nate's rebound, even if both of them had been in denial about that for most of the relationship. His brokenness had appealed to her; his attempt to pretend he was fine, when he was anything but. She'd never been the woman who felt the need to fix guys, and at the outset he'd just fit her usual, basic, criteria – single, hot (both physically and professionally) apprentice rider. She'd honestly just wanted her typical short-term gig. But despite thinking he'd go for that early on, he'd turned the tables on her when she hadn't been able to reel him in on the first cast. She'd been intrigued. The chase was going to be a little harder this time. She'd thought it might be fun. Maybe it was for a while.

Fake champagne and the music helped numb her. She didn't care at the moment how she was getting home. She'd come with Dean, assuming Liv would give her a ride. Dean had left ages ago – hadn't even waited to see the band. Her big brother kept an eye out for her, but he wasn't a party kind of guy. He knew someone would get her home safe, because she wasn't going to adhere to his old-man hours. Em was responsible; it would probably be her. But Faye saw a fresh challenge before her now. Will would be a fine chauffeur. She could think of several ways to thank him. She didn't even know the guy, and she already had plans for him tonight. Seemed like as good a way as any to break out of her slump.

They were playing covers, from oldies and 90s stuff all the way through to current tunes. *Oooh, that one's perfect.* The Flys' *Got You Where I Want You.* She snagged Will's eyes as the hum in her continued – or was it a coincidence that he'd looked at her just then? She gave him a smile anyway, like the song demanded, slow and sultry. Closing her eyes as she swayed, she let the distance between them vanish, in her mind, at least, trying the idea on.

When the song ended, her little fantasy blew up, because Nate was next to him now, grabbing the mic. It was annoying as hell that he'd messed up her escape. But him being there meant Liv was hiding out somewhere.

Faye didn't owe her anything.

But for eleven years, Liv had been her best friend. And Faye was *not* standing up here now that Nate was singing.

She turned her back on the band and weaved through the bodies amid whoops and whistles as Woodbine's freaking Golden Boy – Plate-winning jockey, last year's Sovereign and

4

Eclipse award-winning apprentice...and breaker of her heart — started in with Panic! At the Disco's *Victorious*. Of course.

The kiss from her Prince Charming had not miraculously transformed Liv into an extroverted princess. She stood on the fringes, just enough apart from everyone to look her awkward self, too afraid of her own body to even step in time to the music's beat. She probably didn't even dance when there was no one around. Faye had given up trying to drag her into it, because it had just started to feel cruel.

Right this moment, Faye wished Liv wasn't her best friend. She wished she could either ignore her, or let fly with the barbs poking in her brain. But she probably shouldn't even acknowledge that she'd seen anything, because Liv would only be embarrassed. And Liv didn't mean to hurt. It wasn't her fault that she and Nate were better suited than Nate and Faye ever could have been. *Nice guys are wasted on me anyway.*

She hoped Will wasn't a nice guy.

She sidled up to Liv, looping arms. "They're good," she said. "I'm impressed. Too bad Nate had to join in." *Couldn't you have distracted him just a bit longer?* Just a bit of snark. She couldn't help it.

"Too bad security will probably shut them down any time."

You're probably looking forward to that. But Faye said, "Gotta make hay while the sun shines then, sweetie!" She started bopping around, even if it was to Nate's voice. Liv smirked as Faye jostled her, but none of it was rubbing off on her.

Wait — that wasn't another horse reference, was it? Making hay? *I need to watch that.*

Nate was on to *Finding Out True Love Is Blind* now, which was a little risqué for this venue, but damn, Faye loved that song, even if it was older. He liked older stuff, the Golden Boy did. And as Nate's taste went, this one wasn't actually that old.

"Where did Em go?" she yelled at Liv over the music.

"No idea."

"She'd better not have left." Faye had already growled at a couple of guys who'd thought they'd try their luck with her, so it was time to secure her ride before she got any drunker. She spotted Em. "Sorry, sweetie, you gotta excuse me."

At least it was the backside, and not a dance club, so Liv could always slink back to the shed if she wanted and commune with one of the horses. Faye wasn't worried about her fending for herself. Even without the Nate development, men had always backed off from Liv for the most part, between the anti-social veneer she'd perfected and her status. Liv would hate hearing it, but she was kind of racetrack royalty: daughter of the owner of a prominent stable. She worked hard, but it hadn't hurt her any to have that behind her.

Faye reached Em just in time to scream out the last lines of the song, and they collapsed into laughter. Faye grabbed the plastic glass out of Emilie's hand and downed what remained of the golden liquid in it. Then Nate was back to Panic! At The Disco, *Collar Full*, and he only had eyes for Liv, who had not, surprisingly, retreated. The song was kind of perfect for them. Faye would have loved it if she didn't hate it. Em probably didn't notice, whereas Faye felt like Nate might as well be sere-nading Liv under a window. She needed more fake champagne.

It was a relief when it was over and he relinquished the mic, giving Will a man-hug before leaving them. She and Em squished their way back to the front as Will started a new song, all gravelly voice and guitar. He was singing Blue October's *Soar*. That wasn't actually the name of the song, but it's how Faye always thought of it. Once again she obeyed the lyrics he sang, smiling at him, looking up, and there was no question this time that Will was returning the gaze, his eyes dark but soft and seeing her. It sent a warm rush through her, on top of the vibra-tion of the deep-down hum, and in that instant she felt like this was her destiny. *He is my destiny.* Then her head went dizzy and pain shot up the side of her neck. She dropped her chin and jammed a thumb into the overstretched muscle. *This is why I don't date tall guys.*

There was a buzz of activity behind them, and Faye turned sideways – because her neck hurt too much to just glance over her shoulder. Sure enough, a security guard stood talking to Roger and Nate and Liv. Nate made a gesture with a finger across his throat to Will, and the band stopped playing. Em pushed out her lower lip and headed towards Nate and Liv while Roger wandered to the food and drinks, where a couple of the grooms were starting to pack everything up. The Triple Stripe crew would eat well for a few days.

Faye followed Em slowly, concentrating hard on negoti-ating the lawn as her heels poked through the grass, in no hurry to join the lovebirds. In her advanced state of inebriation, she couldn't be trusted to maintain a filter.

"Oh well, we had a good run," Nate was saying with a shrug.

Faye grabbed Em's arm and pulled her to the side. "Can I catch a ride home with you?"

Em glanced at Liv, whose head was tilted into Nate, and Faye couldn't help watching them. They weren't touching, but there was an intimacy there, and it hurt. *I need the pain to go away.* Which meant either more alcohol, or getting out of there.

"Em?" she hissed.

"I came with Liv," Emilie said apologetically.

"Maybe she'll go with Nate, and you can take me with you in her car." Liv was still Liv, so Faye didn't imagine Nate driving her home would end with her in his bed, but wouldn't they want to prolong this disgustingly magical evening?

"This is my sister we're talking about. I'm sure we can give you a ride."

Which would be all sorts of awkward, even with Em there. Faye sighed. "Let me know when you're leaving." What choice did she have? She could just ride in the back seat and pray she passed out.

Em went to help with the food, Liv went to check on her horse, and Nate went over to the band where the guys were loading equipment into a van.

Was it too late to make a play for Will? It was desperation, not destiny. Destiny was not a real thing. Even if Nate and Liv made a pretty good case for it.

Nate glanced her way, but she was beyond caring enough to try to read his expression. He said something in parting to Will, and headed for the shedrow. He and Liv had to tuck their precious baby in together, right?

Well. *Hello.* Will was headed in her direction. Maybe the night wasn't a complete failure. There was no more music, but the hum rose up again as he got closer. Okay, truth be told, it was probably the fake champagne.

"Will, wasn't it?" She was conscious of pronouncing her words, and hoped it wasn't obvious. She didn't offer her hand, because she at least remembered she'd done that earlier, and it would seem like she was trying too hard if she did it again. She wasn't the girl who fell over a guy, no matter how much she needed him to help her get over Nate Miller. "That was fun." *And that was lame.*

"You're–" He stumbled over his tongue before taming it. "–Liv's friend."

Nice recovery. Sort of. At least she wasn't the only one who was less than smooth tonight. If he and Nate were real friends, he would know exactly who she was. Would that be a problem? Was there a code? Would Will think it was wrong to sleep with his friend's ex? Did guys care about that? She couldn't worry about it. She'd never been Nate's property, and couldn't let her past with him dictate her possible future. Drive on.

"So what do you do when you're not, you know, rocking the backstretch?"

"You're assuming this isn't a full-time gig?"

"Well, I haven't heard you on the airwaves, so..."

"Maybe I don't normally play the kind of music you listen to."

"Do you know what kind of music I listen to?"

He looked like he was thinking hard, thumb and forefinger resting on his chin. "The poppy side of Alternative, I'm going to say. The Killers. Maybe City and Colour. Bastille."

"Not bad. Are you mocking my musical tastes?"

"No. Everyone has their own taste, and just because mine might be different, it doesn't mean that it's better than yours."

"That sounds very diplomatic. Do you mean it, or are you just saying it?"

He chuckled, the crimping of fine lines around his eyes and those tasty-looking lips as he smiled making him even more attractive. She wished she had something in her hands, because suddenly she didn't know what to do with them, because they wanted to grab his t-shirt and pull him down, press her mouth to his, and see if he really did sizzle. "I knew Nate had secrets, but how did I miss you?" It came out breezy and breathless. Maybe she was laying the sultry on too thick.

"He's a busy guy. And our schedules don't exactly mesh."

"So we're back to, what do you do, when you're not rocking –"

"The backstretch – is that what you called this? What does that even mean."

"Damned if I know."

"Want to grab a coffee?"

Faye's eyebrows shot up. The biggest party night of the year for the racing crowd and this guy wants coffee? But she smiled, coyly, she hoped. Considering she'd thought she'd gotten nowhere at all, she would not stick her nose up at this offer.

"Sure."

She'd found her ride home after all.

So, this was Nate's ex.

She was...lovely. That's the word Will had used when he'd seen pictures, instead of the more raw reaction her appearance inspired. Not that Nate had exactly shared them, but she was obviously a social media fan, and tagged him relentlessly. Nate did have his own accounts, though Will didn't really know what for. To torture himself about the past, mostly, was Will's bet.

Picnics. Dancing. Downtown. Hashtags galore. But Will had never met her. Nate had brought her out to their jam sessions like the other guys sometimes brought their girlfriends. It wasn't as if she'd been a secret, but he'd kept her in a weird bubble – like the rest of this bizarre horse world.

Will had dated horse girls in Calgary. Ones that rode those jumping horses and had dreams of the big classes at Spruce; ones that rode barrel races and were determined to compete at the Stampede. Where did racetrack horse girls fit? Nate's ex was forward, that was for sure. She'd had her eye on him all night.

She was still Nate's ex.

Before she'd been Nate's ex she'd been his rebound, and Will knew one thing for certain: he wasn't going to be hers. He'd do this favour for Nate, and make sure she got home safe – even though it was wildly out of his way – so she didn't have to ride with his *new* girlfriend (as of the last minute, apparently). Even though the two women were supposed to be best friends. The whole thing was strange.

Nate had offered to let him crash at his place, but Will was used to late nights, and this one was not late. It was only just getting dark. He could do this little thing, for his oldest friend, and still be home earlier than he would have been on a work night.

She'd been looking all forlorn over there, now that things were winding up and she was left on her own. The look didn't quite fit her. She didn't look comfortable with it. And that made Will feel sorry for her. So, he'd walked over there like it wasn't planned; enjoyed her face as it brightened.

She was trying to play it cool, hide that she had an agenda, which Will was pretty sure was to use him to make herself feel better about the obvious fact that Nate was totally – though apologetically, because he was Nate – into someone new.

Her expression when he suggested coffee had been priceless. He saw a lot of drunk people in his line of work, and she'd had enough alcohol tonight. And while there was something about the whole damsel in distress thing, she was likely the type who would punch him if he called her that to her face because she'd be too proud to admit she'd found herself in such a position. This wasn't the real her. It caught Will off guard, but he found himself wanting to know the real her. The her that had drawn Nate in enough to stay with her for eight months.

"C'mon," he said, motioning to his Chevy as the other guys tucked the last cords into the van. She teetered on heels that looked dangerously unstable for a sober person, let alone one in her tipsy state. She slipped into the passenger seat, and he swung the door shut.

"Is there some pact that guys from Calgary have to drive beat up old vintage cars that are probably older than they are?"

she asked, her eyes travelling over the Camaro's dash with one eyebrow quirked. Despite her level of impairment, she looked classy. Classy and smart. The alcohol was merely a coping mechanism.

"Is there a problem with that? What do you drive?"

"Let's see if you can guess that like you did the music."

Will pulled on his seatbelt and put his foot on the clutch. "You're going to have to tell me how to get out of here, because I'm pretty much lost."

She directed him to what he recognized to be Highway 27, but heading north, instead of south back into the city. He figured she was a Starbucks kinda girl, but wondered where the hell around there would be one of those. It seemed like solid Tim Horton's territory.

He shouldn't have worried. She probably had an app that told her the location of every last franchise.

Even under the dwindling influence of too much cheap champagne, she had a quick smile and a thank you for him as he held open the door and let her walk through. The rich smell of coffee overtook the subtlety of her perfume, and he breathed it in, the sharp blast of pressurized steam frothing milk punctuating the background buzz of seated patrons. It was one of his favourite things, the quiet atmosphere of a coffee shop – at least if they served proper espresso.

Faye ordered a cappuccino – double-shot Venti. Seemed a good choice.

"Same," Will said. "Want something to eat?" He looked down at her, but she shook her head. "I'll have one of those brownies." They'd cleared the food by the time the band had been done playing, and he was kind of hungry, but the savoury stuff wouldn't have dealt with being almost a day old as well as the sweets would have.

He reached for his wallet, but Faye waved her phone in

front of him. "I'm buying. I collect rewards. And the least I can do is pay." She glanced up at him with one of those cute smiles she'd been giving him all night, then flashed the phone in front of the reader.

They lucked out with a table, someone leaving just as they picked up their order. The place looked to be populated predominantly by students, tucked behind laptops looking either intent, or bored, or in some cases, asleep.

Faye stood out, and it was more than because of the way she was dressed – the fancy outfit, the makeup that had withstood the day's events. She had an air, though it seemed a little deflated, a light that was running a few watts lower than it should be. Anger poked at him, catching him off guard. Nate had done this, to this beautiful person. Nate said she'd broken up with him, but that didn't mean she hadn't suffered for it.

"Is there a school close to here?" he said to make conversation before he lifted his cup.

"Humber College's main campus is just over there." Her chin lifted, indicating the direction.

She reached for the brownie, long fingers breaking off a chunk, and placed it languidly on her tongue. Didn't want something herself, but had no problem scavenging his. Her lips closed, savouring, in her own little world for a moment before she swallowed and chased it with the cappuccino.

"So why did you come to Toronto? Were you running from something too?"

She was talking about Nate, of course, but he hoped his flinch wasn't visible. It wasn't like Nate, the reason he'd left. Nate's impetus had been all angst and drama – not that it hadn't been warranted. "I came on a scholarship to U of T for music."

"Wow. So it's a serious thing for you. Did you finish your degree?"

"And started a masters."

"Wow." She was still a little drunk, he could tell; more impressed than she should be by that. "What do you plan to do with that?"

"Nothing. I mean, I could teach, but I'm not a teacher."

"How do you know?"

She had him there. Cue subject change. "So this Queen's Plate thing is a big deal?"

Her laugh came easily, a clear timbre behind her vocal chords that made him wonder if she could sing. "You don't know that? It's Canada's most famous horse race. It's the longest continuously-run sporting event in North America. During war time when the Derby wasn't run, the Queen's Plate went on." She could have done a commercial for the event. "The Plate is special. I love the Plate. It's when Woodbine dresses up and shines. I get to wear a hat." She put another piece of brownie on her tongue, and Will fixated on it until she pursed her lips and looked perplexed. "I have no idea where I left my hat."

He hadn't seen the hat, but she was ridiculously adorable. Her dark hair had probably been a bit tidier when she'd been wearing it. Definitely before the band started playing. The way she'd been swinging her head around as she danced had left those wavy tresses in sexy disarray. Not that he'd been watching her dance. No, not at all. He blinked it out of his mind.

"Your brother works on the farm?" Will was picturing a straw hat and suspenders; combines and hay rakes, maybe a few beef cattle. In other words, his childhood memories of his grandfather back in Alberta.

"He does some stuff, but he has a live-in manager to run things. Technically he's a trainer. He has a public stable here." She gestured in the general direction of the racetrack. "Well, there. About twelve horses, mostly for clients he inherited from my father, and a few of our own that he bred – again, the result of my father's breeding program. Some of them he's had to sell pieces of here and there to keep things going."

"Pieces? Like an ear? Or a tail?"

Faye smirked. "A comedian, I see. Do you really know nothing about racing? Like Nate doesn't tell you anything?"

"I think getting together with me and the guys to play some music is his escape from it, to be honest."

She looked slightly bewildered. "Huh. I never got the impression Nate felt it was anything he needed a break from."

Will shrugged. "Maybe when he was with you, you gave him that break." He thought of those social media posts, a picture record of their time together, and made a mental note to check to see if she'd deleted them, erased what she could when the biggest reminder was an unavoidable part of her life.

She looked completely sober now, her face impassive as she seemed to absorb that thought. The flicker in her eyes was a little nostalgic.

"Well if so, he's gone full immersion now." She straightened, stealing another morsel of brownie so that there was only a tiny piece left. "Let's not talk about my ex, all right? That's just bad manners on a date."

"This is a date?"

"It would be weird if we dated, wouldn't it?"

"I don't know. Because our friends are involved? That's just life."

"I suppose. Besides which, Nate and Liv are far too engrossed in their own lives to probably even notice, right?"

There was a touch of bitter there. A hint of resignation. He felt bad for her, that she'd happened to fall for someone who, plunked into different circumstances – a different time, a different place – might have really loved her. Will didn't understand the racehorse world or its people, but he'd been around enough horse girls to understand that their priorities were a little skewed. The racetrack seemed a level deeper, a place where you just ended up with someone you worked closely with because you were together all the time anyway.

"Sorry. I'm doing it again. I am so not that girl. I apologize for embarrassing myself."

Will waved her off, and tipped back his cup to catch the last drops. "Don't worry about it. I don't date horse girls anyway."

Her laugh this time was a spontaneous burst. "You think I'm a horse girl?"

Will narrowed his gaze. A fair assumption, wasn't it? "Ready to go?"

He hoped he said it in a matter-of-fact, *hey I'm just getting you home safe* way. She nodded and rose, picking up the empty cups and napkins and depositing them in the trash on the way out, leaving him to watch the sway of her hips under the fabric of her dress. She knew what she was doing. She might be down, but she was not out. She was probably never out. She was *that* girl.

Casual, impersonal, conversation about nothing carried them all the way to King City, Faye interrupting to give him directions when needed. They talked about last week's incessant humidity, and he answered her questions about Calgary's weather, where the higher altitude made that a non-issue. How did he like Toronto? Had she grown up out here? There's Triple Stripe, Liv's dad's farm, also where Nate lived; the farm where Faye lived a little further on. Up a short driveway between fences, to a century home. Her brother's truck next to the house. A little Corolla beside it. Hers, most likely.

He escorted her up three steps onto a deck. Outside the back door, she turned, gazing up under dark lashes with one of those smiles, standing bathed in yellow light. He caught his breath, gave her a quick kiss on the cheek, and left her there.

Back in the car, he waited, watching her. She waited a beat too, watching him, before opening the door and disappearing inside. She was still too much Nate's ex, and not enough whoever she'd been before him. He wanted to meet that Faye – because this suppressed, trying-not-to-feel-everything-she-was-still-feeling person, was not her. He wasn't going to be her rebound, he reminded himself. He wasn't going to think he could put back together what Nate had torn apart. And he didn't date horse girls.

CHAPTER TWO

THIS SHOULD HAVE BEEN the time she slept through the sounds of Dean getting up, but no. Her face was so imprinted on her pillow she was glad there was no need to lift her head, or open her eyes, which seemed to be stuck together. At least *she* didn't have to get up at dark o'clock and head into the racetrack. She wondered again where her hat had ended up. *I liked that hat.*

When she heard Dean's truck rumble out the driveway, she rolled over with a grunt, her mouth dry and vile, but sleep beckoned her back before she could reach for the water bottle on her bedside table.

It was the bathroom calling her that made her finally drag herself out of bed. The sun was aggravatingly all bright and cheery in a cloudless sky. Someone needed to turn it down. Where were her sunglasses? Probably wherever her hat was.

The face that met her in the mirror was not an attractive one. *Not a good look, Faye.* Crusted mascara, creases on her cheek from her pillow. That humming that had enchanted her last night had been replaced by an incessant pounding behind her temples. She should have just kept drinking, then she wouldn't have this headache. This – face it – hangover. Damn Mr Straight-Laced musician. How did that even make sense? Coffee and a chaste kiss on the cheek. That's what he'd left her with. At least she'd got her tongue down Nate's throat the first time she'd kissed him.

I have lost it. I've lost my touch.

Either that, or she needed to avoid these Calgary boys. They were too *good*. How boring. She shuffled back to her room, guzzled some water, and stared at her bed. This was not how it was supposed to go.

In the sobering light of the morning after, it probably hadn't been a good move, trying to land Nate's best friend. It irked her as much as it hurt, that Nate had landed squarely on his feet – winning the big race, getting the girl, living the dream – while she floundered. She wasn't the girl that did that. She'd dropped him. Why was it taking her so long to recover?

And how did she still know nothing about his friend? She knew music wasn't his full-time gig, that was it. He lived in Toronto. He was educated. He had to pay the rent somehow, didn't he?

He hadn't even asked for her number. Then again, neither had Nate, after her initial play. But Nate had known where she lived. Knew many ways of finding her. So there was that. This Will character could track her down, quite easily. By asking Nate. Now that was just...she didn't know how to feel about that.

She wasn't holding a torch for Nate, honestly she wasn't. Just a whole hell of a lot of resentment. Mostly that she'd let herself fall, for the first time in her life. Damn Mr. Straight-Laced, again, for not helping her get back on track. Well. She had to do something about that. Enough was enough. She needed to find another project and regain her form. One good thing about the racetrack, it wasn't a matter of finding someone to sleep with, it was just a matter of whom.

Thank goodness she didn't have much to do today. She always planned ahead, so the day after Queen's Plate was relaxed, in case she did run off a bit at the event itself.

It appeared she couldn't help the horse racing metaphors. Something else to get over. Maybe it was fair Will thought she was a horse girl. She hadn't had the chance to tell him he couldn't be more wrong.

There would have been many pages this morning at Woodbine from employees citing mysterious "car trouble." Not Nate and Liv though. They'd both be there, dedicated souls that they were, riding the high of a big win and shiny new feelings. A year ago, those kinds of feelings for Nate had been starting their drip of lies to her. *Maybe this time will be different. Maybe you can fall in love.*

Wrong.

She needed a shower, then, breakfast. Coffee and Advil would be about right. On second thought, drugs first, then shower, then coffee.

A couple of Liqui-gels and some scorching hot water later, her headache began to ease. The clatter of nails on hardwood met her when she reached the bottom of the stairs, and Gus scrambled over to greet her. She trusted her head enough to bend and take his big Golden Retriever head in both hands, and planted a kiss on top of it. Satisfied, he wandered back to his spot near the back door, tail wafting lazily back and forth, and collapsed into a fluffy lump of long, yellow hair.

The pot Dean had brewed hours before waited on the counter, a dreadful, dark concentrate of its former self. She drank it black, its harshness enough to kickstart her brain so she could generate a proper cup. That life-saving aroma of fresh grinds filtered by steaming water in her French press made her think of Will. He'd seemed relieved at her choice of coffee options, and hadn't said a word when she'd eaten most of his brownie. He might be a catch, if only he was looking to be caught. Which he obviously was not. At least not by her.

She reached for a bottle from a cupboard by the sink, and added a shot of Baileys to her mug – for medicinal purposes, of course. Now she could take on this day. A day for accepting reality – at least when it came to her non-existent love life.

Not a lot had changed in the farmhouse in the last eleven years. The office still displayed photos of her father's greatest training wins, and a framed image of the family old enough that Faye was scooped up in her father's arms. There were no recent photos save for in Dean's office at the track, where she'd been in some of the win pics of horses he'd trained. He didn't bring them here. Didn't think they were worthy of holding court alongside the accomplishments of Ed Taylor.

Gus joined her as she parked herself in front of the computer and went right to the spreadsheets, just in case Facebook showed her things she didn't want to see. Things she already couldn't unsee. It was the end of the month, so she started by invoicing Dean's owners. Touch and Go running second in yesterday's Plate to Liv's filly wasn't anything to be embarrassed about – a million dollar purse, second was worth twenty percent. Dean owned a third of him, and as trainer got ten percent of the other partners' pieces. Faye calculated in her head quickly. That would pay the bills for a bit. The numbers helped her, got her mind off less tangible things. Like how the two of them would probably grow old here, die here. Dean the quiet farmer bachelor, Faye his spinster sister. She'd be a hot cougar spinster though. There would be no bun and dowdy clothes for her.

Her mother had taught her how to do the bookwork, a way she could contribute to the family business when it became obvious she had no interest in the horses. She took after her mother. But at least her mother had been capable enough to pitch in when needed. Brave enough. So Faye learned the books, and learned how to cook, and to bake her father's favourite dessert, forever trying to make up for not being a horse girl.

When her phone rang at eleven, she'd accomplished enough to ease the annoying thoughts in her brain. She grabbed for it. Liv? Calling her? It kept ringing, and Faye sighed. She couldn't not answer.

"Hey, sweetie, what's up?"

"Everything's fine. Yes, I know, me on the phone. Do I need to come over with a defibrillator?" Liv typically only used the actual call function of her phone in dire circumstances.

"You might, actually. To what do I owe the honour?" She tried to keep her tone light, instead of tired. "Tell me again that everything's okay."

Though on some level, she was hoping it was not, that things had already gone south with Nate. Because with Liv, that was totally possible. She was an expert at removing herself, all with perfect justification. The animals would always come first; relationships could be collateral damage.

Stop that.

Besides, Nate would always adapt, because he was, Faye was quite sure, very much the same. He would gentle that resistance in Liv, with all the patience and compassion he showed the horses he partnered. And the boy had enough of his own hangups; the two of them were probably just as perfect together as Faye feared.

"Everything is fine," Liv repeated. "How are you?"

Faye didn't know how to answer that. Did she tell the truth? Instead, she redirected. "How is the filly this morning?"

Faye asked because she had to. It was proper etiquette,

unforgivable not to, especially after a hard race like yesterday's. Even if she didn't have the same draw to the horses, they were the reason Faye had the things she did. They'd always been what fed and clothed and sheltered her. She would forever acknowledge and be grateful for them, for that reason. Plus, being best friends with a bona fide horse girl – or the daughter or sister of a trainer, or the girlfriend of a jock – one began to ask such things out of habit.

"Good. A little tired, no surprise."

There was an awkward silence between them. Because why was she calling? Liv had a history of avoiding Faye, and for once, she had an excuse Faye could go along with. But the small talk wouldn't last long. Liv wasn't one to talk for the sake of talking. She needed a purpose. Faye usually drew it out, but she wasn't sure she had it in her this time. Heaven forbid she was asking for advice about something delicate.

"Can we get together?" Liv said, finally.

Faye tried to sound casual, but was afraid just a little bit of frost crept in. "Are you coming over?"

"Am I still welcome?"

Faye sighed. "Of course. If you bring cappuccino, that is."

She thought she could feel Liv's slight smile.

"I can't today...if I don't go for a run this afternoon I'll explode–"

There had been a time when Faye would have mentioned glibly that there were better ways to relieve tension, but given what that would imply in the new state of things, she didn't want to think about it.

"–and I have some stuff to catch up on at the farm. Tomorrow though, for sure? We could meet at Lucy's at noon for lunch. On me."

"Of course on you. You just won the Plate."

"It's a date."

"See you tomorrow."

Liv hadn't said it, but that run she was so desperate for was a date too, of sorts, because Nate would be running with her. There were trails on the Triple Stripe farm, but one day last week, Faye had caught a glimpse of them on the road. One of the little clues that tipped her off that something was closer to happening, despite Liv's protestations. Liv ran alone. Period. Except now she did not.

Faye sighed, a heavy release from her too-tight chest. She had twenty-four hours to prepare for whatever Liv felt they needed to talk about. And Lucy's didn't serve alcohol. Or cappuccino, for that matter.

On that note, another coffee was in order. The mention of Lucy's made her crave something sweet to go with it. Gus followed her to the kitchen. She wanted to think it was loyalty, but it was really just because he hoped there was something in the trip for him.

The selection was a little sparse today – Dean usually picked up groceries after morning training on one of racing's dark days, so he'd be restocking soon. Then she heard his truck. Gus did too, leaving her feet to scramble to the back door.

Their reunion was joyous, like they'd been separated for weeks instead of hours. Dean cooed goofily at the dog, setting down grocery bags to give a proper hello. Faye wasn't jealous, because Gus lavished the same excitement on her. Or anyone, for that matter.

Dean picked up the cloth bags and set them on the counter, while Gus ran off to retrieve his ragged, once-plush, squirrel toy. The dog bounded back into the kitchen and dropped the drool-soaked mass proudly on Faye's toes. She shuddered, and edged it carefully away.

"You good for coffee?" Dean asked, picking up the rinsed-out carafe.

"I was just about to make some." Gus tossed the filthy squirrel at her, and Faye pushed it away again. "You left early last night."

"Well, you know. Too much hullabaloo."

Who said things like that anymore? Dean, that was who. All the time. It was so silly it was endearing. It reminded her of her mother.

"It was a tough one to swallow, losing like that." He leaned back against the counter as the coffee maker started gurgling, and Faye began to put away the groceries. "Though of course if we were going to get beat, I'm glad it was Liv. That's one gutsy filly."

Faye wondered if he'd stayed long enough to see what had transpired between Liv and Nate. Little known fact: her brother had a crush on Liv. He'd never outright admitted it, but Faye knew. It wasn't hard to figure out. He brightened in her company. Got even more awkward than his normal awkward.

"How's the colt this morning?" Faye asked. Duty, again.

"Tired. That track took a lot out of him."

"That's what Liv said about Chique."

"You talked to her?"

Faye nodded, and opened up a package of shortbread fingers.

"I'm proud of her," Dean said, like the big brother Liv saw him as – a perception he stoically accepted. The coffee maker made its final hiss and sputter, and he pulled out clean mugs.

Liv was oblivious to his suffering, of course. Look what it had taken for Nate to get through to her. Faye certainly didn't plan to tell her, especially not now. It would fry her already over-taxed mind. And if Dean did know about Liv and Nate, he wasn't saying. He probably wouldn't – he'd just quietly endure. He and Liv were a bit too much alike in a lot of ways.

"Should be able to cut more hay tomorrow. Looks like the

weather's going to be good for the rest of the week," he said, taking a sip of the brew.

Faye didn't know how he could drink it that hot. "Don't forget about the concert tomorrow night."

"Right." He threw back the rest of the coffee like it was water, then rinsed out his cup. "I'm going for a bike ride."

She could tell he was pondering a way to bail, and haying would be a legitimate excuse, but who would she take? Not Liv, not right now. Em would probably be game.

"Figure out if you can still come with me while you're riding. Have fun." How she'd ended up with such a sporty group of friends, including her brother, was beyond her.

So, note to self, round up haying help. Because if she found enough of it, she wouldn't have to fight with the bales herself.

"I didn't expect to see you today."

Will opened the door wider to let Nate into his loft before wandering back to the kitchen and extracting a couple of beers from the fridge. He held one out.

Nate accepted. "Thanks. It was kind of a surreal night. I needed to come here to keep my feet on the ground."

"Didn't get to see much of you. Other than your little cameo. Man of the hour. And I can say I knew you when."

Nate's lips twisted, the bottle's cap gone with a quick flick of his wrist. "Think my dad will be impressed?"

"I'm betting he didn't call to congratulate you."

"You would win that bet." Nate gravitated to the keyboard, like he always did, sliding onto the bench and setting his bottle carefully on top. He started warming his fingers up with scales, traveling easily over the keys, head moving to the tempo he set.

"So, made some progress with the boss?"

Nate glanced sideways, missing a beat before carrying on, a smile of simple contentment on his lips. "Like I said, it was a little surreal. Speaking of –" He dropped his fingers from the keys, one hand closing around the bottle, and spun a hundred and eighty degrees. "How'd it go with Faye Taylor?"

"I made sure she got home safe. Rest assured I behaved like a perfect gentleman."

"Much to her disappointment, I bet. She's probably pissed as hell this morning that she went to bed alone. But thank you."

"Anything to help ease your conscience, buddy."

Nate was too wrapped up in his new happy to even take offence to that. Disappointing. People in love were so annoying.

"What if I told you it was nice?" Which was true, but Will was still hoping to get a rise out of him.

"Like visiting with your grandmother? I wouldn't believe it."

"Like I like her company. Like maybe I like her." *There.*

Nate took a slow pull from the bottle. "That would be interesting."

"Would you mind?"

"It has nothing to do with me anymore."

"But I'm getting a vibe, like you're still a little protective of her."

"Because I feel bad about what happened between us. She deserves better than that."

Thank you. Will didn't believe it had been intentional, whatever Nate thought he'd done to Faye. Nate was probably being harder on himself than he had to be, but he was like that. He held onto things. But he was obviously getting better about it, because after Cindy, his first girlfriend back in Calgary, he'd pined for four years, and whatever had happened with Faye hadn't kept him from starting something new with Liv a few months later. Maybe that's what he felt bad about – that he'd moved on while it was pretty obvious that Faye had not, despite what she might want everyone to think.

"So you really wouldn't want me to ask her out?" Will had no intention of doing so, but it was entertaining, watching Nate stew about it.

"I don't know. It's your call. But it might be in everyone's best interest if you don't."

"Why?"

"Because if things don't work out, then both of you are going to be mad at me. Right now it's only Faye. And well, if you do go out with her, you're bringing something pretty significant from that world into this world, and this is supposed to be my break from that."

"So this really is about you, then."

"Fine, all right? Do what you want. Just keep me out of it. And at least for a while, can you keep her out of here? Just let me have my little sanctuary, at least until the two of you figure out if it's more than just a passing thing."

"You've got a lot of demands, don't you?"

"Can we just play some music? Where are the others, anyway?"

"Who knows. Late, obviously. We can start without them."

Nate started pounding the keyboard with *A Song For the Dumped* like it was in any way relevant to his life. So Faye had dumped him, and there was some toxic residue. But he had this shiny new thing, and this fancy life, so he needed to get on with that and stop worrying about things that weren't his to worry about anymore.

"The real question is..." Nate turned away from the keyboard abruptly. "...do you really want to ask her out? Because I will tell you what I was told. Faye doesn't like to get attached. Though it didn't exactly play out that way, with me."

"Women get attached to you, Miller." Even if he hadn't

intended it with Faye, it was just in his DNA. Will, on the other hand...

"Ha. Hardly. If Cin had been attached we'd be married right now."

"And Liv?"

"We'll see about that."

"She looked pretty attached to you last night. Physically."

"Funny guy."

Will moseyed over to his guitar, parking himself on a stool. "Last night was fun but that whole scene was a bizarre experience. It's a different world, isn't it?"

"Oh, definitely."

Which is why whatever impression Faye had made on Will didn't matter. Their paths crossed due to a series of events that wouldn't likely be repeated. The only reason he ever saw Nate was when they got together like this, which was pretty rare. Will had never been to the country where Nate lived – until last night, when he'd driven Faye home – and he lived an hour away in the city. So what were the chances of him ever seeing her again? And after he'd treated her like a sister last night, he didn't imagine she'd be all that warm towards him in the unlikely event he did decide it wasn't too strange to get her number from Nate. She obviously had a good dose of pride, however fragile it might be at the moment, and he'd injured it last night. Not that he'd do things differently. It had been an interesting encounter; that was it. He'd leave it at that.

"Do you think you'll make it down a little more consistently now?" Will started tuning the guitar. "Even if it seems kind of backward that being more famous might suddenly give you the inspiration to make time for it."

Will had thought they might pick up again as friends when Nate had made his own way east, but their worlds were opposites: early racetrack mornings versus Will's late nights at the restaurants. It would be good for Nate to make the effort, create a balance with the all-encompassing nature of his job. He didn't get to leave it behind like Will did. When Will left work – at whatever time he managed to get out at the end of the night – he didn't really think about it again until his next shift.

"I'm not famous. But, yeah. I want to make a point of it. And Liv's going to be her usual preoccupied self leading up to Chique's next race, so it's probably best if I give her space. Coming down here will distract me from the fact that we're always one step forward, two steps back, you know?"

"How long is that for?"

"Three weeks. And if she wins that, another three weeks till the last race of the series. I know it'll fly, but still."

"Not so good for you, good for the band." Will grinned.

"So we're a band now?"

"If you keep showing up, we will be."

"Can we be a Switchfoot cover band?"

"I don't know about that. But maybe we can have a show that's not at a horse barn."

"I'm still going to Florida for the winter."

"Then we'll have to practice by Zoom."

"Y'know," Nate said, a slow smile taking over his face, "that might actually work. Because this is going to be the winter where it all comes together."

He started playing that Blue October song Will had done last night, singing the bit about not being able to wait to see what was around the corner. The guy was really an optimist at heart; it had been hard to see him so squashed by what Cindy had done. This recommitment to music was probably as much about getting beyond that as needing a break from the pressures of his dangerous job. Not that Will was a psychologist or anything.

"Do you think you'll ever spend the winter up here again?" Will asked.

"When there's the option of going south? Are you kidding? Do you remember what it's like to work on a farm in the winter? It's bad enough I have to stay here till the middle of December. Especially when I'm betting Liv will be gone with the first load of horses in November."

"But do you really even work on the farm anymore?"

"If I didn't go south I would be. You think I'm going to sit on my ass all winter and still live there?"

"Florida's made you soft, buddy. Remember when we used to be on the slopes in Banff every chance we got?"

"When we weren't on the ice?"

"What happened to us?"

"Life, I guess. Though it's worked out all right."

"For you, maybe."

Nate looked at him carefully, cradling his bottle. "What's up?"

"What happened to me, then? I'm stuck in this job I hate, living in a city I hate." Will set the guitar down and wandered back to the kitchen, grabbing an apple from a bowl on the counter. "After I dropped Faye off last night, I drove past this 'For Rent' sign in front of one of those places in town there, on King Sideroad. A coffee shop, I think."

"Lucy's? It was probably one of the other places there. Lucy's an icon, albeit a crusty one. I can't imagine her leaving. King City would fall apart without her."

"I'm pretty sure it was for the coffee shop."

"That's crazy. Everyone within twenty-five kilometres of King knows Lucy's, there's no way she's giving it up. Unless she's found a better place, but I can't imagine where that would be. She's right on the main strip, and that big parking lot is great."

"It just made me wonder what it would be like to get out of the city, and start my own thing."

"It would be cool to have you out that way."

"Didn't you make enough money to buy a house yesterday? We could be housemates."

Nate laughed. "Oh, I'm not giving up my apartment now. The girl next door and all that."

"Next thing I know you're going to be married, and I'll still be stuck in a dead end, if I don't make a change."

Nate's brow was furrowed, watching him. "It scares me that Faye Taylor inspired all this."

"She didn't." Did she? "And just so you know I was having you on. I'm not asking her out. Remember I don't date horse girls."

Nate laughed, much the way Faye had at the same statement. "Well, Faye Taylor is no horse girl. The closest I've seen her to a horse is next to the groom in a win photo. She's terrified of them."

Will raised his eyebrows, and took a bite out of the apple. He still wasn't going to ask her out.

CHAPTER THREE

THE MEMORY of the day Faye had met Liv remained distinct, a solid stake in the survey of her life marking where the property line had changed.

She hadn't expected the school bus to slow, then stop, at the big farm just down from hers. Upgrades had been going on there since the sale had closed that spring – fences repaired and painted a classic white, evidence of a major reno happening at the house – but it wasn't until a slight, dark-haired girl around her own age climbed aboard that Faye realized a family had moved in. The bus was packed the first day of a new school year, when attendance by the rural kids seemed to be at its highest. Something about the new girl grabbed Faye, because Faye felt as much a stranger on this bus as that girl was. They stared at each other for a beat before the girl scanned front to back. Faye picked up her bag and moved it onto her lap. New Girl's gaze swept the seats again, but Faye was the only one making space.

The girl's eyes flashed sideways as she slipped onto the bench, hugging her backpack to herself.

"I'm Faye," she'd offered. "I live at the farm just down the road. We've got Thoroughbreds too."

New Girl ventured a small smile, and Faye felt bad that she'd be disappointed when she found out Faye was not really into horses.

"I'm Olivia. Liv."

There was a certain cadence to the syllables – French Canadian? Her loss might not have been as drastic as Faye's, but she was grieving something just the same. Her old home, and old friends, and lost confidence faced with all the new? Whatever it was, Faye found herself softening. She felt like they saw each other.

The admitted attraction of the prospect of a friendship with Liv was that she didn't know Faye before the accident. She just knew this Faye, unlike her former friends and classmates, all of whom had drifted away during Faye's lengthy absence from school. And behind Liv's reserve, those spooky grey eyes, was something unknown, like she carried around her own darkness, so she wouldn't be turned off by Faye's. Faye had suspicions now that something had happened in Liv's childhood that was buried deep in her subconscious, but it was only a theory. Faye hadn't made any attempt to extract it, because it might have meant exposing her own dysfunction. That was one of the best things about Liv; she didn't probe, because she didn't want to be probed. Okay, sometimes it was exasperating.

They were total opposites for the most part. Liv was as quiet as Faye could be outspoken; Liv dressed to blend into the background while Faye liked to stand out; tastefully, of course. Maybe it was a youngest child thing. She'd adored the brother she'd lost, Shawn, but he was the family's bright light, and even though he complained that Faye got away with too much because she was the cherished baby girl, Faye still had to do her bit to get attention. Especially as her father's was always shared in a lopsided fashion with the horses.

So, unlikely as it might've seemed from the outside, they became fast friends. But not in the usual, teenage girl way. They were always just left of popular, admired by those much lower in the pecking order, hated by the cool girls. Faye had been one of those cool girls before the accident, but death had taken that from her, too. But the best part? None of that mattered to either Liv or Faye, one bit.

This, today, was new territory for them, though. They'd never been in a place like this. Faye glanced at the clock on the kitchen wall. Time to get ready.

The farm landline sidelined her, ringing out from the office, and she rushed to grab the receiver and check the number. Her biggest client, a powerhouse on the Ontario circuit. And, it was the boss-man himself. She gulped her last swallow of coffee, wishing it was something stronger, and listened while he delivered one more thing to make her life just a bit more miserable. Her cell buzzed on the desk with a text from Liv as she hung up.

Running late. 1PM okay?

For once, she got how Liv felt about such get-togethers. *I don't want to go.* But she keyed in, *Sure. See you then.*

Faye showered; dried and styled her hair; put on makeup. This whole funk she was in would *not* keep her from looking good. Lucy's was a drab place, so she found some bright turquoise capris and her favourite cap-sleeved blouse, a cheerful pattern of flowers on a background of white. Now she felt prepared for whatever Liv had on her mind, a mystifying place at the best of times.

Liv was waiting outside. She was still in her barn clothes, her t-shirt mostly clean, faded jeans cinched at her tiny waist to keep them from sliding down practically non-existent hips. She was still feminine, even without curves, with perfect skin and dark hair and lashes. Her slate eyes were always so studious, and still her most startling feature. Faye had never been able to convince Liv to wear makeup, but the truth was, she didn't need it.

Faye put on a smile and clutched Liv's shoulders in a quick hug, catching the familiar whiff of racetrack: dust and leather and horse. "Shall we go in?"

Liv nodded, and swung open the door. It didn't matter how many times they'd been here, they both approached the café's counter with trepidation. Lucy burst out of the back, wiping her hands on her flour-dusted apron, five feet tall and half as wide, her hostility thinly veiled, from her dark, close-cropped curls to her sturdy feet. Dean called her the Angry Hobbit, and Faye couldn't see the woman now without thinking it. She bit her lower lip to keep control of her features.

"What can I get for you?" Lucy said brusquely.

Faye almost ducked, the words punching out into the air. "Coffees?" she said, like she was asking permission. They would not get cappuccino here, and Lucy wouldn't have let them in the door if Faye had asked Liv to pick some up on her way back from the track.

Liv nodded silently.

"And I'll have the chicken wrap," Faye said, gaining a little confidence.

"Me too." Liv quickly took the path of least resistance. "And a butter tart for each of us, of course."

"Only one left," Lucy barked.

"We can share," Faye said, sliding Liv a sideways look. Liv wouldn't look at her – Faye had the impression she was at risk of breaking out laughing too.

Lucy served up their coffees in ceramic mugs and

presented the revered butter tart on a plate. "I'll bring your wraps out when they're ready."

They retreated to a table with thanks – to Lucy, and for the dismissal – after doctoring the coffee. Faye cut the butter tart neatly in half, and didn't ask about Chique again. She waited, cautiously taking a sip from her cup.

"I'm worried," Liv said, finally, staring intently at her own mug, clutched between her hands. She glanced quickly at Faye.

One of Faye's eyebrows crept up. "About what?" she asked, slowly, thinking her worst fears about a request for delicate advice was about to come to pass.

"About us. We're broken. This thing...is messy. With Nate."

Faye sighed, and stared at the butter tart, pondering if she should just eat it now. She could use the sugar high for this. "I told you not to use me as an excuse. I'll deal with it." Even if she hadn't been doing a very good job, something last night had made very clear.

"But I need to know...we need to, somehow...we can still be friends, can't we? Because this friendship is more important to me than whatever might happen with him."

Oh, don't say that, sweetie, Faye wanted to say. *You have to put him first now, if you want it to work.* But Liv had a point. It shouldn't have to be one or the other. Faye had always believed guys shouldn't get in the way of friendships between women. Romantic relationships came and went, but it was your female friends who were always there waiting to pick up the pieces. Or should be. There was nothing that irked her more than women who disappeared when they hooked up with a new guy, all in love. Worse yet when they crawled back heartbroken and lonely when it didn't work out. Until the next time; the next guy.

And now there was this. Liv hadn't done anything on

purpose to hurt her. She'd tried very hard to spare Faye's feelings, at the expense of her own. And really, Nate hadn't broken Faye either. She'd been messed up for a long time before he came along. It was just more satisfying at the moment to ignore that fact.

"We can't let a guy get between us. Not even Nate." Liv stared Faye down, and Faye wanted to believe in that conviction. "We have to do better."

She's growing up, my backward little friend, talking to me like this.

"Okay. But first off, you don't get out of this Nate thing because of me. I won't let you. You suffered in silence to protect me for longer than I know, I would bet. I've had my pity party and I'm getting over it, as of this morning. Mostly because I hate hangovers like I had yesterday." She made a feeble attempt at a smile. "You deserve all the happy. The great career, the great guy. And, a great friend, so I will do better."

Lucy interrupted, bringing over two more plates with their wraps, then leaving wordlessly.

"So when does that start?" Liv asked.

"Now, I told you. I mean it."

"All right." Liv nodded resolutely. "So tell me what happened with Will."

"Sadly, nothing. We went for coffee. I didn't even really learn anything about him. He left me on the doorstep." She spared Liv her recollection of that similar scene with Nate which pushed its way immediately into her brain.

"Too much sad girl?"

"Apparently I'm not a very good actress."

"Are you supposed to be?"

"'Fake it till you make it?'"

Liv didn't debate the concept; in fact Faye felt she was quite familiar with it.

"I just badly need to break out of this funk," Faye continued. "I was hoping he could help with that. I guess I picked a bad spot." She was going to need a cattle prod to make the horse racing references stop.

"Maybe you're supposed to go forward instead of backward."

Because you're suddenly an expert on life? Faye bit the words back before they made it out. She didn't want advice from a friend who hadn't even kissed a guy before – oh, wait, like a year before Faye had learned about it? "I have to ask you something, then. Not to rehash old news, but I'd like to understand. That New Year's Eve, in Florida, when you guys kissed, why didn't you tell me?" If she'd shared that little event, maybe Faye would have spared herself the whole Nate Miller fiasco.

"Do you remember where my head was then, Faye? How screwed I was? I told you nothing happened, because it didn't count. I thought he was just feeling sorry for me. And sorry for himself. Trust me, even if I'd known then what I know now, it would not have been a good time to start something between us."

"I should probably agree with that. Like throwing myself at Will was a reasonable thing to do. Even though I'm still disappointed with how that ended. A sensational non-event." Faye shook her head slightly, then zeroed in on Liv, determined to play her part in this new friendship dynamic. "But your evening was not." The corners of her lips curled up, if only because she forced them.

Liv's eyes swept to hers, then back to her mug. "It's too weird to talk about that with you, Faye. I feel too bad about it."

"This feeling bad has to go out with my feeling sorry for myself. All that ends right here, okay? Tell me you're happy. You get it now, right? You're excited about what comes next, if a little terrified?"

LINDA SHANTZ

"What comes next is I'm taking Chique to Fort Erie to train until the Prince of Wales."

"You're what?" Faye snapped. "Why the hell would you do that?"

"Because it's the right thing to do for the filly? To give her the best shot at success?"

The Queen's Plate-winning filly was, as Nate liked to call her, a bit of a wild child. She tended to be nervous and quirky. So, from that point of view, giving her plenty of time to get used to her surroundings, instead of shipping in on race day, made sense. But that would put almost two hours between Liv and Nate. Not such a good thing for a budding relationship. But this was, Faye had to keep reminding herself, Liv, the spooky, green, filly. It would give her time to process, and the ability to focus on what still mattered most in her world – Chique.

"Speaking of moving forward, that's not going to do it. Have you told Nate about this plan?"

"Of course."

"And he's okay with it?"

Faye thought she was going to say, *What choice does he have?* And it made Faye feel just a little sorry for the guy. He had his work cut out for him with this one. But he'd ride it out. He'd ridden out worse.

More horse references. Did they have a cattle prod at the farm? Her parents had kept a few Limousins for a while.

"He'll come down to work her," Liv said, like that answered the question. "It's only three weeks," she added, frowning when Faye kept silent. "And just because something has started between us, doesn't mean I'm going to let it get in the way of my job. I'm not going to change who I am."

"Oh, you don't need to explain. You forget I'm not new around here." Faye had been born into that kind of logic. Her mother had come to accept it. Faye wasn't sure she ever would.

40

"But you have to stop avoiding my questions. You are happy, right?"

The look on Liv's face managed to both tug at her heart and frustrate her. It was soft, except for a little wrinkle of tension between her eyes, the upward turn of her lips faint and uncertain.

"It's still so new. I've gone twenty-six years without these kinds of feelings. I can explain it away however I like – like it's just the chemicals in my brain, but I can't control them. And yeah, that's scary."

"Only you would try and dismiss love as science."

The soft disappeared, Liv's lips pressing into a line, her eyes defaulting to a more familiar skepticism. "It's a little too soon to be using labels like that."

Faye laughed and wrapped up the rest of her lunch for later. "Whatever you say, sweetie." She reached for her half of the butter tart. "Just give it a chance, okay?"

"You too."

"Which means?"

"Maybe don't go falling back into old patterns quite yet."

"Why not? It was a winning formula, before Nate. It's hard to mess with that."

Liv scowled at her. Easy for her to say, wasn't it? Old habits died hard, especially when the one time you deviated from them it ended up a disaster.

The lingering taste of the tart made everything right with the world for a delicious moment, and Faye eyed the other half. "When do you leave?"

Liv scooped it up possessively and took a bite. "She'll ship down tomorrow. I'll see how she feels Wednesday morning, and maybe take her for a jog and let her see the sights." She sipped her coffee, then finished the butter tart. "Are you sure we're all right?"

"We're fine."

They left their dishes on Lucy's counter, Lucy herself nowhere in sight, and slipped out, standing in the middle of the parking lot. Faye's eyes wandered, the *For Lease* sign on the marquee out front catching her eye.

She turned back to Liv. "I got a bit of bad news today. McIntoshes are getting out of the industry."

Liv frowned. "I'd heard rumours, but hoped they were just that. It sucks, on so many levels."

"My biggest client. I did everything for them. Books, their website, social media." Faye sighed. "I might have to find a job if no one comes along to fill that void."

"I'm sorry, Faye. I'll keep my ears open if I hear of anyone looking."

"Thanks, sweetie." Faye gave her a hug in parting. It had been a good thing, this. No small thing, either.

"Oh!" Liv's eyes popped wide. "I almost forgot. I have your hat." She grinned.

"Thank goodness," Faye said, following Liv to her car. She'd take all the good news she could get right now.

Dean hunched behind the wheel of the Corolla, angles folded awkwardly, but it was a more economical choice for a trip into the city than his big truck. Faye had offered to drive, but in the end they'd agreed to split it – she'd drive home, because he'd be half asleep by then, long past his usual bedtime.

"We'll be okay, Faye. Maybe we can beat Liv's filly in the Prince of Wales. She's not invincible. But if I have to, I'll sell a piece of Ride The Wave."

She'd told him about MacIntoshes. His words pained Faye, knowing how much he was in love with that colt. And if Faye

42

could have feelings for a horse, it would be for Ride The Wave. The two-year-old, as yet unraced, was one of the last foals sired by Catch The Joy, the horse their father had won the Canadian Triple Crown with. She was used to Dean taking on partners for the homebreds to keep things afloat, but selling a piece of that colt would feel like selling a slice of their hearts.

"Don't do it yet. You know he'll be worth more once he runs." Or not, but she had to at least pretend to have the same faith in the colt's potential that Dean did.

They were waved away from the lots nearest the concert venue, already packed, and parked on the other side of Lakeshore Boulevard, in the Canadian National Exhibition grounds. In another month the CNE would be its own kind of mayhem, but for now it was a concrete ghost town, so there was plenty of room.

A warm breeze blew off the lake, seagulls dive-bombing to snatch up bits of food discarded by the gentle flow of people drifting into the Amphitheatre. Faye was attached to Dean's elbow, mostly because she couldn't remember where their seats were, and he held the tickets. It didn't hurt to have him as a shield, either, to deflect the occasional cluster of rowdiness in the midst of the otherwise well-behaved crowd.

"Faye!"

There was something familiar about the voice that reached her over the drone of voices around them. She scanned, staying tight to Dean. A wave caught her eye. Oh, no way. It was Nate's friend. She looked around him nervously. Nate had given her the tickets for her birthday back in March – a couple of weeks before they'd split up – but it wasn't a stretch to think he'd still want to come, and would be with Will. And just because she didn't see him didn't mean he wasn't here, somewhere.

Dean gave her a strange look when she stopped in her

tracks. Running didn't seem to be an option at the moment, so might as well face it.

"Oh, hi Will," she said, unenthusiastically, though the sight of him sent an involuntary shiver through her that seemed to ignite her nerve endings, leaving her with an embarrassing glow, that stupid humming sound starting up. So random to run into him down here, and she wondered fleetingly if the Dave Matthews Band qualified as "the poppy side of alternative." Then a blonde peeked around him – a relief, really because it made a Nate ambush seem less likely – except she was taller than Faye, and younger, too, a high ponytail swinging across her elegant neck. *So I was both too old and not blonde.* Whatever. Faye took a cleansing breath, and her heart rate tempered. One step closer to being the foxy spinster, hanging on the arm of her bachelor brother.

She dislodged one hand and swept it in front of Dean's torso, maybe a little too dramatically.

"This is Dean," she said, and left out the part about him being her sibling. Will didn't need to know that. Faye and Dean looked different enough that the fact they were closely related wouldn't be immediately apparent.

The men shook hands, and Faye hoped she didn't imagine Will's sudden stiffness. He and Dean were about the same height, both dark-haired, lanky, and handsome. If Will didn't already know the last guy she'd dated was short and blonde, he might be thinking this Dean character was her type, so Will could be, too, making him – hopefully? – a little bit jealous. Why was she bothering to think about it? He was here with the blonde.

Will introduced her as Monique, with no more detail than Faye had provided about her own companion. In order to pre-empt the possibility of that changing, Faye inconspicuously dug her nails into Dean's arm. Dean flinched, his head flipping down to her. Okay, not so inconspicuous. She'd left red marks on his skin.

She smiled up at him sweetly. "We'd better go find our seats. Nice to meet you, Monique!" *Not really!* "Enjoy the show!" She almost shoulder-checked Dean to catapult him into motion.

"What's got you all in a kerfuffle?" he asked, trying to rub his arm. "Who was that?"

"If you hadn't bolted the other night, you'd know. That's Nate's friend, from the band."

"So what's with the animosity? He seems like a nice guy."

"He's the one who drove me home."

"Which seems like a nice thing to do."

"Yep. He's an upstanding citizen. Forget it." Not that Dean didn't end up hearing her stories about men – he was remarkably unperturbed about her bringing them into her home, more like a platonic friend than a big brother – but she'd had enough reminders of her most recent failure to snare that particular one. "Where are the tickets? Give me mine."

Dean separated the laser printouts she'd entrusted to him for safekeeping and Faye plucked one from his fingers.

"I'll meet you there. I'm getting a drink. You want something?"

Dean shook his head, and Faye skulked off, her eyes constantly on the lookout for Will and his blonde. She really didn't need to run into them again. What she did need was to find a willing participant in her plan and clear her bad juju. She tapped a text to Em as she stood in line at the concession. *Please tell me I didn't make too much of a fool of myself the other night.*

Em: You didn't make too much of a fool of yourself the other night. Did Liv give you your hat? What happened with Will?

Faye: Will was a disgustingly perfect gentleman. Also, really, really not into me.

Em: Looked pretty interested to me.

Faye: Well, Dean and I are at the DMB concert, and guess who we ran into, complete with tall blonde? So, I think not.

Em: Sorry.

Faye: We need to go to the races this weekend. I'm clocking prospects. You in?

Em: (laughing emoji) Sounds like fun. Keep me posted.

She made it to the front of the line and ordered her over-priced beer. She and vodka coolers did not get along. Faye handed the plastic cup to Dean as she climbed over the back of her seat and settled into the chair. He took a sip before handing it back.

"Anyone running this weekend?" she asked.

"I'm entering She Brews for Saturday. She should win."

Of course she should. It wasn't often Dean thought his horse wouldn't win, regardless of how realistic it might or might not be. He got points for positive thinking. She made a mental note to ask Liv if the maiden filly actually had a shot. She didn't ask who was riding, guessing it was Nate, because he'd been on her the last time. She could handle him in that context better than any other. It would just be a pleasant surprise if he had another call, and it ended up being someone else.

By the time they were driving home, the buzz from the beer she'd had was a safely distant sensation, the music intoxicating enough to ease the shock of running into Will and his friend. Dean slept soundly in the passenger seat despite looking horribly uncomfortable.

He was a good sport, coming with her. Shawn had always been her go-to for concerts. Shawn was largely responsible for forming her taste in music, sparing her from adopting the pop or country so many of her high school classmates had loved.

These were the times she missed him most. Eleven and a half years, but let her hear Dave Matthews singing *Where Are You Going,* and it was almost as if he was there, singing along with her.

————————

Will hadn't seen her – them – again, but not for lack of searching. Not really surprising, at a venue that held about sixteen thousand people when it was sold out like it had been for a popular band like tonight. It had been so unexpected, a beacon in the midst of the nameless faces he'd taught himself to glaze over, living in a city this size. When he'd realized she was with a guy, yes, all right, he admitted it: it was a blow. Good for her, though. She'd obviously found someone. She didn't waste time. And, it solved the whole *Nate's ex* dilemma. Not that he did like her, or want to ask her out. Okay so he liked her, but did not want to ask her out. Or would not. Which now, obviously, he didn't need to worry about.

Ontario Place emptied out, the crowd still energized from the show, which had been shut down before a proper encore, like his band had been shut down at the Queen's Plate, only a little bit later. Noise ordinances. The new bane of concerts. Though being right on Lake Ontario, music playing at the Amphitheater could probably be heard all the way to St. Catharines.

Monique bumped him intentionally as they were swept towards the parking lot. "Who was that girl?"

Will didn't look at her, just kept walking. "My buddy's ex."

"Uh-huh. That's a problem."

"Why?"

"You're obviously into her."

"Why would you say that?" He didn't mean for it to come out like a growl, but it did.

"Because exactly that. You just snapped at me! And your head's been bobbing all over the place hoping you'll see her again."

"It is not. And I am not."

"You are such a liar. Does your buddy know?"

"I only just met her Sunday night. There's nothing to know." But, for some reason, when he'd seen Nate, he'd felt the need to test the waters. And received a wave of protest back. Not a tsunami or anything, but enough to remind him to back off. "Besides, you saw her. She was with someone."

"That was nothing."

"How can you be sure?"

"I can sense these things."

Will wondered if she was right, and if so, if Faye could sense those things too – if it would be just as obvious to her that he and Monique weren't together.

"She is really pretty. It's too bad. You should have a proper girlfriend, a nice guy like you."

It was slow getting out of the lot, cars inching out of spots and into lines that slowly flowed onto the Lakeshore. Monique turned up the radio, which was so permanently tuned into The Edge that the dial probably wouldn't have let her switch it to anything else if she'd tried. She didn't live far, and he pulled up in front of the house she shared with friends.

"Are you going to be at work tomorrow? You've been missing a lot of days lately."

Just two, but still, for the guy who was everyone's old reliable, it attracted curiosity. Maybe it was a sign of his dissatisfaction.

"Yeah. You need a ride?"

48

She shook her head. "Not this time. Thanks though! See you then."

He waited until she disappeared inside before he drove off. The radio station started playing *The Coldest Night of the Year* which left him with an inappropriate earworm on a perfect summer night. It must have been the *you're not even here* part wriggling things free from his unconscious mind. So, who was it his brain thought should be here?

Not Monique. She was quick to accompany him when he asked if she wanted to come along to shows, waving a free ticket. He didn't plan these things, just always grabbed two when they went on sale for something he wanted to see, figuring out later who his company would be. Who it was depended on his mood. Sometimes he went alone. He wasn't adverse to that, selling the extra ticket to scalpers, or gifting it to a starving student, because he knew what that was like. And truth be told, he didn't feel all that removed from it, even now.

Faye, then? Seeing her with that guy, thinking she'd be more inspired company than Monique. As much as Monique was cute and sweet and funny, anything that occurred between them outside of work had always been superficial, which he was pretty sure both of them had no complaints about. Monique had her sights set higher than the likes of Will. Will didn't really know where his own sights were set.

Which led to, the ghost of missed opportunities past? It was still stuck there, wedged firmly in whatever part of his brain processed rational thought, refusing to budge. Childhood memories weren't to be trusted, especially emotions that harkened back to those early teenage years when hormones started doing their thing. But he still kept her propped on a pedestal, comparing everyone he met to her and gauging their worthiness. Even if he'd never told her how he'd really felt about her. If he had, though, he wasn't sure it would have changed the outcome.

Maybe that's why he'd come to Toronto: more for the noise than the music. He'd grown up on the outskirts of Calgary, where the mountains were only ever an hour away, beautiful and deadly. On the way to them were safer expanses, grassy ranches that he'd loved even more than the tremendous rock faces...not quite still, still changing. All of it – all the space, and the calm – had turned upside down on him, like he'd become agoraphobic. Toronto was a place he could get lost, and hide from the memories that were embedded in every crack in the pavement, every favourite bar, every shadow of those momentous peaks. This was a place where no one knew him.

But the comfort was wearing off. What was the answer, though? The café near Nate niggled at him, but it was really just a fantasy. He couldn't leave his job in the city; couldn't afford to. So the idea of not only trying to pay for, but run, such a place, wasn't realistic.

When he'd finally wound down enough to crawl into bed, he still lay awake, all of a sudden hyper aware of the noise. He supposed Toronto did sleep, but not quietly.

CHAPTER FOUR

FAYE SCANNED names and weights in the program, but not because she was any kind of handicapper. At least, not of horses. She was looking for numbers, little superscripts to the pounds each horse had to carry, because they indicated an apprentice rider, her prey of choice.

Emilie sidled up next to her, eyes going first to the horses. Em might not be as hard-core as her older sister Liv when it came to them, and claimed she was determined to make her career outside of the industry, but she still galloped for her father's trainer on weekends, and whenever she wasn't otherwise occupied with working towards becoming a physiotherapist.

She Brews was in this race, a legitimate excuse for Faye to be at the track besides clocking bug boys, though she stayed safely outside the rail with the public rather than in there with Dean as she probably should've been. It was a perfect summer afternoon, the unbearable hot spell having mercifully moved on, that big storm on Plate Day taking away the humidity and leaving temperatures that were just right. It was the kind of weather Canadians dreamed of when they were complaining about the cold in January. Somehow that cold was quickly forgotten during heat waves like they'd suffered last week.

"So, who do you like, Em?" she said, alternating between the program and the vibrant hues before her. She'd always found the traditional outfits jockeys wore on the silly side – baggy nylon pants and stockings that came up to their knees, slipped into paper-thin patent boots with slipper soles. The silks were nice, though – at least when they were tastefully done – but the helmets they wore were a reminder of the insane danger of the job. Those helmets and the dense safety vests hidden beneath the flimsy colours always seemed inadequate defence against the possibility of life-altering – and life-ending – injury. Small humans dressed up like lawn ornaments and sent out to risk their necks.

"So I asked Nate if Will has a girlfriend," Em said casually.

Faye pursed her lips, and tried to sound disinterested as she responded. "And?"

"Not that he knows of."

"So who was the blonde?"

Em shrugged. "I couldn't ask that, could I, because that would have brought your name into it, and you wouldn't want that, right?"

Faye groaned, and curled the edge of the program between her fingers. "None of it matters. We're here to scout new candidates. Will had his shot, and it was a hard no."

"Don't write him off yet. It might've just been that he and Nate are old friends, so he has to be careful."

"Did Nate say that to you? Because if he did, you need to tell him he doesn't get a say. He can stay the hell out of my life."

"Except, it does affect his life, if it involves Will. But I didn't bring your name into it, remember?"

"Stop making so much sense," Faye grumbled.

Faye doesn't like to get attached. That was her reputation. Was Nate afraid she'd compromise his friend, or something? Because he surely didn't think Faye was going to let herself fall for someone again, and be around enough to mess up his precious little bromance. He should know better than that. "How good a friend can Will be, anyway? I'd never heard of him."

"Because how much did Nate talk about Calgary with you?"

Faye rolled her eyes and gave her a gentle shove. "Didn't I just tell you to stop that?"

It was true, though, because the original intent of her getting together with Nate had been the same as every other time she'd hunted down a man – something he was supposed to be a willing party to. That had been the deal. They were day-to-day, living in the moment, until it became obvious they should be beyond that. By then they'd gotten way too good at not sharing the important stuff to start.

It had been foolish of her to think she could have a sustainable relationship. She'd always been the one to break hearts instead of waiting to have her heart be broken. Until Nate had made her think perhaps it was time to evolve. She hadn't figured Liv into the equation, though. That had come out of nowhere. Had it, though? Had she just refused to see it? There was probably a lot about Liv she failed to see.

And here she was, back to seeking out a non-relationship. So much for evolution. Well, evolution happened over millions of years, right? *Take it a little easy on yourself.*

She studied the riders for likely candidates. A few of them, of course, were in the lines of her past performance, journeymen now. It was this time last year that she'd connected with Nate. No, she definitely would not let something like that happen again. She would be on alert at every turn to nip any possibility in the bud.

The paddock judge's *riders up* call rose over the hum of conversation, interrupting the crowd's collective watchfulness. Groups inside the walking ring broke up as the horses formed a line with their grooms, and trainers lifted feather-light bodies onto bunched muscle. Even Faye couldn't watch impassively; it sent a little shiver through her each time, anticipation and apprehension all bundled together.

Nate was on She Brews as Faye had expected, and stuck his tongue out as they went by before firing off one of his dazzling smiles.

"This looks like trouble," he said.

Faye kept her face neutral and said, "Good luck," to keep herself from snarkier retorts, because Dean owned all of this filly, so Northwest would get the full sixty percent winner's share – less Nate's portion, and the stake money Dean would allocate to his crew for their hard work. Nate's mounts always went off at shorter odds than they might have with a less notable rider, but that wasn't always an indication of the kind of chance the runner had. So Faye turned to Em, who was actually quite a shrewd handicapper.

"Are we getting our picture taken today?"

"I think she has a decent shot, but Extra Blonde has run second, like, five times in a row, and Watanabe needs just one more win to go to lose his ten pound bug, so he's extra hungry right now."

Literally.

Faye had noticed Jiro Watanabe's name in the program, thanks to that number ten superscript, and eyeballed him from a distance, pinning him as a definite possibility for the *Faye Gets Her Groove Back* project. He was a recent import from Japan. Maybe she could learn a new language. She remotely heard Em cooing *she's pretty* as Extra Blonde danced past, and had her own appreciative thoughts about the rider.

Very cute. Yes, he would do nicely.

She had to play along as a tradeoff for Em's company, following as the horses left the walking ring on the way to the track. They took the escalator to the second floor, meeting Dean at the seats outside. He was in trainer mode, binoculars locked on She Brews instead of acknowledging their arrival.

The Northwest silks were the original ones, her father's simple design, Faye finding them easily. They could use an upgrade – old school checkers, a red and white version of the famous Meadow Stables colours Secretariat had carried – but Dean would never change. He'd feel it was dishonouring their father, even though their father and Dean hadn't exactly got along.

She let herself admire Nate, despite their history, his posture perfect without tension, his easy-going manner coming through even from this distance as he chatted with the pony rider. Then Faye moved on – because she was moving on – to peruse Jiro Watanabe. Even though Faye had never taken up riding, as much as her father had tried to inflict ponies upon her as a child, it was easy to see Jiro was comfortable on a horse. Her admiration effortlessly shifted from Nate to him as Extra Blonde's escort initiated an easy gallop around the clubhouse turn.

Her attention faded as the horses got farther away, and she scanned the apron below them instead, searching it for interesting people.

"Em – who's that with the baby?"

Emilie pulled her binoculars a few inches away from her eyes, and followed Faye's gaze. "You're not up on the gossip? Where have you been? That's Pat Simon's girlfriend."

"And baby?"

"Yep. She's one of MacIntosh's grooms."

"What happened to the wife?"

"I guess he fell madly for the groom last fall. I heard they were together all last winter in Florida. Though obviously the baby was in progress by then." Em gave her a sly grin.

"You're right, where have I been?"

Pat Simon. He'd been top apprentice what, five years ago? He'd been fun, then married his next love interest. And here he already had a failed marriage and baby with a new girlfriend, while she was still chasing bug riders. It was like he'd lived several different lifetimes, while she'd been looping through the same one. Same old, same old. Not that she wanted something else. Did she?

The horses were in the gate now, just in time to distract her from that depressing train of thought.

She Brews broke on top, keeping her head in front of Extra Blonde as the field raced along the backstretch. *You're helping Dean with the farm.* That's important.

They zipped around the turn, and Extra Blonde pushed her nose in front at the quarter pole. *Dean needs you. He came back to take over Dad's horses and abandoned a masters to do it, so he could take care of you. You owe him. And you owe Mom and Dad, to maintain their legacy. Besides, you were supposed to be in that car.*

The two fillies – and riders – were locked in a battle down the stretch. Faye leapt to her feet at the same time as Dean and Em, and started screaming.

"Come on Brew!" *Come on, Nate. Dean needs to win this one.*

That kid Watanabe was pushing insistently, the left-handed rhythm of his stick measured, coming every third stride. Extra Blonde was pouring out a huge effort, like she was done being a bridesmaid. It was just a nose at the wire, but that's all she needed to deny Nate and She Brews.

"Well. He can ride." Faye watched the two fillies gallop out, still side by side, Nate reaching over to congratulate Jiro. His fifth winner. Ten pound bug no more.

"Told you he was hungry," Em quipped.

"I'm sure that was delicious." Faye was kind of hungry too.

Her plan of attack came so easily it was laughable. She followed Dean down to the apron, Emilie behind her. "Maybe if you get him on She Brews next time, that five pounds will make the difference."

Dean glanced over his shoulder. "You're suggesting I fire Nate?"

"Not because it was his fault. It's just a business decision. He'll understand."

And she would have an innocent excuse to meet Jiro Watanabe.

They weren't all that busy tonight, which was a good thing, because Will's head wasn't in the game. He kept getting stuck on seeing Faye with that guy, a bruise that should have faded by now. So he didn't want to take her out, but apparently he didn't want anyone else to take her out either. Like he had any right to feel that way. They'd seemed very comfortable with each other, Faye and that guy. He could ask Nate who it was. Except that would piss Nate off, because he'd think Will wanted to take her out. When he didn't.

Busy or not, the chef, Gerry, was in a mood, and Will was supposed to be the buffer between Gerry and the staff. He had to get his mind back where it belonged.

In the blink of an eye, the guy could go from inappropriately teasing the female servers to tearing them apart for the slightest transgression. For some unknown reason though, the women put up with it. Worse, they seemed to like it. And Gerry rotated through them after hours like the specials on his menu.

The chef's behaviour often meant Will was the shoulder some very pretty women cried on; shoulder being a figure of speech, of course. He'd been the beneficiary of Gerry's castoffs on more than one occasion, Monique being one of them. They were always temporary, which was probably just as well. *Don't play where you work.* Nate had dipped his toe in that pool, with his new relationship. The waters were perilous, but it was hard not to fall in when it was your most viable option.

Faye popped into his head again, like she stood for something important, something he was supposed to figure out; the answer to getting off this merry-go-round. It wasn't a job he'd felt worth sharing with her. She hadn't told him what she did for a living either, so they were even.

Maybe she didn't have to work. She lived on a farm in King City, after all. The land up there was worth a ton. The farmhouse hadn't been fancy from the outside, but her family owned racehorses. Racehorses – even pieces of them – cost a lot of money, he knew that much. Will couldn't even afford a cat, with the cost of small animal vet medicine these days. Goldfish might not even work with his budget right now. So why was he building café castles in the air?

Tonight, Brenda was having a bad time. One of her tables had a real jerk of a guest, and she never did well with that sort of thing. She was one of the newer servers, her bright face and cheery, chatty personality usually making up for her lack of experience, but not with this guy. The more her anxiety escalated, the more mistakes she made, and Gerry was going to blow soon. When that happened, they were all going to pay.

The answer? Dessert was Will's favourite thing. Because, really, what couldn't be solved with sugar?

"Here, take them this," he said, handing her slices of cheesecake and carrying out complimentary cappuccinos.

Brenda breezed back into the kitchen. "You saved me again." Her sweet face was starting to look a more normal colour than the extremes he'd seen in the last half hour – from flushed to pale and back again.

"All part of the job description," he responded.

"He told me I wasn't pretty enough to be that bad at my job." She was controlling the quiver in her voice, and Will would bet the time she'd come back on the verge of tears had been when the asshole had said it.

"Never mind him. I'm sorry we wasted that amazing cheesecake on him."

She smiled. "I hope you saved some for me, because I'm going to need a piece."

She was more than pretty, really, so the guy had to have been blind. She'd take dessert over alcohol to console herself, which wasn't a terrible thing. Faye Taylor, though...liked both, Will recalled.

At the end of the night, disaster averted, Gerry was chatting Brenda up. Will sat at the bar and watched her leave with him.

"Why do you all go for that?" he asked Monique, who was trying to hide the fact that she was disappointed Gerry had a new flavour of the week. Last week, it had been her.

She slid her long lashes sideways, and slapped a couple of shot glasses down. "It's called charisma, Will. It covers up a lot of stuff that really should revolt us."

This was such a toxic place. But he was stuck here, for now. Because Gerry was one of the top chefs in the city, and if Will could put up with him just a little longer, gleaning what knowledge he could, and leave on good enough terms to get a decent reference, he could find a job – out of the city somewhere. Or make the big move, and open his own place. The number for that spot for rent in King City was behind a magnet on his fridge. Maybe he could work on the farm Nate lived on. Will didn't know anything about horses, but he could shovel shit and drive a tractor. They needed guys like that, didn't they? Even if he didn't swing an apartment like Nate had, it had to be cheaper to rent something out there than it was in the city.

He tossed back the tequila Monique had served him up. He'd let Brenda have the last slice of cheesecake. His loft wasn't that far; he could walk home.

He should have slept like a log, after the tension and the tequila, but he only tossed and turned, and wondered how his escape east had become just a different kind of prison.

CHAPTER FIVE

SO MUCH HAY. A good thing for the farm, but horribly bad news for Faye. Her arms and back still ached from last night, and there were still three more wagons to be unloaded and stacked in the barn. It had to be done today, because there was a sixty percent chance of rain in the forecast. At least the way Dean was going on about the yield this year, they probably wouldn't have to supplement their supply with outside sources.

Haying was one of the best justifications for keeping the male of the species around – besides sex, of course. Manual labour. Unlike Liv's anything-you-can-do-I-can-do-better attitude, Faye was more than willing to concede men were stronger, and it was important to take advantage of that fact. At times like this, she needed more than a bug boy; she needed the entire jock's colony at Woodbine.

In the absence of finding a magical genie to conjure that up for her, Faye had shamelessly begged a favour, and Emilie had promised to steal some help from Triple Stripe. With enough people, it would go quickly, so she was hoping Em would bring a busload. That way Faye's job could be serving up pop and Gatorade for her hot, sweaty saviours. Unfortunately all the workers at Triple Stripe right now were young and female – other than the older guy who'd taken on the farm and stallion manager position, and Em wouldn't try to recruit him. So, no eye candy for Faye, though any guy who had ever helped stack hay knew better than to do it bare-chested like in some Facebook meme. Still, Faye had a pretty good imagination.

The fridge was full of cold drinks and there were stacks of ice cube trays in the freezer. She'd done the groceries this week, stocking up on all manner of snacks, from healthy to not and in-between. Apples and oranges, granola and protein bars, various kinds of chips and dips. Hot dogs and burgers to grill after, a thank-you bonus barbeque on top of the $20 an hour – cash – Dean would dole out.

Her phone pinged with a text from Emilie. *On our way.*

Thank heaven Em was going to come through. Maybe the farm girls had boyfriends who would see tossing hay bales around as the great workout it was, if you were into that sort of thing.

She dumped ice in the cooler and jammed it full with bottles of water and Gatorade, then hoisted it to her thighs, using her butt to push open the screen door.

"Perfect timing," she said as Dean tromped up the steps to the deck. "Drop your tailgate so we can drive this to the barn?"

Dean went one step better and relieved her of the weight, so Faye scooted around him and ran to the truck, just as a couple of cars pulled up. One of them she knew far too well. She threw her weight behind the tailgate to close it, then leaned back against the bumper, arms crossed.

"Well...this is a surprise. Em, you've outdone yourself."

Em climbed out of her red Honda, grinning. Yes, there were three girls from the farm, but she'd also recruited Nate...

and, out the passenger side of that familiar, decrepit, Mustang, Will.

"What did you have to promise to get these two to come, Em? I will have to take a pic for Liv, because there is, apparently, no end to the niceness of Nate Miller."

"Now, don't be snide," Em said.

"Beggars can't be choosers." Nate threw Faye a crooked grin, and she gave him a withering look in return.

She forced herself to be civil. "I'm sorry if that sounded ungrateful." Her eyes fell on Will, who was even dressed appropriately. She wasn't going to complain about the way his jeans fit, or how his t-shirt fell from those shoulders of his. There would be eye candy after all. "It's nice to see you again, Will. You've met Dean...my brother," she said slyly.

Will's lips curved slowly into a smile, his eyes locking onto hers for a moment before he nodded and pulled them away to send a far less sexy expression to Dean. "Hey, Dean."

"Nate must be a really special kind of friend, to introduce you to the horrors of haying," Faye said, letting her gaze wander over Will again.

"Will's an old pro," Nate said. "I sat on my first pony at his grandfather's ranch. We were the child labour there for a lot of summers."

Will and Nate grinned at each other, and Faye recrossed her arms. Grandfather? So they'd grown up together. She wanted to sit both of them down and tear them apart with her questions, but it was too late to do that with Nate, and too soon to do it to Will.

"Could I maybe talk you both into taking your shirts off for the photo?" she tried instead, sweeping her phone from her back pocket.

"Liv would know that was fake." Nate smirked.

"True. But that doesn't mean she won't still appreciate it.

No? Fine," she huffed when they refused to comply, and settled for a far less entertaining image.

The three girls behind Emilie silently watched Nate and Will with sparkly eyes, looking as if they were on the verge of giggling. Faye stopped herself from barking at them that they'd better keep their minds on the work, because a) they weren't her employees, and b) she still might be slugging bales alongside them, which would require her to follow the same order. It would be very easy to stand back and watch two gorgeous, muscly men at work.

Emilie slipped on her gloves, slapping her hands together. "Let's get this party started."

Dean tossed Faye his truck keys. "You want to drive it back? Conserve your energy." Even Dean was getting into the teasing. "Faye doesn't like to perspire."

"He's allowed to say that. I'm not." Nate's grin had lost its effect on her forever ago, and now Faye just wanted to smack him.

She flicked her hair over her shoulder and pulled it into a ponytail as she walked to the cab. She heard the tailgate come back down, and Nate and Will hopped up to sit on it. *Oh, brave, brave boys.* She resisted the urge to accelerate over potholes as she drove back to the barn, passing Em and her farm girls. It wouldn't be nice to break Liv's boyfriend. And other than her wounded pride from Plate night, she had nothing against Will. Unfortunately. She'd like to stretch against him, from lips to toes. The truck lurched, bouncing her up off the seat, Nate's curses reaching her ears as she heard cooler and men scrambling in the back. She glanced sheepishly in the rear view mirror.

"Sorry!" she called through the window in the back of the cab. It didn't look like either of them were any worse for her distracted driving.

The first wagon was already backed up to the hay barn, and Faye pulled in adjacent to it. She put the truck in park and sighed, tugging on her gloves, feeling the shift of weight on the tailgate as the guys hopped off. Nate gave her a sideways look, clearly thinking the rough trip was intentional. Will just grinned, like he might be enjoying their little squabble.

Dean began snagging bales with a hay hook, throwing them off the wagon until there was room for him to climb on. The minions set to work. Em grabbed the first bale; the guys, of course, took one in each hand because they had to be all manly and toss around as much testosterone as possible. Somehow they were back for more before Faye had managed to grab even one. Everyone was faster than she was. She dodged a wild throw off the wagon from Dean, and rammed right into Will's – quite solid – chest, his hands coming up to catch her by the arms.

"No offence, Faye, but you're kind of just getting in the way." Which, coming from Nate, was completely offensive.

Like, in the way of getting the job done, or in the way of your bromance?

She dragged the back of her hand over her brow, already dusty and sweaty without having really done anything, and stared him down as he stared back, lifting the corner of his shirt to wipe something out of his eye.

Will's hands were still on her shoulders. "There are plenty of us here. Why don't you grab the cooler?"

Faye twisted out of his grasp, pulling off a glove and brushing hay dust, and his touch, from her arm. "You just can't help coming to my rescue, can you?"

He looked back at her like he was doing a full appraisal. Was she flirting, or was she being snappish? She wasn't sure herself. She hated stacking hay, could barely lift the damn things, and half an hour ago would have jumped on getting out of it, but damsel in distress was not naturally in her repertoire. She certainly didn't appreciate being dismissed.

Dean hadn't stopped unloading the wagon, and Em and the farm girls cleared the accumulation. Nate held up a hand to keep Will from grabbing the next two, looking happy to escape.

"Seriously," Will said. "I'm pretty sure you're not getting paid to be here, like these guys are."

"Nate better not be getting paid for this," she grumbled. He owed her in more ways than she could count, in her not-so-humble opinion. *Fine.* She went back to the truck and lifted the cooler out, setting it nearby. They almost had the wagon empty, and everyone would be ready for a water break while Dean moved it out of the way and parked a new one.

She decided she couldn't stand there and watch them toil, so she went back to the house and cleaned, to feel like she was doing something almost equally abhorrent, but necessary. Emilie texted her when they were done, and she wandered back with Gus, finding the group of them draining bottles and cans and looking tired and grimy, but somehow still smiling.

Dean tossed his empty water bottle into the open cooler. "I'm going for a dip in the pond."

"Pond? How did I not know you have a pond?" Nate asked.

Oh, there is so much you don't know, and so much I don't know, because we never asked. But she kept those thoughts to herself.

"Wait up Dean," Nate called as her brother marched away, Will grinning and following. Em and the farm girls trailed, more out of curiosity than intent to join them, Faye guessed, because that was definitely what motivated her.

And there was her photo op. She whipped out her phone, and swiped it to video. Dean was already in, clothes dumped in a heap on the ground, Gus launching after him, like the self-respecting water dog he was. Gus loved a good pool party. The other two boys stripped down to their skivvies – such a disappointment they stopped there, but maybe a little modesty was appropriate in the company of the farm girls. They both leapt in like a couple of crazy adolescents. Faye shuddered at the thought of that water, but it was amusing nonetheless.

"C'mon Faye."

That was Will, taunting her. *Dream on, buddy.* She hadn't gone swimming in the pond since she was fourteen, that last summer, before the accident. It was fine, then. She and Shawn, laughing and tossing a ball around, or floating on old tractor inner tubes. Memories of her lost innocence, back when boys had only been friends or brothers. At her age, now, it wasn't fitting. She was too old for that. She didn't exactly consider herself demure, and let's face it, Nate had seen her naked, but Will was a stranger.

"I'll pass thanks. I was working inside in the air conditioning while you all got dirty and sweaty. I'll just watch." That prospect turned her on, just a little. Okay, a lot.

She kept videoing, then quickly edited it, and sent a clip off to Liv. *You're missing the fun.*

The reply came back quickly. Late afternoon, Liv had probably just finished feeding Chique, and had nothing better to do than check her phone. Her response was brief.

Damn. There was an ROTFL emoji attached.

Will climbed out, tilting his head like he had water in his ear. He walked over to Faye, and shook his wet hair on her like a dog. She jumped back, protecting her phone.

"I should go get you boys some towels," she said, taking in the way the water made his pale skin glisten. He needed to spend more time in the sun. Farm work would look good on him.

He grinned, then snatched the phone, tossed it at Em, and scooped Faye up.

"Hey! Put me down!"

Will just chuckled, heading for the water.

"Oh, no way. Don't you dare."

He wasn't stopping, even though she tried to twist out of his hold, and grab at his hair. It was too damn short. She kicked hard enough with her feet to send flying the sandals she'd slipped on at the house, but that was about it. Will waded in, then tossed her, fully dressed, into the water.

Her head went under, and she kicked herself to the surface, coming up sputtering. "You bastard!"

All of them were laughing at her now, Will looking pretty proud of his childishness. She shook her head, clawing her hair away from her face, and started treading water – keeping her knees high, which made her beating legs less effective at keeping her buoyant. The pond wasn't deep, but the silty, reedy bottom creeped her out. Things lurked down there. Things she didn't want to think about.

She scissored her legs, and with a few crawl strokes made it to the shore, shuddering at what she felt between her toes as she clambered out, dripping. Now she really wished she had some towels handy.

"Oh, you're kidding me," she said, scowling as Em waved her phone. Of course she'd captured the whole scene. "If that goes beyond Liv, you are so dead, my dear friend."

Em's smile was full of mischief. "You know Liv. She's discreet."

Some things one could count on in this life.

Em relinquished the phone, and there was already a response to a text Em had sent to Liv – extensive video evidence included – and added Faye on.

Liv: *I am so missing out.*

Faye texted back. *You are. See, this is what you get for going on a retreat to Fort Erie with a horse. And like I said to your sister, if that video ends up anywhere outside our circle, they won't find your bodies.*

Liv: *It won't be me.*

Faye glanced over to Em. It wouldn't be her, either. She texted Liv back. *Those boys can't be trusted, though.*

Liv: *Em didn't share it with them, did she?*

Faye: *I don't think so, but Nate's powers of persuasion are dangerous, as you know.*

Liv: *True.*

Faye felt Liv's coy smile in that single word, and it made her smile too as she pushed back a sodden dread of hair. The boys were clambering out now – one soaking wet Golden Retriever included – and for what Will had put her through, Faye figured she'd earned the right to freely check him out. He didn't have Nate's zero body fat, finely-tuned physique, but, well, she wouldn't kick him out of her bed. If she could just get him in it.

Shower. She really needed a shower. She didn't know Will well enough to invite him to join her, did she? She'd have to let her imagination run with the idea.

"Everybody back to the house. I've got a ton of food. Dean, you can get the barbeque started up."

She fully intended to have that shower to wash off the pond slime first, and left them to fend for themselves. Afterward she felt human again, piling her damp hair on top of her head, and she skipped downstairs in shorts and a tank top.

Bursting onto the deck with a salad in each hand, she felt Will's eyes land on her, drawing her own. He looked a little goofy with his hair sticking up in a couple of places, wet splotches on his t-shirt because he hadn't been completely dry when he'd pulled it back on, but that gaze was totally grown-up. A bit too much for this farm family gathering, if she was reading it right. The same humming she'd felt the night of the

Plate vibrated through her, from her toes right through to her ears. But there was no champagne here, no music, so she couldn't blame either of those things.

She pivoted abruptly on her toes, and set the salads on the table. Dean had the grill fired up, and he'd passed around beers to the boys. Em and the farm girls had glasses of lemonade. Faye avoided Will, recalibrating, and poured a glass of lemonade for herself. Sipped, and sighed.

This is how farm work should be done. It made her a little homesick for her childhood.

Will's shoulders ached; his arms, too. But it was a good ache, a satisfying ache, the kind born of old-fashioned physical labour. As a kid working on his grandfather's farm, he'd cursed haying season, but yesterday afternoon reset the memory, making him miss that kind of honest work, the camaraderie of sharing it. Those few hours had been as good as a vacation – and a trip to the gym. Funny that Nate's escape was to come to the city, and Will was being drawn back to the country. Was it just the country?

The whole experience might have been made all the more enjoyable due to his discovery that the guy he'd met at the concert was Faye's brother. That new knowledge had fed his actions, imbued him with a long-repressed feeling of being care-free and reckless. He might have taken it a bit too far, tossing Faye into the pond, going by the way she'd avoided him after that. But all of it had been about more than reliving his youth. He hadn't had that much fun in forever. It had made his day-to-day a bit more bearable; refreshed his sanity.

Which he was going to need for lunch. He'd taken another day off for this. Such a waste – if he was going to miss work, he'd much rather it be for more farm work – but it couldn't be avoided.

His father was late, of course. Refreshed sanity aside, the beer Will ordered while he waited was probably in everyone's best interest. It would take the edge off a meeting he wasn't convinced deserved his best behaviour, but he should probably strive for that anyway. One of them needed to be a grown-up.

By the time Will spotted dear old dad, he was striding over to the booth, his smile, no doubt intended to be warm, looking just as fake as ever. Will didn't stand to welcome him, even though his father hesitated, arms held out slightly from his sides, palms at forty-five degrees like he was hoping for a hug. Where he got that idea, Will had no idea.

The server scurried over, and Will gave her an affable smile, then looked at his dad. "What'll you have to drink?"

"What's on tap?" he asked, making the server ring off the list before settling on exactly the same thing Will was drinking. He turned back to Will. "Nice to see you, son."

The words grated on him. He was determined to be civil, though, and not say the things that came to mind. This meeting wasn't on the schedule. He saw Dad at Christmas when he went back to Calgary when they endured each other's company for a single meal out – in the name of being blood relations – and that was it. To what did he owe this honour? Flying across the country for lunch seemed suspect.

"It was a surprise to hear from you," Will responded, trying to keep out the irritation out of his voice. "What are you in town for?"

"I've..." His dad hesitated. "I've met someone. Here in Toronto."

The server came back with his father's beer just in time to distract Will from the immediate feeling of *here we go again*. As she set the glass down, Will caught her eye. "Uh, can you bring me another of these?"

She gave him a warm smile and nodded. "Sure thing."

"We met online," his father was saying, as if Will had asked. "I've been here a couple of times, and she's flown out to Calgary a couple of times."

So, great, how often had he been to town, and not once called Will? Just come for his trysts and slinked away. And why would he look so far afield for a new partner? Will finished the last of his drink and the server, who he'd decided was an angel, appeared with the other and removed the empty glass.

"We're getting married."

If Will had taken a sip from his pint, it would have been spewed all over the table. He set the glass back down and tried to loosen his jaw because his teeth were clenched so hard it hurt. "Does Mom know?"

"Not yet. Please don't say anything. I'll tell her, I promise."

When his parents had split, it had been the typical man having a mid-life crisis and leaving his wife for a sexy co-worker story. Which had seemed insane to Will, because his mom was the mom his buddies had to stop saying lewd things about, deflecting to *that's your mother? She looks amazing!* But Dad had gone all-in, abandoning them and moving to Vancouver with the woman. That first relationship had fizzled out after a couple of years, and Will had hoped his dad had got it out of his system. When he'd moved back to Calgary, he'd naïvely thought there was a chance his parents would get back together. Nope; his father had just started what had become a cycle of younger and younger girlfriends. Was it any wonder Will stayed single? If there was any possibility he'd inherited that tendency, he did not want to become that man.

Now, his mom was far too smart to take Dad back. But this?

"I'd like you to meet her, Will. Would that be okay?"

72

The edges of Will's eyes hurt, he was scrunching his brows together so hard. He sighed. "Yeah, sure."

His father half-rose in his chair, waving someone over. *She's here?* Unbelievable. Hiding at the bar, waiting to execute the surprise attack.

She was tall, slender, with shoulder-length strawberry-blonde hair. Almost a younger version of his mother, Will realized with horror. *How old is she?* He came way too close to blurting it out. Ratchet that cliché up a level, Dad. She looked like she was Will's age.

His father rose, and Will did too, his shock not enough to override basic manners. Dad kissed her and Will swore she purred.

"This is Ashley."

Her hand was small and damp – she was nervous about this, apparently. Her smile made Will think of an Invisalign commercial. Dad helped her with her chair, and the angel server magically appeared with a glass of white wine.

"So nice to finally meet you, Will."

Nice. Yeah, not the word he would use. He went along with the small talk, keeping his voice level, and resisted the temptation to check his watch or his phone. This would be a great time to get a call he had to take, any excuse to get out of here.

"Come to the wedding," his father said magnanimously, like Will would feel left out if he wasn't invited. "It's just going to be small. It's here in Toronto next month. Bring a friend."

Will's mouth opened, then closed.

"Are you seeing anyone?" Ashley asked.

Will shook his head. Maybe these two could give him dating advice.

"It would mean a lot if you'd come," his father said, seeming to realize Will was going to take some convincing.

"Please come," Ashley said, placing her hand over his father's. His father flipped his palm upwards and wrapped her fingers around hers. *Ugh.*

"I'll have to let you know. Friday nights are busy at work."

"Bring Nate. It'd be good to see him again. Each of you can bring a plus one, if you like."

Will wondered in passing which would be worse for Nate, coming to Will's father's wedding, or Nate seeing his own father. Beat-up vintage cars and fathers they liked to avoid: it was the little things that drew old friends together.

He prayed his father's brand of stupidity skipped a generation. His grandfather had been so solid and faithful, something lost in a bygone era, but that was what Will would hold out for. Not this.

CHAPTER SIX

IT TOOK a lot to get Faye up early enough to watch a horse train in the morning – like maybe Dean admitting he'd taken her advice. Jiro Watanabe was going to breeze She Brews, and his agent had told Dean to give them the call next time he entered the filly.

Not that she'd come in with Dean. Oh no. The work wasn't until eight, so there was no need.

The crew liked it when Faye came. She always stopped at Tim's to buy bad coffee and pasty doughnuts for them. Her travel mug contained something more palatable, and she couldn't eat before ten AM, so the doughnuts didn't tempt her.

She set them in Dean's office, because it was open season on the shed. Racetrackers could smell doughnuts as soon as they hit the east gate, but Dean's office was off limits. Hotwalkers and grooms – okay exercise riders, trainers – from other barns wouldn't go in uninvited. Leave them on a foot locker in the shed though, and word would travel. They'd be gone in no time, usually before Dean's own staff had had a chance to grab something themselves.

Faye hadn't seen Dean yet – he was probably out with a set – so she hid out in the office. His crew was okay, but it was too early for the kind of inane conversation that went on out there. The peace and quiet in here while she finished her coffee – brewed from a fresh roast from Java Works – would suit her just fine. What did people do before cell phones? She would have had to resort to reading one of the old *Daily Racing Forms* Dean had stacked on his desk. Instead she could use social media to avoid looking at the win photos that wallpapered the walls, many of them old enough her parents, and Shawn, were in them. Dean would never take them down, but they were an unwanted reminder for Faye. *She was here, and they were not.* No amount of therapy would erase that.

She jumped out of those thoughts when the door popped open, and scowled a little too readily at the intruder. "What are *you* doing here?"

Nate grinned, heading straight for the box of doughnuts. "Good morning to you, too. Why do you think I'm here?"

"To eat the doughnuts I brought for the crew. Get out of there!"

He ignored her reprimand and selected a glazed sour cream, breaking off a piece and popping it in his mouth. "I know what *you're* doing here."

He was tall for a rider – taller than her by an inch – so how did he not have to watch his weight? He'd been an apprentice when they'd been together, and he'd needed to be more careful then – but that designation had run out in the spring, and apparently the extra five pounds it afforded him meant doughnuts – no doubt in moderation – were a reasonable choice, on occasion. The guys in the room who had to sweat off pounds – and far worse practices than that – must hate him. Faye still wanted to hate him, and sometimes she still did.

Graduating to journeyman status hadn't slowed him down

at all in the local ranks. Still leading rider at Woodbine. Queen's Plate-winning jockey. A smooth transition. It was probably just as well she'd broken up with him. Journeymen didn't fit her M.O.

"So why do you think you know why I'm here?"

"Because I remember last year, you'd be here pretty much every time I worked a horse for Dean, and Nikki would tell me she hadn't seen you around that much since the last bug rider who'd caught your eye. It's a well-known fact you don't come to watch the horses go, Faye. And well, you're not here to see *me* now, are you?"

Faye heard the buzz of his phone, and was grateful when he unzipped a pocket to retrieve it instead of waiting for a response from her. Oh well. His words were true. Own it, girl.

The smile on his face made it pretty obvious the text was from Liv, and not something he felt the need to share with her. His finger swiped some more, his face returning to a more professional state of interest, and he tucked the phone back in his pocket.

"Let's go. Jiro's here. Maybe a leg up will be the start of your next great encounter." He smirked as he held the door open for her.

The morning was cool, the sky a uniform grey, and she was glad she'd been nursing her coffee so she still had some. "There're doughnuts in Dean's office, Nikki," she said to Dean's assistant after glancing around to make sure there weren't extra ears around.

"I'll have to take my chances, because I'm coming out to watch these two. You didn't tell anyone you put them there, did you?"

"I didn't, but you'd better make sure Nate keeps his mouth shut."

Jiro was waiting down the shed. He looked even better in

jeans. Downright edible, in fact. He was probably the same height as Nate – though he looked small with Dean towering over him, of course. Similar build to Nate too, which was not a bad thing at all. He was just skinnier, if that was possible. Faye quite enjoyed this chance to study him as he exchanged words with Dean, and didn't mind that her brother was horrible about making introductions. Once Nate was on a horse, he ignored her, but she felt a small thrill of victory when Jiro gave her a quick smile as Dean led him past on his mount.

"Come on." Nikki set off after them, power-walking. "I'm not going to miss this."

"You seem pretty excited about going out to watch a couple of maiden claimers."

Nikki snorted. "I'm going to watch for the same reason you are. Nate Miller and Jiro Watanabe."

"If I'd known Nate was coming I might not have been so quick to make the trip," Faye said wryly.

"Ooh, yeah. Sorry."

"Don't be. I'm over it." She was just going to keep telling herself that, and before long, it would be true.

They followed the horses through the tunnel and up to the gap, Dean turning Jiro and She Brews loose, Nate, jogging the other filly up beside them to back up. Nikki and Faye shuffled along to find a spot on the rail.

"Have you talked to Dean yet this morning?"

Faye shook her head and glanced sideways. Faye knew better than to bother her brother when he had workers, so she'd left him alone. She'd done no more than hand him a coffee by way of good morning.

"No – what's up?"

"Touch and Go. We think it's just a stone bruise, but Dean's going to do x-rays later. I think he's out of the Prince of Wales either way."

"Ouch. That sucks." Could they have worse luck this year?

Faye saw an injured horse for how it affected their bottom line. A horse on the farm didn't bring in as much money as a horse at the track, where owners paid trainers a hefty day rate. Then there was the possible lost income from missed purses, especially with a nice horse like Touch and Go, last year's champion two-year-old in the country. Not that that part was in any way guaranteed. Dean, on the other hand, would feel the disappointment and heartache. Maybe it was how he paid the bills, but Dean was in the game for love.

"But Wampum's training great, so here's hoping it's not too long before he's back at the races."

Wampum.

That colt's name sent her mind hurtling back to April, in Kentucky. The terror she'd felt watching the accident, Nate and Wampum both going down, and Nate's confusing aloofness afterward. It had given her painful clarity about their relationship. Her reaction to Nate's brush with death made her realize she was in much, much too deep.

So yes, she'd been the one to end it. Yes, she'd used Liv as her scapegoat, not that the whole kindred spirit thing between those two hadn't been a growing issue. But if she were honest – as hard as that might be – it wasn't *the* issue. *The* issue was that she couldn't have feelings for someone who loved to do something that had the potential to put him in a morgue as a result of a simple misstep by one of those insane, if beautiful, beasts. It didn't make acceptance any easier. It didn't hurt any less. But it was why she'd have to let Nate off the hook eventually.

This wasn't really the best place to watch horses breeze – the bleachers would have been a better choice. Faye would act like she cared – okay she did care, just not with the same passion her brother did. Horses were horses, and her eye for them wasn't as keen as his. Her eye for good-looking men, however...and those two boys going past, poised just so with their acey-deucy irons? They provided quite a pleasant view. She tucked her now-empty travel mug under her elbow, keeping her arms pressed to her sides as she lifted her phone and snapped a pic, which, with the delay of the shutter, pretty much just caught their butts. Not that that was exactly disappointing.

When the workers disappeared behind the tote board in the stretch, Nikki waited just long enough to see them reappear on the other side near the wire before she nudged Faye's arm.

"I've got to beat them back to the barn. Catch you later."

There was bath water to be made ready, and stalls to be finished up, if the others hadn't stepped up in her absence. Sometimes they did, sometimes they didn't. Faye was in no hurry to get back though. She watched them gallop out, getting another good look at them while Dean shuffled by so he'd be there to meet them coming off the track after they pulled up.

Faye went in the other direction, a few vague *good mornings* and half-smiles coming her way as she went. She carefully negotiated the steps and made it through the tunnel before Dean and the horses.

It wasn't far to Barn Twelve where Dean's stalls were, and the walk back warmed her up again. Really, where was that heat from a couple of weeks ago? A little moderation would have been nice, instead of going from one extreme to the other. This was just a weird summer across the board.

With the bland look of disinterest she'd perfected, she waited for them to come back. Nate was on the shed first, steering the filly he was on into one of Nikki's stalls. Faye didn't know the horse's name, and felt guilty for not attempting to find out. She moved a little closer, deciding part of being over Nate meant carrying over the *do better* initiative to him.

He came out of the stall, tack draped over one arm, bridle

in the other, and dunked the bit in the water bucket hanging on the rail before depositing the tack in an organized heap next to it.

"So I know you don't care how the horses looked; how did we look?" he said, cheeky grin and post-breeze adrenaline flowing.

"You're in fine form, Mr. Miller." She gave him a smirk.

Nate glanced a few stalls up where Jiro emerged from She Brew's stall. "Hey Jiro? Have you met Dean's sister?"

Faye controlled her expression, because why not? Jiro came up, Faye's appreciation growing the closer he got. She offered her hand, smiling just the right amount. *Enchanted, I'm sure.* She didn't say it out loud, because the nuance might be lost on him, but definitely not on Nate, who was looking a little smug. Faye didn't quite understand that, but she wasn't going to waste time trying to figure it out.

"Faye," she offered, because Nate had forgotten that part.

Jiro smiled and nodded and said, "Nice to meet you," with his adorable accent, then apologized for needing to leave. Both the riders had to keep moving, of course – in-demand enough their agents kept them hopping all morning long. Which suited Faye perfectly. All she'd wanted to do was plant a seed.

There was no need for her to stick around, so she walked to her car, parked in the lot by the kitchen, and sent Liv the photo. *Just in case you're missing him. I'm calling it, "Breezing Butts."* Then, on a whim, she dialed. And Liv, miraculously, picked up.

"It says a lot about our friendship that I'm answering, you know," Liv said.

"I'm so proud of you. You're learning to adult."

"So what are you doing at the track this morning? Nice picture, by the way."

"It's okay if I still admire his butt, isn't it? It's the other one I'm interested in now, though, so don't worry."

"I'm sorry, I don't recognize it," Liv said wryly.

"Well why would you? You've only got eyes for Nate, and it took three years for you to admit that. Jiro Watanabe worked She Brews for Dean this morning. Don't ask me who Nate was on."

"So that's who you're clocking these days, is it? All right."

"He fits the profile nicely, I must say." Faye paused. "Touch and Go's out of the Prince of Wales."

"Oh no, Faye. I'm sorry. Tell Dean too, okay?"

"I will."

"But you'll both still come down for it, right? Please?"

"Sure." Faye was always up for a party, and Fort Erie did a good job. With any luck, Jiro would be riding down there that evening. She needed to build on the progress she'd made.

She stopped at Starbucks for a cappuccino on the way home, badly needing a cleanse from exposing herself to track coffee – not that she'd been drinking it.

"A brownie, too please," she said, and it made her think of Will, and that night after the Plate party. She'd eaten most of his brownie when they'd come here. She should probably make him a pan of them to apologize, and to thank him for helping with the hay. Though he had tossed her in the pond, which really should erase any debt she might feel she had.

———

The cappuccino was so hot, she was almost home before she could safely sip it. Except for a few nibbles, she'd saved the brownie, so she pulled it from its brown bag and set it on a plate, then planted herself in front of the computer to catch up on some web work. The internet seemed to have other ideas about that plan.

Faye hit reload again, with the same result. Nothing but an

inadequate apology from the browser. Rural Canadian internet was something even third-world countries couldn't comprehend. In this day and age, someone should have come up with a way to provide reliable service, even when you lived in a location where tall trees and rolling land made line of sight a challenge. She sighed, and gave up, putting the brownie back in its bag for later, and grabbed her coffee.

"Hey Gus! Wanna go for a walk?"

Like the answer was ever *no* to that question. The Golden was bouncing at the back door, tongue lolling, before Faye even got close to her shoes.

They wandered beyond the pastures where the mares and foals grazed to the hay fields, the new growth looking like a green brush cut. It needed to warm up again so they got a decent crop of second cut. She zipped her jacket up to her neck, grateful the cappuccino in her hand was still warm. It was ridiculous to need a fleece in the middle of July. No one would have been so quick to jump in the pond if they'd been putting up hay today. Except Gus, of course. He launched right in as they got close, then swam happily back to the edge when she called him, bounding up to her and stopping to give himself a good shake.

"C'mon, goofball. Thanks to that shower, I'm going to need to change before I freeze out here."

Dean's truck was parked outside the barn where he kept the layups, and she followed Gus into the dark interior. Gus tracked him down. He was in a stall grooming a big colt, a task that was the farm manager Stacey's job, but this particular colt was Ride The Wave, who Dean loved with optimistic devotion. There had been no more talk of taking on a partner.

The fact that the colt was here and not at Woodbine was not a good thing. Two-year-olds. *Ugh.* Maybe if Dean would take him into the track, he'd get some more interest, as much as

Faye struggled with the idea. But Dean was treating the colt with kid gloves, determined to do right by him. Ride The Wave was a big, growing thing, and Faye feared, left to his own devices, Dean wouldn't get him to the races until he was five.

"How's your baby?" she teased.

"You think I'm an old fuddy-duddy." Dean sneezed at the dust rising from Wave's muddy coat.

Faye choked on a laugh. "You are an old fuddy-duddy."

"This colt is the last of Dad's legacy, Faye. He's got to be good. I mean, look at him."

"Because I know what I'm looking at." It was a good way to deflect Dean's hopefulness.

He raised an eyebrow as he switched sides. "You do. You just don't want to admit it."

"Well, it doesn't matter. I lack credibility because if I get any closer than this, I start having a panic attack."

"Don't worry, I'm not suggesting you start helping with the hands-on stuff." He grinned. "I still think you could be a blood-stock agent or something like that."

"No thanks," she said. Just because she could, didn't mean she wanted to. "The internet was down again when I got home. If it's not back up, I'm heading into Lucy's."

No surprise, the connection at the house was still dead in the water. She packed up her laptop and headed for civiliza-tion. Or Lucy's, at least, where she'd have access to free WiFi, and if she was lucky, a butter tart.

Lucy's ire was more subdued this morning as she set Faye's coffee and tart down and rang it up, so Faye took a rare stab at conversation. "I guess you'll have a new neighbour soon. Who's leaving?" The *For Lease* sign had been out front for a couple of weeks now.

Lucy frowned. "Me."

"What? No, Lucy, you can't go! Why?" While Faye

guessed the coffee shop wasn't the most lucrative business in town, it has survived while other places had not. She hoped the landlord wasn't doing something crazy with the rent. She couldn't imagine Lucy not being there.

The little quiver that came with Lucy's sigh shocked Faye. It was the first time Faye had seen any sign of vulnerability in her.

"My mother's very sick, and needs a lot of extra care. I just can't manage the business and that right now."

"Oh Lucy, I'm so sorry." Faye didn't know what more to say, but then the wheels started turning. "What if someone took it over for you? You'd still have an income, which I'm sure would help out right now. And we wouldn't lose this amazing place you've built."

Lucy's eyebrows went up slightly, with an expression Faye almost might have called hopeful. "I don't know how I'd find someone like that."

"Well it just so happens..." *What are you doing, Faye?* "... That I'm looking for an opportunity."

Lucy's head tilted, like she was pondering the likelihood of Faye having the necessary skills. Faye tried not to be insulted. It wasn't as if Lucy could have any idea what she did for a living, or what her interests were. Faye just needed...something. Something more productive to do with her life than deciding who her next boy toy would be.

When Lucy didn't speak, Faye jumped back in. "I'm a business manager for some of the farms around here." Okay, glorified bookkeeper, whatever. She did have the degree that would qualify her for such a title, though. "And while my baking isn't as wonderful as yours, I've been doing it since I was little, helping my mom. Why don't you think about it for a while? Here's my number." She pulled one of Dean's business cards out of her purse, and scribbled her name and cell number on the back. "Just give me a call, or, I'm in here enough, tell me you want to chat if you see me. I'll make the time."

Lucy actually smiled, all the hard lines of her round face softening so that Faye barely recognized her. "Thank you. I'll do that."

Faye nodded, and handed her a ten-dollar bill.

Lucy waved her away. "On the house."

"Thanks, Lucy. We'll work something out. Something to buy you some time before you give this up."

She parked herself at a corner table, opening up her laptop and logging into the WiFi, then looked around the shop. It was surprisingly big. The things she could do with this place, after a fresh coat of paint. She created a new Word doc, and started brainstorming ideas while they were fresh in her mind.

CHAPTER SEVEN

Two HOURS WAS TOO long to keep Dean folded into her little Corolla, so they took his truck to Fort Erie. Dean was like a kid, all but bouncing in his seat on the way down, as if because he wasn't running a horse in the big race himself, he didn't have to be serious. When they got there, he insisted on going to the barn first to see Liv and Chique. Faye couldn't protest; it was the right thing to do.

The Fort Erie backstretch had seen better days. Faye had never known those days, but walking around the run-down barns always made her want to find paint. Her father had always called it Saratoga North, but he'd been around in the days when the A meet in Ontario had shifted to the border track for the summer, much like Saratoga hosted a boutique meet in New York state.

Dean pulled up outside the shed where Chique had spent the last few weeks, and Faye immediately saw Liv outside the stall, fussing over the filly while Jo St-Laurent stood to the side with a controlled expression. *Yep, we're in the right place.* Liv was dressed up, wearing a pretty blue-print sundress – did she ever wear anything but blue? It covered her scary-strong shoulders, but not the flex of the just as scary muscles in her arms. It also left her well-defined calves in full view above blue flats – Faye had never seen Liv in heels. Ever. Just as well, maybe, because those calves in heels? She could probably do one of those swimsuit fitness model competitions, or whatever they were. The ones where the contestants got spray-on fake tans and wore tiny bikinis.

"Thanks for coming!"

Liv's words sounded artificially bright, like she knew she had to say them but was too distracted to actually mean them. Not that Faye doubted her sincerity, just her ability to focus on anything other than the horse. Faye navigated the uneven shedrow in her heels and wrapped her arms around Liv, making herself a human Thundershirt. Liv stilled.

"Now breathe," Faye instructed, and she felt the exhale. Chique snorted behind them, then yawned, and Faye dropped her arms and stepped back. "Better."

"Anything I can do?" Dean asked, probably dying to help out because he wasn't comfortable watching anyone else work while he stood by.

"Stick around in case I pass out or have a panic attack?" Liv quipped, which might be a legitimate concern.

On a normal day, it was easy to forget Liv had only had her trainer's licence since April, and this was only the third time she'd saddled a horse – but today the jitters of inexperience were putting on a parade. Liv had always wanted to be a rider – and had been, until a freak accident in Florida last winter had put her in the hospital. Faye didn't know all the reasons behind Liv's decision to take over as Chique's trainer of record in the spring. By then she'd been feeling a disruption in their friendship, suspicious something was developing between Liv and Nate, and it kept her from asking either of them. Now it didn't really matter.

"It's still a couple of hours till post time. You two should go over to the buffet," Liv said, crossing her arms and grasping her elbows. Chique tossed her head up and down, her long forelock flying, and Faye wanted to laugh. It was like the filly herself was telling Liv to calm down, because she was making them all nervous.

"If you were a normal trainer, you'd come with us, and leave Roger's very capable assistant to do her job and get the filly ready," Faye said with a smirk.

Jo snorted, and Liv shot her a look, but admitted, "Because I could eat right now? You can go with them if you want, Jo."

"I have strict instructions to stay right here in case you do, in fact, self-destruct."

"If that happens, Jo, call 911 first, and then call us. Dean can help you with the filly, and I can help resuscitate Liv."

Liv rolled her eyes. "Would you two just leave?"

Dean put an arm around Liv's shoulders and gave her a squeeze. "You'll be fine. See you over there."

Fort Erie was a happy place, despite its tumbledown state. It was a tighter community than Woodbine, made up of smaller outfits. The people here had to be in it for love, because there wasn't a lot of money to be made. Those A meet glory days were several decades in the past now, the present-day racing dates going from May to the end of October and offering an option for horses that weren't quite competitive enough for Woodbine. The eternal optimism shared by everyone who called The Fort home was at odds with a reality that couldn't help but depress Faye on those rare occasions she walked this backside.

That was another reason she'd been surprised Liv had wanted to spend a couple of weeks here. It was the last stop for some of those animals, and at the end of the season a number of them were sold to trainers who went south for the winter – but not to warmer destinations like Florida, New Orleans or Arkansas. The ones who survived the season at Fort Erie went to places like Pennsylvania and West Virginia where they could run on medications that weren't legal in Ontario. Dean never let his horses go like that. He retired them, and let Emilie and Nicole – who galloped and ponied for Triple Stripe but had a network of riding horse friends – find appropriate homes and second careers.

On Prince of Wales Day, though, Fort Erie shone, at least on the front side. Faye scanned the food trucks, patrons lined up as they waited to grab a quick bite before watching the horses in the nearby walking ring. The paddock was rustic, more intimate than Woodbine's, which had once upon a time been similar, but suffered modern upgrades. The old trainers liked it better than the new one at Woodbine; the younger trainers didn't know any differently until they came to the Fort and someone told them this is how it used to be. How it should have stayed.

While Dean grabbed a program, Faye texted Em. *We're here. Where are you?*

Em: *Upstairs. We have a table. Come up!*

Faye: *We?*

Liv's parents, perhaps. But Em didn't answer before Dean was swallowed by the grandstand and Faye had to pay attention and stay close, latching a hand onto his elbow so she didn't lose him in the crush of people packed on the lower level.

Faye didn't know this grandstand like she did Woodbine, relying on her brother to lead the way: up some stairs to where a buffet dinner was set up, tables crowding the room that looked out over the pretty infield. The lake there had a story, and the picturesque little bridge was a popular spot for weddings – at least racetracker weddings. Beautifully-maintained landscaping surrounded the old tote board that declared *Alive And Kicking*, the track's motto. Because Fort Erie had, indeed, fought hard to stay alive and survive in the post-Slots-At-Racetracks climate in Ontario.

Em waved as soon as they pushed through the door. There was someone sitting with her, but it wasn't her parents.

Oh. Will. Smiling a charming smile. That stupid humming started, overriding the din of diners' voices.

Well okay. She could do this. She could accept that not every guy was going to go for her. Nothing to be embarrassed about. Will stood as Faye and Dean approached.

"Nice to see you again, Will. You remember my brother, Dean?" she said coolly, as if Will hadn't already endeared himself to Dean by helping with the hay. Faye carefully took off her hat – because she never missed an excuse to wear a hat – and seated herself across from him.

Dean grinned as they exchanged a handshake across the table. "You're becoming a regular part of the gang now."

Like they were the Little Rascals or something. Faye caught an amused look on Em's face.

"I am sorry I missed hearing you play at the Plate Party." Dean settled into his seat. "I keep hearing how good you were. I hope we can get away with having you again next year."

"You have a horse in it next year?" Will said – sounding like he was just being polite.

"I hope so."

"You hope so every year," Faye said with an eyeroll, but Faye hoped so too. Dean's eternal optimism always brought out her fondness for her brother. Sometimes she had a hard time believing they were related.

"So who's that, Dean?" Emilie said.

"A son of Catch The Joy out of Avalanche. I doubt I'll even get him to the races this year – he's a big colt, awkward as anything. But he sure is bred for it."

Em looked suitably impressed. "Catch The Joy was trained by Dean and Faye's father, and won the Canadian Triple Crown, *and* was second in the Breeders' Cup Turf Classic, *and* was Canadian Horse of the Year for two years. He went on to become one of the top stallions in Ontario."

Will looked blank, and Faye had to take pity on the poor guy. "So you've heard of the Kentucky Derby, right? And if you've heard of the Triple Crown, it's probably the American one. We have one too. The Queen's Plate is the first race, and this race today – the Prince of Wales Stakes – is the second. Then in another three weeks, the third one is back at Woodbine. It's called the Breeders' Stakes, not to be confused with the Breeders' Cup, which is two days of races and pretty much accepted as the world championships of horse racing...even if it's mostly only horses from the northern hemisphere that compete."

"You really have missed your calling, Faye," Em interjected. "You should be volunteering for the Canadian Horse Racing Hall of Fame. You're like an ambassador."

"I'm not exactly looking for philanthropic opportunities right now, Em. If you hear they're hiring, though, let me know, all right?"

"So kind of like the World Series is really just an American thing, not a world thing?"

Dean laughed. "Kind of. Though a lot of horses from the UK and Europe come over."

"How do they get here?" He looked genuinely puzzled.

"They fly," Dean said.

"Do I want to know what that costs?"

92

At least he hadn't made a crack about Pegasus. "Best not to think about it," Faye said. "Are we having wine, Em? Or did you drive?"

"Will met me at Woodbine and I came with him. He drove." She smiled.

Faye nodded. "Wine it is, then."

Well, that was cozy. Faye stopped herself. Em wasn't acting like she was interested in Will, though Faye wasn't sure if she'd recognize if Em *was* interested in someone. In that way, the sisters were a lot alike; Em just wasn't systematically opposed to the idea of male companionship like Liv had been – historically, at least. She'd wondered early on if Em liked Nate – it was from Em she'd learned about him, not Liv, after all – but the two of them had fallen into a cute brother-sister type relationship. And though Em was the youngest of their group, sometimes Faye thought she had a better head on her shoulders than all of them combined, the common sense she'd demonstrated steering clear of romance with Nate Miller being a case in point.

Faye reached over and snapped the program from Dean. "What race are we on?" Will's presence had distracted her. She needed to check if Jiro had any mounts.

The buffet wasn't as fancy as what they'd had at Woodbine on Plate Day, but the atmosphere was down-home, and hey, it was free. It would have been better if Touch and Go had stayed sound, but it had been nice of Liv to invite them. Faye nibbled as Dean nattered about the race that had gone off, Will valiantly trying to follow what he was saying. His utter confusion was adorable.

"I need to stretch my legs. I'm going down to the paddock for the next race." Faye scooped up her hat and gave Em a pointed look. "You coming?"

She felt bad abandoning Will to Dean, but they were

grown-ups. She was sure they'd find something to talk about. Dean could discuss things other than horses. Like hockey. Nate liked hockey, so probably Will did too. Like any self-respecting Canadian boy, right? Was it wrong to make that assumption? All Faye knew was she needed to get her mind off Will and back to a more suitable target.

"I don't know, Faye," Em began as they started down the steps. "I think you should give Will another chance. He seems so nice."

"First of all, it's him who would have to give me another chance, because it's him who turned me down. And second, nice is wasted on me."

"Are you really going to let what happened with Nate taint your view of relationships forever?"

"You're not exactly an expert, Em."

"Oooh, snippy!"

"Sorry." Really, Emilie didn't deserve to take the brunt of her frustration. "I think we need Pie In A Jar, Em. Yes? That might be the best food truck I have seen in my entire life."

"Caramel apple with ice cream? Count me in. I'll stand in line, you grab a spot."

"You're a good friend, Em. I do need to maximize my viewing time." Faye adjusted the angle of her hat. "Am I too old to play paddock girl?"

Emilie laughed. "You've been too old for years, Faye. When have you let that stop you?"

Few of the spectators gathering outside the walking ring were as dressed up as she was. She sidled next to a man with a *Form* propped in front of him, giving him a smile and a *thank you* when he made more room for her. Using her elbows to take up extra space, she typed a text to Liv while she waited. *How are you holding up?*

The response came in a remarkably short time. *Counting the minutes.*

Down to the seconds, no doubt.

Em squeezed in beside her, pressing a mason jar into Faye's hands. "Cheers."

"This looks like sheer brilliance." Faye dug her plastic spoon into its depths.

"I agree."

The pie was so good, Faye almost forgot to look for Jiro. It seemed wrong to be stuffing her face with dessert while ogling a guy whose survival at least partially depended on his ability to starve himself. With sunglasses and her hat, in the midst of the crowd, maybe she'd blend in. She almost laughed out loud. If Liv or Em had heard that thought, she knew how they'd respond. *You never blend in, Faye.* And did she actually want to blend in? No. She needed to keep Jiro aware of her. Maybe finish up the pie before he saw her, though.

"So why," Faye said, in between mouthfuls as she worked to scarf it down, "is Will here?"

Em shrugged. "Nate asked him. I told Nate I'd make the drive down with him."

"So he wouldn't get lost?"

"Or feel lost if he didn't get lost? He's being a good sport." Emilie gave her a sideways glance, her own spoon dipping into the jar with less frantic frequency. "There he is."

Both she and Em zoned in on Jiro. *The guy you're supposed to be interested in, remember, Faye?* She forced herself to admire the view in front of her, instead of contemplating the intruding thoughts of Will floating through her mind. Jiro's stereotypical square, crossed-arm stance, whip tucked neatly under his arm as he listened, nodding, to the trainer. The way he moved, fluidly, as he walked up to the horse, and hopped weightlessly into the saddle with only the slightest aid. His beautiful hands as he knotted the lines, then reached forward to stroke his mount's neck. There was no humming sound here though; no tremor that ran through her leaving her both thrilled and maddened. This fruitless attraction she had for Will was getting in the way.

Faye chickened out and ducked her head as Jiro went by, like a bashful teenager, but Em gave him a full-on smile. He knew Em from the mornings though; she could get away with it. Em got away with so much.

"We'd better go rescue Will from my brother." Faye nudged Emilie with her elbow as the horses headed for the tunnel under the grandstand on their way to the track.

Will and Dean looked as if they were doing okay; not best buddies or anything, but getting along as well as fish-out-of-water Will could be expected to with a horse-centric like Dean. Faye and Em's return didn't bring relief to his face though. Why would it? Em was a horse girl, try as she might to deny it, and he'd already shunned Faye. It didn't stop that damn humming sound from coming back, blocking her eardrums from everything else for an instant so all she heard was her own erratic heartbeat.

She still had wine, thank goodness. But she'd need another glass. She took a photo of the refill and sent it to Liv. *I'm having one for you.*

It was a few moments before Liv answered. *You're the best.*

Faye grinned at the phone screen, feeling the sarcasm through whatever magic transmitted SMS messages. *What are friends for?*

"You know what they're going to do, right?" Dean was starting in on his prediction of how the Prince of Wales would be run, his plate replaced by the program he'd reclaimed from Faye when she'd returned. He'd left his *Form* behind, at least.

Her brother needed to get a girlfriend; one who was into

racing. Liv really would have been perfect. Sure there was an age difference, but Liv had always been too mature for her own good, and she got along so well with Dean. The two of them probably had one of those pacts; the ones where they promised if they were still both single in their 40s, they'd get together. That would put Faye's sexy spinster plan out the window, though, so she'd better root for Nate.

She realized Will was staring at her, and hated to think what weird expression she'd had on her face. She smiled at him, hoping the look she sent back was more, *I understand, I've always felt like an outsider too with these people*; a civilian hovering at the fringes of the frontlines on which they battled.

Faye had grown up in a horse racing family. She'd come to understand the ins and outs by osmosis; it couldn't be helped. It didn't hold her interest, but she felt obligated on some level to have some idea of what was going on. But Dean was the only one of their group who really paid any attention to the race that was going off. Em normally would have watched too, but she could at least set her interest aside and do her part as Will's escort as assigned by Nate. They were talking music, Will looking way more comfortable. Faye just observed, thinking about how he'd guessed what her musical tastes were, and for a moment, feeling just a little bit left out of everything.

When the race was over, she hopped to her feet, quickly draining what was left in her glass. "Okay. We all have to go down for this. And watch the race with Liv, so make sure you have everything. We probably won't be back."

The horses were already in the saddling enclosure, and there was no hope of seeing Liv and Jo and Chique with the crowd that had gathered. Well, Dean and Will might be able to; they were tall enough. Faye and Emilie squeezed up to the walking ring rail instead, leaning forward over the hedge inside it. Faye glanced over her shoulder under the brim of her hat, catching Dean's intent expression as the horses started to appear. She could feel Will, so close the heat of his body was like a warm shawl on her back. Maybe someone would run into him and press him against her. *Oops, so sorry!* Her pulse drummed in her ears. *Okay, breathe, girl, and at least try to pay attention to what's in front of you instead of who's behind.*

The early evening light hit Chique's bright white shadow roll first, then caught the glint of her eye against the cut of the blinker cups. Nate and Liv followed, spotting their cheering squad. A little four-fingered wave from Liv, a toned-down grin from Nate, then their heads were back together, strategizing.

"Chique's behaving," Em said. "Though with her, I'm not sure that's a good sign."

The little dark bay filly might be tough to manage, but her crazy seemed to enhance her performance rather than hinder it. It was really a credit to Nate she'd accomplished as much as she had. He'd insisted the pre-race treatment most trainers would use to settle an anxious horse was taking too much away from her. He was the one who had to ride her crazy ass, so Liv had gone along with it.

With the riders up call from the paddock judge, everything started to move. Trainers and riders, horses and grooms; their activity choreographed in the small confines of the walking ring. The outriders on their decorated ponies led the procession to the track.

"*Aweille!*" Em said the word like a war cry, shooing with her hands and pushing into Faye to get her point across.

When Em lapsed into French, you jumped first, and asked questions later. Faye stepped back quickly to get around the person next to her, and felt her pointy heel sink into something softer than pavement.

"Ow!" Will gasped.

Faye spun around in horror, seeing Will's scrunched-up

face, and grabbed his arm. "I'm so sorry Will! But, um, suck it up, because we have to catch Liv. We can't miss this race."

With Em leading the way, serpent-like, through the sea of spectators, they reached Liv as she exited the horse path.

Faye squeezed her elbow. "Okay?"

Liv looked at her sideways with a smirk. *Right.* Don't ask a control freak that when things are out of her control.

"Filly looks great," Dean said.

"What do you think?" Em asked.

"It's Chique. Anyone's guess, right?" Liv answered wryly.

The sun was setting over the beautiful old track, giving everything an orange glow as the horses warmed up. Faye made sure she wasn't next to Will, wedging herself between Emilie and Liv.

When the gates opened, Nate didn't gun Chique for the lead. Dean, on the other side of Emilie, was nodding, muttering, "Good, good. Let that speed horse go. You don't want to get caught up in that." By the turn Nate had Chique tucked on the rail, saving ground behind the pacesetter.

"See, what did I tell you?" Dean nudged Emilie hard enough Em dominoed into Faye. "They'll try to keep her boxed in, spoil it for her."

Shut up Dean. But Liv would know that. Faye glanced at her just the same. Liv's jaw was set, but if she was worried, Faye couldn't tell.

"Nate's cool, though," Emilie said. "And Chique looks surprisingly chill."

"She's really grown up," Dean said.

On the backstretch, nothing changed, and Faye was starting to sweat. Her palms damp, she clutched Em's hand because Liv's were wrapped resolutely around her binoculars, fixated on every stride her filly took. But Chique bullied her way out as they turned for home, Nate threading her between horses the moment the sparest of holes opened up. And once Chique was clear, she was gone.

They were all on their feet, screaming, like everyone else there, so it made sense for Will to scream too, feel part of the excitement. And it was exciting, the way it looked like the little horse was stuck and wasn't going to get out, and then she was breaking free, and running away. The fact that that was Nate on her – that this fast and nervy sport was what he did for a living – was pretty cool. Nate had always had a bit of an edge; always been a bit crazy on a snowboard or on the ice, the scrappy little dude who everyone liked just enough to not punch in his perfect teeth.

Em was whooping as she and Faye enveloped Liv in a hug, then Dean hugged Liv too, though Liv was soon breaking out of it to push Faye in front of her and rush away. Will wondered if he'd thought quicker, if he could have gotten away with hugging Faye, but there'd been no smooth opportunity for it, because she'd stayed way on the other side of Liv.

Emilie reached for Will and dragged him behind her, with Faye's brother bringing up the rear. Down the stairs and right to the racetrack. Amazing how fast these women could move in their fancy shoes, through the deep sand of the racetrack that he was having enough trouble with in loafers. Emilie braced him, laughing and pulling again.

It had been sweet of Em to take him under her wing. She was easy to be around, too. She was cute. She was young. Too young. Plus, she seemed to be Nate's adopted baby sister, so that made her a definite no, even more so than Faye. Faye was still a no, right?

Liv broke away from their little conga line to meet Nate

and the horse, reaching up to grab his hand, Nate pulling her close enough, and leaning over far enough, so he could kiss her. It was like something from a movie, and it did seem like all of it was coming together for Nate. He'd worked hard, professionally and emotionally, to make that happen.

Em led him to a semi-circle where they crowded with Faye, an older couple Will guessed were Liv and Em's parents, and the woman who had been with the horse at the barn, whose name Will had already forgotten. They stood in a line, waiting while Liv positioned the horse with them, a blanket of yellow and purple flowers now hanging over the horse's neck. A photographer captured the scene before Nate hopped off, all smiles as he undid things and took the saddle off the horse.

"We can go now."

Faye's sultry voice, and the very familiar way she looped her arm through his, unnerved him. He was tempted to lean over and whisper in her ear, *Where are we going?* But he kept the words to himself and the sensation of her touch at bay, obediently going along.

It wasn't until they were back across the track and Faye led them up to Dean that he realized Dean hadn't been over there. Dean seemed unfazed by the way Faye still had her hand on Will's arm, small and warm, the brim of her hat every so often brushing his bicep.

"We're going back to the barn, I assume?" Dean said.

"We'd better." Faye nodded, then looked up at Will. "You can come with us. We can drop you at your car afterwards. How's your foot, by the way? I can't believe I did that."

"It's all right." To be truthful, the excitement, and now her nearness, had distracted him from that pain.

"You sure? I could get a wheelchair for you."

Her cheeky smile made him want to scoop her up right

there, in the middle of everything, and wipe it off her face with a kiss.

"I think I can make it," he answered dryly, though he did think about putting an arm around her shoulders, using the excuse of needing the extra support. She still had hers wrapped around his elbow. That was probably as much touching as he should be trusted with right now. "You going to be okay on those shoes?"

Dean had a beast of a four-door black Chevy pickup, parked far enough away he did become more aware of his foot. He didn't know how Faye managed not to be crippled in those shoes.

"Nice vehicle," he said as Faye released him to climb into the back.

"Are you guys going to talk about the virtues of Chevrolet now?" Faye peeked at him between the seats, her hat still poised on her head.

"Not a fan?"

"My choice of vehicles is evidence of my black sheep status in the Taylor family." Her eyes, like milk chocolate, went from him to Dean and back, teasing. "You never did guess what kind of car I drive."

"Toyota Corolla. Really not what I'd have thought."

"Of course you saw it at the farm. Well that's no fun. What should I be driving, then?"

He thought for a moment. "An Audi RS 5."

"Hmmm. I like that. Hear that, Dean? Can we buy me an Audi?"

Dean laughed, and drove up to a small booth. There was a security guard inside, and Dean just nodded as the man waved the truck through.

"So I don't have to write my name in blood?" Will quipped, remembering the paperwork and photograph Woodbine had required for him to gain admittance to play after the Queen's Plate.

Dean shook his head. "They're a lot more relaxed here."

Maybe that was because things were...dilapidated. Dean drove slowly down one of the rows between the barns and pulled up in front of one that bore a vague resemblance to the stable at Woodbine where Will had played the Plate party. He got out slowly. Except for a couple of scruffy-looking types down at the end of the barn, there was no one around.

"So –" He hesitated. "Where's the party?"

"I think you're looking at it," Faye said. She didn't seem to care how out of place she looked with the backdrop of the peeling green paint and weathered wood railings, the dirt on the barn floor hard and uneven.

"They're at the test barn," Dean said, as if that explained everything.

What the hell was a test barn?

Faye clarified as if Will had said it out loud. "That's where the winner of the race, and usually the second place horse, and/or maybe a badly-beaten favourite, go for drug screening. The horses are walked around in circles to rehydrate and cool out, and when they're done – which is basically when they stop drinking water – the attendants take a urine sample, and a blood sample for horses on Lasix, which is most of them, and also, randomly, a second blood to test for bicarbonate."

"So that was mostly a foreign language to me. How do they do that?"

"They take a blood sample from the jugular, which is pretty easy to access on a horse, and they whistle at the horse to get it to pee, and collect it in a cup."

"They – you're joking."

"Not one bit."

"They pee on command."

"Yep."

Will looked at Dean. "She's having me on, right?"

Dean shook his head. "We start teaching them that when they're just babies. Simple association, a conditioned response. Whenever they urinate, you whistle. Over time, for most of them at least, you whistle, they urinate."

"You'll never think of whistling the same, ever again." Faye grinned.

What a funny little world this was. Faye didn't quite fit; it was as if she was mocking it when she elucidated, while at the same time loving its weirdness. The more he listened to her, the more he watched her, the more she fascinated him.

Emilie joined them – had she walked here? It wasn't really that far, but she was all dressed up too, even if she wasn't wearing quite the heels on which Faye teetered.

"I don't imagine Chique will take long – she was barely breathing hard after that." Em said.

She and Dean started talking about things that were way over Will's head, like Dean had gone on about how the race would develop – and, apparently, had. Faye seemed to appreciate he was out of his element here, and gave him a quick smile.

"We should at least find some beer. We have to make some attempt to mark this as a celebration. There must be a bootlegger around here."

"A – bootlegger?" Where were they, the Wild West?

"There's always someone who will sell you beer on the backstretch." Faye elbowed Dean. "You've got to know who?"

"Sorry."

"Those guys will then." She tipped her head towards the other end of the barn, where the two scruffy guys he'd noticed still sat on overturned buckets. Then she started walking – on those high, strappy shoes, over the rough terrain.

He called after her. "Want me to come with you? They look kind of..."

Faye snorted. "Oh, please. I'm fine."

Will watched her navigate the dips and ruts expertly, hips with an extra swing, hair flouncing, hat still set just so on her head. Totally out of place, and completely at home. The two men didn't seem to be at all affected by her arrival, and Faye appeared to chat with them with the same ease she did anyone else. One of them gestured; Faye nodded and smiled, saying something with a laugh – and disappeared around the corner of the barn. Will took a step – did she really think it was safe to parade around here? But a hand on his arm stopped him.

"You don't have to worry about Faye. She can fend for herself." It was Emilie, a slight but very amused smile on her lips. "Of course, we'd be very worried about you, if you tried the same thing."

"I live in downtown Toronto, and I'm kind of intimidated in this place," Will admitted.

"You didn't catch the sign by the stable gate? Mostly harmless."

"What?" He'd found himself saying that a lot around here.

"I'm kidding. And, did you somehow miss reading *Hitch-hiker's Guide to the Galaxy* growing up?"

Faye returned with half a dozen bottles of Molson Canadian. Em rushed up to help her, handing one to Dean, and one to Will.

"We can share, Em," Faye said. "I'm hiding the other three so we don't attract scavengers. Though I'm willing to bet Liv won't want one." She stashed them in a box in front of one of the stall doors, closing the lid then sitting on it as she cracked open the beer and took a swig.

So, that seemed to be how Faye Taylor operated. Sweep in, take charge, make things happen. Proactive, not reactive.

Everyone was quiet – such a different scene from after the other race, when this one seemed to be pretty important too. Faye took another sip of beer, then offered the bottle to Emilie; Dean stood with one hand tucked in the pocket of his dress pants and the other wrapped around his bottle. Then the horse appeared, with the short-haired woman who had led her to the grandstand and taken her away when Nate had got off her. Liv was right behind them, and with the influx came a fresh injection of energy.

"What's her name?" Will whispered to Dean, feeling awkward for not remembering, if he'd even been told.

"Jo St-Laurent. She's the assistant trainer for the stable Liv's father owns. Liv's been taking care of the filly while she's been down here, but Jo came to run her."

Faye piped up. "That means she brought Chique from the barn here to where Liv put the saddle on, then brought her back after the race. I'm guessing she walked her – to cool her out – too, because she wouldn't let Liv do it in a dress and unsafe shoes. Which Liv probably tried to do, despite the stupidity of it."

"Oh come on, Faye. She probably had running shoes in her car." Emilie grinned.

"I knew I should have brought one of the hotwalkers with me," the woman named Jo said, walking Chique outside. Chique looked at the scrubby grass and Will swore she gave her a look of disgust. It didn't look all that enticing, he had to agree. "Liv had to hold the filly for me to bath her."

"Track speak, Will. They bath – not bathe – horses. Never, never, 'wash'." Faye gave an exaggerated shudder. "Unless you want to stand out like a sore thumb around here, say bath not bathe or wash!"

"You should probably just stay next to me while I'm here to act as my interpreter."

Faye blinked before she smiled, like she wasn't sure. Was he flirting? Maybe he was. Or just trying to be funny? He hadn't decided yet. And she didn't come over to him, which he realized he'd been hoping she'd do.

Will recognized Nate's car pulling up, and the horse abandoned the grass hunt, her head popping up. Nate went right to her, feeding her something and scratching her neck.

"You're just in time, Nate. She's ready to do up," Jo said.

Nate laughed, and Will just automatically looked at Faye now.

Faye smirked. "So, first you have to know, that's a groom's responsibility, not part of the jockey's job description in any way, shape or form. But if you don't already know this Nate – which I kind of gather you don't – after the Plate, he helped Jo do up Chique. Liv took a photo and posted it on Instagram, and it went a little bit viral." She rolled her eyes. "What it means, literally, to do up a horse, is cleaning out her feet and putting some cool mud on her soles to draw heat out, then putting a similar kind of mud on her front legs for the same reason – all to help prevent or reduce inflammation. Then the legs are bandaged – you just have to look at those to know what that means, because I don't even know how to explain it. It's sure not what you'd put on a paper cut. Then for Princess Chique here, they'll bandage her hind legs too, likely with a sweat underneath, which is kind of the opposite of a poultice, because it creates heat so makes everything feel nice and warm after all that exertion. Anyway, all of it to say, for him to help do all that is a remarkable display of humility and his way of honouring Chique. Sound totally weird?"

She looked like she might admire Nate for all that, even if it killed her just a little.

"Now you're embarrassing me, Faye. But you should have a YouTube channel or something." Nate threw out that high-watt grin of his, and Faye pressed her lips together, giving him a withering look, apparently no longer affected by its radiance. "Put her in, Jo, and I'm there."

Faye's head turned to look at something somewhere behind Will. He glanced over his shoulder, and saw a very new, very blue Toyota 86 pull up. Nice. A guy, skinnier than Nate, and Japanese, climbed out.

Dean turned, "Hey, Jiro!"

Nate was taking off his suit jacket, and said to Liv, "I invited him to stop by before he drives back to Toronto." Then he gave Faye a pointed look.

Faye extracted the beer from the box. "We have domestic beer, or we have domestic beer." She passed one to Jo, and one to Nate. "I'm assuming you're not going to want one, Liv, which means I must've got this for you." She gave Jiro a winning smile.

A beer might take out a guy that size. But it looked like Will had lost his interpreter. Faye was casual about it, but moseyed over to stand opposite Dean, eyes settling on Jiro with that same look she'd given Will when they'd met at the Plate gig. So the last few hours had been a game for her, or the sense of obligation she'd felt to babysit the outsider fulfilled, and she was clocking out.

Dean tipped his head back slightly to take a swig from his bottle, and Will muttered at him, "I'm feeling like a giant around here." All the women were pretty much the same size, give or take an inch, so he and Dean seemed to tower over all of them. "Do you get used to it?"

Dean laughed. "I guess. I don't even notice it. Stings a little though when they always seem to get the women, though. Like what they lack in height they get back double in attractiveness."

Will looked at him sideways, and wondered what that meant. Was Dean trying to tell him something? Like *don't waste your time, buddy; my sister is going to end up with that guy, not you.*

Faye was engaged in what looked to be a slightly humorous, if a bit clumsy, conversation with Jiro, thanks to a language barrier. Nate and Jo were probably with the horse in a stall doing whatever doing up was, with Liv and Em close by. Why was he here again? Dean was friendly, but not exactly talkative when horses weren't a subject option.

It was a relief when Nate finally came out of the stall. He said something in Liv's ear before coming over with the beer Faye had left on the railing for him.

"I bet you're bored stiff." Nate looked apologetic.

Will shrugged. "Just out of my element."

"You think?" Nate laughed. "Sorry, sometimes I need someone else to remind me."

"Congrats though, buddy. On your success."

Nate touched the neck of his bottle to Will's. "Thanks. And I really do appreciate you coming out."

"So who is that guy?" Will motioned towards Faye. "And why did you invite him? I know his name is Jiro. And that Faye is obviously into him." He tried to keep the disgruntlement out of his voice.

"I feel bad for him sometimes. It must be tough, coming to a new country, especially one where no one really speaks your native language." Nate paused. "And you sounded a little jealous there. Just remember what I said."

Will narrowed his eyes, but took the hint. It was okay if the guy nobody really knew got together with Faye, but not him. How, exactly did that make sense again?

Faye was laughing, brushing her hair off her shoulder. She was obviously making sure she didn't misplace her hat tonight, because it remained securely on her head. Jiro was enjoying the attention; Will had yet to see him take a drink from the beer.

Jiro nodded at Faye, saying something, then handed her the bottle and stepped back, waving.

"Thanks, Nate! See you!"

There was a collective "Bye Jiro!" chorus that Will didn't join in on; he was just glad the guy was leaving. Liv, Em and Jo joined their little circle, but Faye watched Jiro drive away, then turned and lifted Jiro's bottle to her lips, her eyes steady on Will as she did it. Was she trying to drive him crazy? Because it was working.

When she came over, she squeezed in between him and Dean, her elbow touching his hip, a bottle in each hand. He looked down at her, but she ignored him, scanning the circle.

"This feels a little kumbaya," she said, the usual wry humour in her voice.

"We could sing," Nate said, grinning, and catching Will's eye.

"Oooh, acappella!" Em almost bounced on her toes. "Would you?"

Nate had never needed much of an excuse to sing, and an invitation? He wouldn't turn that down. He started singing *Elements Combined*, a song by Fiction Family, and Will joined in with the harmony just because it was habit, and the song demanded it. Nate could hold a song on his own, sure, but it sounded that much better with the both of them.

Nate was singing to Liv, her face pinking under his attention. Will had been around for part of his relationship with Cindy, the girl who'd ripped his heart out. He was looking at Liv like that, which was maybe a brave thing for Nate to be doing. Liv, from what Will had gathered, wasn't nearly the open book that Cindy had been. Though when all was said and done, Will could argue a good case for her lack of transparency. What had she really been doing with Nate? Playing games. She was just more subtle about it than the likes of Faye Taylor. With Faye, it was more of a sport.

But was Faye over Nate? She'd latched onto Jiro like he was Nate's gift to her which was a little messed up all on its own. Will wasn't really sure he wanted to play this sport. Maybe Nate had been trying to protect him as much as Faye by trying to put Will off.

Jo was the first to speak into the quiet that followed the song. "The musical interlude was beautiful and all, but we should probably get your filly loaded and back to Woodbine." She glanced at Liv

"You're taking her back tonight?" Faye said.

Liv nodded. "Jo brought the van down."

"Let's do it, then," Nate said. "We'll have a real party after she wins the Breeders.'"

"Hush, Miller," Liv hissed, and Nate just laughed at her.

Nate and Liv looked like quite the couple, him in his suit, her in her dress, putting up the ramp after Jo had put the horse on the van. Nate grabbed Liv's arm and kissed her before she rushed off to jump in her car to follow the trailer as it pulled away.

"So that's it?" Will asked as Nate rejoined them.

"They're all up past their bedtimes," Faye said, that little smile toying with her lips.

"Exactly. Time to hit the road." Nate pulled his keys from a pocket.

Dean stared at his phone, then typed something. "Hey Faye, would you be able to catch a ride back with Nate? A friend of mine down here asked if I wanted to go for a drink. And if I do that, I'll just stay over and leave early to get to Woodbine."

Faye stared daggers at him. Will was a little stunned by how clueless her brother was.

"How about this?" Emilie chimed in. "I'll go with Nate, if you don't mind taking Faye, Will?"

"Not at all," Will said, probably a little too quickly, but Faye looked relieved.

"Have fun, Dean. Let's go then, Em. Drive safe." Nate raised a hand and Emilie followed him to the Mustang.

"We can go now," Will murmured, and Faye's eyes flashed to his. Now where was his car?

CHAPTER EIGHT

HER FEET WERE KILLING HER. Hindsight: she should have asked Nate to give her and Will a ride to Will's car. She could have dealt with being in the Mustang for that long. But thank you Em, for avoiding the prospect of two hours back to the farm with him. Sure she was over him. But that was asking too much.

"You okay?" Will said.

She was too stubborn to ask him to slow down. "I'm fine," she muttered through gritted teeth. One day she'd learn that comfort was more important to fashion. Too bad it hadn't been today.

"There it is." Will pointed into the darkness.

It wasn't hard to pick out the car. It was one of the only ones left in the big lot, and it was unusual enough that Faye remembered it. She folded into the passenger seat with a sigh, throwing a grateful look up at Will as he swung the door shut, and immediately unbuckled the shoes. So pretty, but so painful. Then she removed her hat, set it in her lap, and ran her fingers through her hair to put some lift back into it.

"You know how to get out of here?" she asked when Will ducked in the driver's side.

He nodded, zooming around to point towards the highway.

So here we are again.

But she was distinctly aware that, regardless of the little moments of zing she thought they'd shared today, he had yet to seek her out, and the only times they'd had contact was because of mutual friends. Well, Nate, specifically. The thought that Nate might have anything to do with Will keeping away made her seethe. Between her aching feet and watching the evening's exchanges between Liv and Nate – she hadn't wanted to let them get to her, but they did anyway – she was exhausted. Just drive, she wanted to say. But she wasn't good at silence.

"So what did you think of the whole Prince of Wales experience?" She tucked a foot into her lap and started kneading it.

Will turned down the music on the radio – it hadn't even registered with Faye that it was playing until he did.

"It was different, being there. I've seen big races on TV, but it's like hockey, you miss so much. Miss hearing and noticing things, because all you ever see is what the cameras decide to show you."

"But this wasn't your first ever time at the races. You were at the Plate."

He shook his head. "Nate arranged whatever credentials we needed to get in, and we went right to the stables."

"Just as well. I love the Plate, but for an authentic racetrack experience, Fort Erie on Prince of Wales night is a better bet."

"It's kind of – shabby," Will said. "But it was cool. Except maybe for the last part at the barn."

"The Fort's backstretch has seen better days, that's for sure."

"So how big a deal is it they won that race?"

"It's pretty big. Liv isn't the first female trainer to have won both the Plate and the Prince of Wales, but she will be the first to win the Triple Crown, if Chique wins the Breeders'. We might be more progressive here in Canada than in the States – we have a number of successful female trainers – but it's still a man's world."

Faye stole a glance at him, when she could have easily stared for the whole two hours home. He was that good looking. It was such a shame things weren't happening between them. She'd tried her best to chat up Jiro, but even that hadn't been satisfying, because she'd kept wondering if Will was watching, and if it bothered him in the least.

"So what was with Dean ditching you like that?"

Faye laughed quietly. "My brother is the most solid, reliable guy on the planet, ninety-nine point nine percent of the time. If on occasion he wants to play, I don't say anything. It's good for him. He needs to do it more. But he could plan better." She sent Will a half-smile, and tried not to think of how valiant it had been of Will to realize how awkward it would have been for Nate to drive her home. "Thank you. How many times have you rescued me now?"

"If he'd done it like half an hour earlier, you could have gone with that Jiro guy."

Oh, well, that was interesting. That wasn't an innocent comment. It was a good thing she was sober, and tired enough not to be firing off-handed comments. "Jiro's just an amusement."

"Like me after the Plate Party?"

Ouch. But guilty. "Is that why you didn't play along? Because you thought that?"

"That, and I wasn't about to trust your judgement when there was cheap champagne flowing, and your ex – my friend –

making ground with someone new. Not to mention that that friend would kick my ass if I behaved dishonourably."

Ah, so, Nate did have something to do with it. "Why would he do that?"

"Because despite how things turned out, he cares about you."

She snorted. "What a guy. You're both too kind. I can take care of myself." This was going famously. Maybe she should have gone with Nate. At least a fight with him would feel good.

"So why are you so mad at Nate? You broke up with him, didn't you?"

She knew exactly why she was mad. She also knew, if she was honest with herself, she wasn't mad at Nate. She was mad at herself. It just made sense for that to manifest as anger towards him. It wasn't exactly a new strategy in the history of the world. "Why do we always end up talking about Nate?"

"To help you get him out of your system."

"Therapy isn't really my thing, if that's your angle. I can think of a far better way to get him out of my system. And I'm sober this time, so you can throw out that excuse. Nate can deal with whatever objections he has to it. I promise not to hold either of you responsible." She switched feet. "You have another hour and a half to think about it. And just to prove I'm not holding a grudge against Nate, the two of you, that acappella duet – wow. Please tell me you're going to do something more than backstretch parties with that."

"I've been trying to talk him into it. We do kind of have opposite schedules. At least our days off match up." He hesitated, fiddling with the volume on the stereo again. "You should come down sometime and hang out while we play. Bring Em with you if it'd be too weird because of Nate."

"Now that I am mad at Nate about. That he never brought

me down. But he never really shared the best parts of himself with me, so I shouldn't be surprised." Maybe just as well, because what he had shared had been hard enough to let go. "He never sang to me, like he sang to Liv tonight. That was sweet, you know?" So it had hurt, burned, pierced, wounded.

Will didn't respond to that. She was opening up too much, bringing Nate right back into it when she'd been so determined not to.

"I don't even know what you do," he said, thankfully steering away from anything that involved Nate. "For work."

"Likewise," she said, a little cheek coming back to her voice. "You first."

"All right. It's very glamourous. I'm a bookkeeper. It started out just being for the farm, and Dean – payroll and taxes and such – then he got me a few more clients. I always thought that I'd get a real job after graduating, but...I don't know. Maybe I'm just an underachiever."

"What's your degree?"

"Commerce. Your turn."

"Almost as glamourous. I work in a restaurant."

"What do you do?"

"Sous-chef."

"A sous-chef with a degree in music. At least my job is remotely related to my education."

"Working in the restaurant business seems to go hand-in-hand with working in the music industry." He grinned, and the hum fluttered back up through her. "But I actually find I like working with food. So I'm thinking about sticking with that."

"Like going to school for it?"

"Yeah. And we need to talk about something other than food, or we're going to have to stop somewhere for something to eat. That buffet was hours ago."

I could eat, she almost said, wanting to prolong this, because hovering around the hum of attraction was something less familiar: contentment. He was going out of his way again to drive her home, though, and she didn't want to take up even more of his time.

"So you aren't a horse girl at all?"

"Oh hell no." Her laugh was automatic. "Everyone thinks I must've been born into the wrong family, because the horse gene skipped me. I let Dean deal with the hands-on. The books – and the odd bale of hay – is as close as I get."

"Guess I can't use the horse girl excuse either, then, can I?"

She smirked. *Don't toy with me.* "What restaurant do you work at? Would I know it?" Food was something she could talk safely about. While Liv was always too busy for forays into the city, Em was usually up for it.

"Mysticus. Right downtown?"

"Ooh, fancy. I have never been. I don't quite frequent those circles."

"I thought your family owns racehorses."

"Parts of racehorses, remember. There's a joke about owning horses. Do you know how to make a million dollars in horse racing? Start with two million."

"That doesn't –"

"Make sense. I know. You're supposed to laugh, not think about it." He laughed easily, and it fed the little happy feeling in her chest. "Dean usually ends up having to take on partners in the best horses to keep things going."

"So did your father retire?"

"My parents and middle brother were killed in a car accident eleven years ago." She was so used to saying it, she never felt the need to sugarcoat, but Will went very still.

"I'm sorry," he said, when his reaction made her feel as if she should be apologizing for being so blunt.

She'd never wanted anyone's pity for the loss. And only Dean might understand how much it had made her the person she was. A psychologist would probably have a field day with her. But sometimes she felt she was hanging onto it all – the grief, the guilt – because who would she be, really, without it? Her identity was built around it.

"Please tell me your parents are alive, or the rest of the drive is going to be unbearably awkward and depressing, and I'm going to end up wishing I had gone back with Nate, as tortuous as that would have been."

Will made a sound that was trying to be a laugh. "Alive and well. My mom's a doctor and my dad's an Environmental Engineer."

"How do they feel about a son who works in a restaurant?" She would definitely not want to be the girl who met the over-achiever parents.

"They're those parents who say, 'as long as you're happy...'"

"And are you?"

He glanced at her, then back to the road. "Good question."

"So if you're not...what would you change?" She didn't usually ask this many questions of the men she wanted to sleep with. She didn't usually care to get to know them that well beforehand. But sex wasn't a foregone conclusion here – Will didn't seem inclined to pull over to the side of the road and ravish here there. Was that legal? So they'd be in this car for a while yet.

"My job. The head chef is an ass. He treats the female staff like shit. I just want to pound him."

"So why do you stay?"

"Because I haven't figured out what else to do with my life, and I have bills to pay."

Huh. They had that much in common. "That can't be fun, standing by when he's treating people badly."

"It's even worse that they put up with it."

"I wouldn't last very long in a place like that."

His laugh was looser this time. "No, you would not."

"So do you have a plan? You're all educated in music, is there something you could do with that? Besides teaching?" She remembered that.

This time when he looked over, there was a little furrow in his brow, a crease between his eyes that flickered with uncertainty. "Music's tough. It's a hard way to pay the rent. And I've always worried that I'd love it less if I had to make money with it. The restaurant biz has grown on me. And this may sound stupid, but I have a thing for pastry."

"I have a thing for pastry too," she quipped.

He chuckled, the deepness of it strumming her strings with a vibration that resonated deep.

"I've learned a bit about it at the restaurant. If I do go back to school, it would be for that, but throwing money at yet more education...I don't know. My mother would insist on paying for it, and I don't want her to do that. So I'm doing what I can online, and practicing at home, and sometimes I get to do stuff at work. What I'd love is to have my own place. Not a restaurant; more a cafe, with books and music and espresso and original art by local artists on the walls. Not necessarily in the city. The city gets kind of old."

"What a great dream," Faye said quietly, thinking of her offer to Lucy, and the brainstorming it had inspired. More common ground. She didn't want to like him as much as she did. She hadn't even liked Nate that much by this point. He'd just fit the profile.

She kept asking questions because it spared Will having to query her. He was probably too scared to, afraid of any more awkward revelations. Did she have more? He knew about Nate. He knew about the car accident. Her approach to relationships wasn't exactly a secret. Maybe all the skeletons were out.

"Do you have siblings?"

He shook his head. "Only child. I grew up down the street from Nate, so he and his brothers were like family to me. I was pretty happy when I found out he was moving east too. Until this whole racehorse thing swallowed him up."

"That's exactly what it does." It was all-encompassing, leaving room for nothing – and no one – on the outside. Race-trackers worked together. They played together. They dated and married within the cult, and made more racetrackers. Sometimes that next generation had the common sense to escape. She'd been one of those. She was most definitely not a racetracker; the backstretch just provided her with a few book-keeping clients, and a consistent supply of prospects for her non-relationships. Things never would have worked out with Nate long-term.

She'd known that, but let herself believe otherwise for a while. She was always surrounded by racetrackers, how could she expect them to be rational? She'd needed someone like Will to come along to make it obvious.

"What about you?" he asked. "The dream thing."

"I'm excelling at being an underachiever, so I was planning just to go with it. We should all do what we do best, right?"

"Oh come on, there's got to be something."

"Then my dream is to be a sexy spinster to my brother's genteel bachelor."

Will snorted. "So basically a cougar?"

Faye looked at him wryly. "I can't quite decide if that's supposed to be an insult. If so, I'm going to reclaim that word for the greater good of middle-aged women everywhere."

"You're definitely not middle-aged."

"No, but we're dreaming here, right?"

He laughed. "So you'll have, like, gentleman callers?"

"Yes. And Dean will continue to do whatever Dean does. Which none of us really knows."

"Try to be serious for a moment. They say the thing you wanted to do as a kid is what you're supposed to be."

"I'm betting you didn't want to be a pastry chef."

"It's no fun when you don't play."

Faye sighed, and wracked her brain. She'd tossed out the idea of dreams so long ago, she couldn't even remember if she had any. She'd always envied that about Liv – that she had such a big dream, to become a jockey, and she'd gone after it. Even if she never went back to riding races, at least she could say she'd done it. Faye had nothing.

"I just wanted to get away from the kind of life I was raised in. I didn't care where, or what took me there. But I'm not going anywhere."

"What's stopping you?"

"Everything. Dean needs me. I mean, look at him. He's closing in on forty. If he found a wife, I'd be off the hook. I could get out of that damn house." She loved and hated that house, somehow. "I don't see that happening, though."

"I bet Dean can take care of himself. We can do that too, you know."

"But the bookwork...that's our deal. I take care of that side of the business, he does the horses and the face-to-face with the clients."

"I'm pretty sure in this day and age you could do that from anywhere."

He wasn't letting her out of this, but she was at a loss. "Clearly I'm going to need help with this big dream thing. We have another hour to figure it out, so let's go."

"Can you sing? You could do vocals for our band. We could

use a female voice. I'm envisioning you and Nate doing Gotye's *Somebody That I Used To Know*."

It felt good to laugh that hard, to throw her head back against the headrest and let go of tension in her chest she hadn't even realized she'd been holding there. "That's a good one."

"So you can sing?"

"I can carry a tune." She couldn't tell him about the painful memories associated with it; how she and Shawn had put on silly mock concerts, how he'd always been the star of the high school musical. How when he'd died, she'd left the singing to others, like her voice had died with him. "All right, that's one. I need more than one."

"Hmmm..." He drummed his fingers on the steering wheel. "Craft brewery? Boutique winery?"

"That would be fun. I could move down this way. Or Prince Edward County."

"Or maybe you could roast coffee beans."

"For your café. You could have your own proprietary beans. To go with the perfect tiny pastries you're going to make."

That sounded a bit too much like they were doing things together, and a little too close to what might be kindling for a dream with Lucy's. If only Lucy would call her.

She needed to redirect. "What do you do for fun, besides play music and bake things? Are you into sports? Please tell me you're not a runner like Nate and Liv."

"No. I played hockey with him growing up, but was never really that good. Used to ski back home. Used to climb."

"Like mountains? You are a badass, then."

"Nope. Not anymore."

His voice was a little flat. There was probably a story behind that, something more personal than she wanted to get into right now. "Just as well, we probably don't have what you'd call mountains around here."

"Your turn," he said, pushing them past the awkward.

"What do I do for fun? You mean, besides getting dressed up and going to the races? I cook. I read." *I pick up bug boys and have my way with them. But in the absence of one of them you'll do nicely.*

"What's your favourite book?" he asked.

The perfect segue. He was well-read, and it kept the conversation going until they were on the sideroad home, and she realized he hadn't asked her to direct him to the farm.

"Do you have a photographic memory or something?" she asked, an eyebrow quirked.

"Just a good one."

He crept up the lane, and for a moment she considered perhaps she should be concerned her remembered where she lived, that his jumping in to drive her home – so far, far out of the way for him – was just a convenient opportunity to execute a plan to slit her throat and leave her to bleed out in her own driveway. Then she remembered he was Nate's friend, and regardless of her antagonism towards Nate right now, would he really have a friend who was a murderer? And if for some crazy reason he did, would he let that murderer drive her home?

She picked up her shoes in one hand – she would suffer those few feet of gravel before she got to the back deck before she'd put those wretched things on again – and reached for the door handle. "Thank you for doing this. On my brother's behalf. For saving me from a fate worse than death." He followed her across the deck. Had he really been a murderer, would she still have been thinking it preferable? What was worth that death? "It's far too soon for me to be civil in private to my ex. I'm impressed with myself for being able to be civil in public."

"And we made it so long without talking about Nate."

She wasn't expecting that look, the light by the back door

catching the upward twist of his lips on one side. His hazel eyes reminded her of champagne, and she let herself feel just a little drunk by them. He leaned in, and it was all the permission she needed to meet him, and his lips did exactly sizzle when they connected with hers.

"Come in," she breathed against his mouth. "Don't make me beg."

CHAPTER NINE

Four AM brought the realization of what should have been there that was not, and what was there that should not have been.

Faye was always aware, if not fully conscious, of Dean rising before dawn, brewing coffee, making toast. He'd eat, then go out to feed the horses on the farm so his manager could sleep later, then she'd hear the roar of his truck starting, the crunch of tires on gravel as it rumbled out the lane. She'd roll over, and sleep to a more civilized hour.

The house was strangely devoid of those sounds. For a groggy moment, she thought she'd better make sure he was up. He never slept in, but there was a first time for everything, right? Then she remembered, he'd stayed in Fort Erie. He'd probably gotten up an hour ago, wherever he'd ended up, and would be on the road to Woodbine to make it by his usual time.

There was an unfamiliar sound in its place, however. This time when she rolled over to reclaim the slumber luring her back, it was to the sight of Will's head pressed into the pillow, hair falling across his forehead, beautiful lashes dark against his skin. The sheet rose and fell with his breathing, his arm free of it millimetres from her own. For a moment, she let herself feel it, the strangeness of it. Any man who had shared this bed had been gone by this time – to risk their necks on those crazy horses. The fact that this one was still here was a reminder that he wasn't one of them. There *was* a first time for everything. But that, in and of itself, was dangerous. Because it would be harder to find excuses to push him away.

If she closed her eyes again, and went back to sleep, he would probably be gone too. That's how it went. And how she wanted this to go. But she watched him a while longer, to enjoy the novelty of it, however brief it might be.

It was light out now. He was still here.

As was Gus, the Golden Retriever, cold nose on her elbow, tail thumping softly against the hardwood.

She put a finger to her lips, *shhhhh*...the least she could do in appreciation of Will not only bringing her home, but also ending her painfully long dry spell, was let him sleep. She threw on a robe and padded downstairs to let Gus out, then back in, then fed him his breakfast before climbing back up to the bathroom. She stopped to look at her reflection in the mirror – the messy hair, the colour in her cheeks – and smiled at it before slipping out of her robe and into the shower.

Oh yes, she was back. For real now.

The man could sleep like a rock. She almost took a photo of him, dozing all cute and dreamy, to send to Em, but thought better of it. That would just be crass. Damp hair soaking through her t-shirt, she pulled on jeans and left him there in search of coffee.

Coffee. Another reminder Dean hadn't been around. The

little bit he always left in the carafe, even if it was burnt and nasty, was how she always started her day. It was one of those little things she loved, because he'd thought to leave it for her.

It got worse. They were out of coffee, period, so there would be none of the French press magic that routinely followed that first cup. Oh well, even less reason for Will to stay. But she couldn't exactly leave him here while she went off in search of some. There was a jar of Nescafé of unknown origin in the back of a cupboard. It would depend on just how desperate he was for that first hit of caffeine.

"'Morning."

She jumped, and spun around, bracing herself against the counter. Then recovered, holding up the jar doing her best display model impersonation. "Coffee?"

"Are you serious?" He laughed, eyes still sleepy, his smile lazy. And he was shirtless.

It was almost enough for her to change her mind about this being just a one-time thing. She could put up a case for it still being part of a single event and meander to him, run her hands over that chest, and help him back out of those pesky slacks. Right there against the doorframe would do.

No, no. He'd served his purpose.

"Normally I'd say no, but apparently we're out of real coffee. The little Prince of Wales foray meant Dean missed his usual Tuesday grocery shop."

"Is there a Starbucks around?"

"Hardly. We don't have them on every street corner around here. There is a coffee shop in town though."

"Do they serve breakfast?"

"Of a fashion. Follow me there? My treat." When he looked like he was going to protest, she waved him off, with a coy smile. "I owe you. You'll need to put on a shirt, sadly."

Getting him out of here was the right thing to do.

Lucy did serve limited breakfast options to go with the only slightly better coffee. Faye wondered if Lucy would be offended if she made some suggestions in that department. If Lucy ever called her, that was.

"What's good here?" Will asked, standing slightly behind her at the café's counter – close enough she could remember the heat of skin to skin.

She took a breath to steady herself. "Everything tastes the same," she whispered, with one eye on Lucy herself, who pressed out from the kitchen, wiping her hands on her apron, her permanent scowl in place. One did not insult Lucy by saying such things within earshot, because those butter tarts were the best in a fifty-kilometre radius, and quite possibly wider. They made up for everything else.

Faye's smile wasn't reciprocated. The reception she was getting made Faye wonder if she'd just dreamed that moment of vulnerability she'd seen in the café owner.

"I'll have an egg sandwich on a biscuit –" she started.

"We're all out of biscuits," Lucy snapped.

"An English muffin then?"

Lucy nodded.

Faye glanced back at Will. "What do you want?"

"That sounds good," he said, his tone hesitant.

"Two of those, then. And two coffees. And half a dozen butter tarts?" she added hopefully.

"Last ones." Lucy nodded, setting the styrofoam tray of tarts on the counter. She rang up the order on the old cash register, and waited while Faye pulled out her wallet and found some bills.

"Well she's terrifying," Will muttered as they sat down, the round metal table tilting when they set the food on it. He pried the plastic top off the styrofoam coffee cup, peering at it suspiciously before dousing it with cream and sugar. He hadn't added anything to his cappuccino on Plate night – that would have been gauche – but Lucy's coffee definitely needed help.

He replaced the lid, took a sip, and shrugged. "I've had worse."

Faye drank hers black, because it would make her appreciate the butter tarts all the more. Will watched her with eyebrows raised as she scarfed down the egg sandwich.

"What can I say, I worked up an appetite last night."

He grinned before he bit into his own, chewed...swallowed...and gave another shrug.

"Had worse?" Faye suggested.

"Yes." He washed it down with coffee.

"Are we food snobs?" she whispered.

"You are, for sure."

"And you're not, Mr. Sous-Chef?"

"Occupational hazard," he agreed.

Faye made a show of opening the butter tarts, then removed two and set one next to Will's plate.

She plucked the other from its tin. "This is why we endure the mediocre."

The filling was crystallized on top and soft in the middle, caramelly-sweet on her tongue, with a touch of sea salt. The flaky pastry melted on her tongue. She closed her eyes and sighed, holding the flavours in her mouth before swallowing.

"Should I leave the two of you alone?"

"You jest," she said, taking a sip of the bitter coffee. "You'll see."

He set the foil to the side, appraising the tart for a moment before presenting it to his mouth like an offering. Would he demolish it in two bites, or three? Would he balance the sweet with bitter coffee? No point in that part, probably; he'd added enough milk and sugar to obliterate the coffee taste.

Two, and *no*.

"You're right," he said, licking his sticky fingertips after the tart had disappeared. "That might be the best butter tart I've ever tasted." He sipped some of his coffee, glancing at his phone. "You should come down Monday. When we play. Nate doesn't usually show up on Mondays."

Little things like that threatened her intent to let this go at last night. He didn't judge her for not wanting to be around Nate. He got that it would be uncomfortable. He didn't expect her to just get over herself and play nice.

"Thank you for the invite. I'll think about that."As much as an alien part of her brain wanted to follow him home, crawl into his bed, make herself a permanent fixture there...no, she would not.

He pushed himself back from the table and stood, coffee cup in hand. "I've got to go. Thanks for breakfast."

She almost said *the pleasure was all mine,* but felt strongly it had been mutual.

"I'll call you," he added

She wasn't going to mention that he hadn't asked for her number, or given her an address. She let him say the things, even if he didn't mean them. He leaned over, his free hand snaking behind her neck as he placed a kiss on her lips that felt anything but chaste. Then he grabbed two more butter tarts with a grin, and walked out. Thief. And he's stolen more than just pastry, he'd nabbed a chunk of her resolve.

"Hi Will."

Oh. That voice was familiar. So familiar Faye could see the dark eyebrows raised, the hair pulled back in its perpetual ponytail, the amused twist to the lips. Faye turned slowly as Liv walked in, rolling her fingers at Faye in a small wave. Will wasn't in view, but he must have held the door open for her.

Liv ordered a coffee, so Faye stayed put. When she asked for a butter tart, Lucy magically found one. She always had a butter tart for Liv. It was like she was trying to fatten the girl up. She almost even smiled when she presented it on its white china plate.

"It's like you knew I was here," Faye said when Liv settled across from her, the seat probably still warm from Will's very fine butt.

"I saw your car out front. And, doing better, right?"

"I think we are. How's the filly this morning?" It was more than rote; she was feeling renewed, the world a brighter place today.

"Good." Liv bit into the butter tart. She was a *three* and *yes*. Faye could tell she was letting those flavours linger before she reached for the coffee. "And how are you this morning?" She drew the words out, eyebrows arcing again.

Faye turned the styrofoam cup slowly, contemplating another butter tart because she was feeling indulgent. A kittenish smile tweaked her mouth. "Good," she said simply.

"It's eleven AM and you're just having breakfast. You never let them stick around that long."

"That's simply circumstance. They always had to be at work before dawn. He doesn't have to be at work till later."

"But you didn't chase him away. And you had breakfast in public."

"You're right. I also shared my butter tarts with him. It might be serious."

Liv's eyes narrowed, like she was trying to glean if there was any truth in the crack.

Faye laughed at her. "So I know one thing for sure. I got more action than you last night."

A tinge of crimson rose in Liv's cheeks. "He caught up with the van and helped unload."

"Is that foreplay? For weird horse girls?"

Liv stuck out her tongue before taking another sip of coffee. "So when are you going to see him again?"

"After the Breeders' Stakes, if things follow their present pattern. Maybe he'll propose then," she quipped. "He did ask me to come down next Monday and hear some music. But no. This was a one and done, sweetie. Mission accomplished. I am back on track."

But a little voice in her head whispered, *the same track? Or a new one?*

———————

Will had never been to Nate's apartment, but for some reason, now seemed like a good time. They were old, old friends; he had to be honest. He wasn't going to keep this from Nate. He texted first, instead of running the risk of wandering aimlessly around that big farm, because that was probably discouraged. Nate texted back, with directions to keep that from happening.

There were gates, which opened as he drove up – no security code needed, though there was a keypad. Tall maples in full plumage on either side of the driveway created a canopy overhead. Nate had said to turn left after the big house – which was mostly hidden by more big trees. He parked the Chevy next to Nate's Mustang and left them there like old friends, catching up.

It was cool inside the barn, and it seemed to be empty. He found the stairs, tromped up, and rapped on the door, balancing the two butter tarts in his cupped palm. Nate's familiar voice called to him to come in.

"Cool space, dude," he said, closing the door behind him. There were shoes on a mat there, so he left his with them. "A real piano, even. How did you get that up here?"

Nate's initial expression of mild surprise at Will's appearance narrowed. "Wait – are those Lucy's butter tarts?" In no time flat he was snatching one, flashing a quick glance up at Will, and heading for the kitchen.

"What happened to the whole jockey weight thing?"

"I'll tack a pound over for one of those. Or put time in the sweatbox if I have to. It'll be worth it." He set the tart on a plate with reverence. "You have to warm them up a little. Make the filling a bit runny." He set the plate in the microwave, beeping in a time. "Here, give me the other one."

Will obeyed, exchanging it for the hot tart Nate handed him. He parked himself on one of the stools at the kitchen counter.

"You slept with her, didn't you?" Nate said, not entirely without accusation, before biting into the hot pastry he'd just nuked, blowing out and fanning his mouth.

It seemed pointless to answer when Nate had clearly already figured it out. Either way, he didn't want to be grilled about it, so he ignored it, deflecting with his own question. "So do I remember you saying you actually don't pay rent here? I'd think you'd actually have to be sleeping with the owner's daughter to get away with that." Will grinned.

"What can I say, they like me." Nate's tone was abrupt "So are you here just to tell me about Faye?"

He wasn't just going to let it slide. "What's there to talk about, really? I wanted you to know first hand. Because the way things work in your tight little world, I'm sure you'd hear about it soon enough. You might already know."

Nate opened the fridge, grabbing two bottles of water. "No. Did you think Faye was going to text me or something? Like, 'take that, you bastard.'"

"You think she's using me? It was some kind of revenge move?"

"No, actually, I don't," Nate responded quietly. "And I

should probably just keep my thoughts to myself. You're both adults."

"Why are you so out of sorts about this? You look like you're happy with Liv."

"I am, okay? I don't know why. Just be careful. For both your sakes."

"You could say we'd been on three dates, so except for the part where you have a bug up your ass, it's perfectly acceptable, isn't it?"

"Three dates?" Nate nudged one of the bottles of water over the counter then opened the other one.

"I drove her home after your Plate Party, which was your idea, as I recall. I came and helped with the hay. I hung out with her and drove her home after the race yesterday. It's more normal that you and Liv. Do you guys even see each other outside of work? I think I have the potential for a healthier relationship with her than what you've got."

That made Nate laugh. "You may be right. Damn, I need to work on that."

"Seriously." Will grinned. He picked up the water, and turned back to the room, scanning the space. "So you think we could come here sometimes? It would give you a break from driving into the city all the time."

Nate shrugged. "There are three of you, and only one of me. Plus not sure the noise would be welcome, with the horses and all. And along the same lines, the only thing that gets me off this place is work, so, balance?"

"Why don't you bring Liv down sometime?"

"Maybe I'll ask her. That doesn't mean she'll come."

"How come you never brought Faye down?"

Nate met the look Will gave him, looking a little grim, a little regretful.

"She told you that, did she?" He paused. "I wasn't really

coming that often when I was seeing her anyway, I guess. My career was new. She was new. Maybe it was something deeper, I don't know. Like I was keeping her in her own compartment, because of what happened with Cindy. What if you two had hit it off then? She would have ditched me a whole lot sooner than she did."

"Would have saved you both a whole lot of grief though, right?" He finished off the tart in two bites. Nate was right, it was way better warm, but that wasn't news.

Nate smirked, like he didn't appreciate Will stating the obvious. "You're a jerk. Can you get out of here? I have to ride tonight, and after being so late last night, I'm exhausted. I need sleep."

Will walked to the door, Nate following. "Oh, one more thing. My dad's in town, to get married, believe it or not. He invited me, and you, and whoever we want to bring with us. It's in a few weeks. Please, please, *please* say you'll come?"

"You're really testing this friendship, you know."

Will slapped him on the arm, and reached for the door. "You're the best, buddy. Talk to you soon."

Will checked his texts as he towel-dried his hair. Monique asking for a ride to work. His neighbour three doors down saying she was away for a few days, could he feed her cat, for the millionth time in the last month. *Yeah, absolutely*, he responded to both. Nate was doing him a huge favour, saying he'd come to the wedding; the least he could do was pay it forward.

The cat's name was Clementine, but Will just called her Lemon. She was a little tabby with white on her chest and extending down her front legs, and was waiting with meow on repeat when Will unlocked the door. He scooped her up and scratched her behind her ears, and she vibrated against his chest.

"What would you like for lunch, *chérie?*" He opened the fridge, found an open tin of wet cat food, and portioned out a couple of spoons into a small dish. "Et voilà! Tuna *tartine.*" Not exactly, but it sounded better than Fancy Feast, which probably had little to no tuna in it anyway. "*Bon appétit.*" His entire French vocabulary was related to food.

He filled another bowl with kibble, gave her fresh water, then leaned up against the counter to watch her eat. He found himself wondering if Faye liked cats. Maybe they just had barn cats. They had a dog, a goofy bear of a Golden. Which led him to wondering if Dean had stayed in Fort Erie to get laid, or just to go drinking with his buddies. Either way, it had worked out just fine as far as Will was concerned.

Lemon finished the wet food, took one sniff of the dry, and wafted over to him, rubbing against his legs with fresh pleas. He lifted her again. "Sorry, *chérie.* Your mom says you have to watch your waistline. It sucks, I know. He placed her back down, and tried not to trip over her as he headed for the door. "I'll see you later. Some of us have to work for a living."

Work. That talk of dreams last night was getting to him. Actually being in that plain old café with the for lease sign, imagining what it could be. What would it be like having a partner? Someone smart and bold like Faye to handle the business side, which he admittedly struggled with. He'd bet she'd do a business plan, and have spreadsheets, and all that stuff that made him shudder. Then he could focus on the creative side. The menu. The right beans. He could handle the kitchen equipment they'd need. Sourcing it. Setting up an SOP. Training staff – when they got that far. Live music nights, a

bookshelf, local ...he needed to call that number, and find out more.

Enough of that. Better get Monique. It would be a bad thing for both of them to be late. Chef would explode.

He was the guy with the car. Few people in the city had them. It made sense – parking was a nightmare, and transit was so readily available. But he'd come east with his, and needed to hang onto it, for the same reason Nate hung onto that Mustang: because it was part of his history. But it meant he was the one his co-workers called on when their usual rides fell through, or transit wasn't going to work, or they didn't have money for a taxi. He was the guy with the car. How did you say no?

Monique was waiting, her blonde hair in a bobbing pony-tail, her makeup perfect. She immediately started chattering away, and he tried to act like he was paying attention, while mostly tuning her out. She seemed extra-superficial today.

"So how was your race thingy? How did your friend do?"

"What?" The race thingy seemed like a different lifetime now. "Good. Great, really. He won."

"That's amazing! My little sister loves horse racing. She probably knows all about it. What was the race name?"

Will relayed the info – actually remembering Prince of Wales because he'd associated it with the Princess of Wales Theatre. Monique keyed something into her phone. Googling it, probably.

"Oh, here it is," she chirped. "He's cute, the jockey. If you like short guys."

Some women do, apparently. Like Faye. Nate, Jiro...that was her thing. And Will had gone ahead last night knowing that. Knowing also he was the rebound, and her way to get past a breakup she'd been clinging to...with his best friend. Maybe he should have heeded Nate's advice.

"That's your friend?"

He glanced at her. "Yeah. Nate. We grew up together, in Calgary."

"That's pretty cool. It says it was like $400,000. Did he win all that?"

"Well – I don't know exactly how it works." Faye could tell him. The way she'd played liaison last night had been pretty damn adorable. "The horse wins it though. But he gets some. He still drives the same old car though, so it can't be that much." Or else he really was just as attached to that old Mustang as Will was to his old Chevy.

Why did everyone want to talk about Nate? Monique didn't even know him, and she'd latched onto the subject. But what else were they going to talk about? No one wanted to talk about work. And he'd never had a conversation with Monique about life dreams or the best books.

He was going to be cool about Faye. He was going to accept that it had been, only, a one-night stand. It wasn't his first. Except...he couldn't shake hoping it was his last.

CHAPTER TEN

"COFFEE'S READY." Dean closed the door on the darkness outside, Gus bringing a current of air with him as he rushed to Faye's feet, like the particles were trapped in his thick coat.

Faye stumbled into the brightly-lit kitchen, eyeing the gurgling brew Dean had initiated before he'd gone out to feed. He poured, then handed her a cup, and she breathed the rich vapour in, wishing she could inhale the caffeine until it was cool enough to drink.

"Toast?" Dean asked, setting up a couple of slices in toaster slots.

Faye waved a declining hand at him instead of speaking, and sipped her coffee gingerly. It burned her mouth a little, but the tradeoff was worth it. She consumed enough of it while Dean ate his toast to help her brain cells start to fire, when by rights they should have still been directing dreams.

Once she was in the passenger seat of the truck, she leaned back and closed her eyes, because Dean, thankfully, wouldn't be looking for conversation. She wasn't likely to find REM sleep in the next forty minutes, but it didn't mean she couldn't rest. Two strange mornings in a row...it was taking its toll on her equilibrium. She let her mind go back to yesterday's more preferable scenario, her bed kept warm by the tasty Will. Just because she was done with that didn't mean she couldn't indulge in some fantasy until someone took his place in her head, did it?

She'd never thought about the future before Nate. It had always been just here and now, because anything could happen to rob you of your plans. She'd gone to school and finished her degree because her parents had set aside money for it, and she'd felt obligated to follow through on the wish they'd had for her. But she'd never thought about what she might do with that degree. What job she could find. As the other students in her program job hunted fervently in the final semesters, she'd rolled along, keeping one disinterested eye on them. Sometimes she scanned the posts on the employment sites, but when she'd graduated, she'd continued to help Dean, who was having a good enough few years to support her under-achiever lifestyle. She took on some local and track bookkeeping jobs to stay out of trouble. Well, mostly out of trouble.

Then there had been Nate. She'd let herself imagine things with him she'd never allowed to enter her head before. Not things she'd ever shared with him – she knew better than that – but they'd worked their way in all the same. A house together. Kids. She'd joked to him once, on the beach in Florida, about being a kept woman. Nate's success probably would have let her be just that. They'd never talked any more seriously than that about it, because about the time she'd realized that's what she was thinking, she'd also realized he'd started thinking that way about someone else. And not with just anyone else. With her best friend.

And truth was, she didn't want to be kept. Like Liv, she didn't want to stop being who she was, and wasn't sure how that would work within the confines of a relationship. She'd told herself, and believed it, that that was why she preferred short-term liaisons. She had Dean to keep her company. Dean had help to work the farm. What did Faye need a man for, but entertainment? Except the older she got, the more it wore thin. The more she wondered if it was actually a subconscious safeguard, instead of what she liked to think of as a feminist stance. That by keeping things brief and unemotional she got out before she exposed herself to the seated fear of losing them like she'd lost Shawn, and her parents.

Liv doing the unfathomable, finally getting together with Nate, left Faye feeling she'd lost her one ally when it came to her perspective on men. Emilie might be single, but there was no doubt in anyone's mind she would have a normal, stable relationship one day. She was the sensible, sane one in their group. She'd take her time and be choosy, and end up with Mr. Right, while Faye continued with an endless stream of Mr Right Nows.

She hadn't answered Will Tuesday night when he'd asked her why she was so mad at Nate, because that would have meant letting it go. Part of it was because she could never be truly mad at Liv. Liv had fought it so long – not just the idea of Nate, but the idea of anyone at all – that it was hard to deny her the prospect of someone who saw her. A someone who wouldn't have ever legitimately been happy with Faye. For some reason that seemed to make her extra-mad at Nate. The nerve of him, making her fall for him. Like it had been all his fault. If she let herself, though, she saw that the relationship with him had opened her up to the possibility of such a thing. So here she was, at a crossroads. Did she close herself back off, or push ahead?

Where had all that come from, when Will had been nestled

so nicely in her head? She was not thinking of a future with him in it. She'd established that already.

Will stirred something else in her, though, like he'd inadvertently issued a challenge. A *dare to dream,* when she'd been so committed to not letting herself do that. To not think *what if.* It was bigger than her relationship goals, or lack thereof. Will had made her aware that she was, just under the surface, dissatisfied with her life. That this was not enough.

How dare he rouse her out of her stagnation, make her think she could have more. More than taking care of her brother. More than being taken care of by him. More than maintaining her parents' legacy. Wasn't that important, though? Who said she got to have her own dream? She'd given that up, accepted it wouldn't be her lot in life just like Dean had given up on his education, something he'd dedicated a lot more to than she had, before the accident that had reduced their family to just the two of them.

She liked her life. How had Will come along, and in one night, made that a lie?

Faye stirred when the truck slowed, and opened one eye as Dean pulled up to the security booth at the east gate. He held his hand out for her license, and she fumbled through her purse, and planted it in his palm. The guard scanned them and sent them on.

"Why are you having Nate breeze Wampum?" Faye mumbled, trying to remember why last night it had seemed important for her to come. Except for some reason the colt's work seemed significant, like it would unlock this future she was so worked up about.

"Because I want his opinion. He knows the colt. He's ridden him every time he's run."

Dean had thrown everything into that horse's rehab,

investing money Wampum had earned back into the colt. Faye had worried he might be rushing Wampum by bringing him back when he had – stress fractures usually meant a solid three months of stall rest – and while Dean wasn't one to take chances, maybe this year had made him feel the pressure. On the farm Wampum had received body work, magnetic therapy, and these funky new patches – so much woo Faye had wondered if they might have some sort of weird interaction and cause more harm than good – but when Dean had sent Wampum for scintigraphy to check how the shoulder was healing, the nuclear scan had come back miraculously clean. Now with any luck, the colt would reimburse him for his diligence. Not many trainers would micromanage like that. But that was Dean, through and through.

"Well he can't ride him this time," Faye felt the need to point out. Because Dean had dog-eared the Breeders' Stakes in the condition book with Wampum's name scribbled on it, and everyone knew exactly who Nate would be on that day. A certain filly with a chance to win the Canadian Triple Crown.

Dean laughed. "I know that. I can't always make my rider choices based on your latest love interest, you know."

"That was almost mean, Dean." She smirked. "Who will you get to ride him?"

"Probably Steve. We'll see how Jiro does with She Brews, but if he doesn't win with her I'm putting Nate back on. The bug might be hot right now, but he is still pretty inexperienced, and the Breeders' isn't just any race."

Faye nodded. Steve Gordon was a nice, uncomplicated choice. A veteran rider who had ridden for their father. Neutral, in the grand scheme of things.

The shedrow was a chaotic, scary place this time of morning, when you were just a little afraid of these unpredictable animals. Sure, some horses walked around quietly, but there were enough crazies to put the fear of God into her. She stood with her back pressed against the metal Dutch doors of Wampum's stall while Dean leaned causally on the bar, looking in. Faye caught Nate's arrival out of the corner of her eye.

"'Morning," he said, his tone businesslike. No smart-ass comments about her unexpected presence.

"Hey." Her eyes didn't quite meet his.

"How's our boy?" Nate asked, and Dean shuffled over so they were both looking in.

"He's been training great," Dean said. "If he breezes well, I'll prep him for the Breeders'."

"He's gonna love the turf," Nate said, nodding. "Not the first time I wish I could ride two horses in the same race."

Last time Chique and Wampum had run against each other had been the Fountain of Youth at Gulfstream Park last winter. *Bet you wish you were on our colt that day.* Wampum had run third, while Chique floundered up the track, letting everyone know her disdain for the sloppy conditions.

"I'm going to watch from the bleachers," Faye said as they went to the track, walking far enough out to the side that she was out of harm's way. She split off from them before Dean led Wampum through the tunnel, and stayed on the paved road, giving little smiles and waves when someone would call out to her. Then she cut across the horse path and up the steps, coming out at the backstretch of the turf course.

She was alone here, and it was a better vantage point than at the clocker's stand where most of the trainers gathered. It was more elevated, and further east, so she had a better view. Not that it really mattered to her; her understanding of the finer points was minimal. She just recognized the extremes. The two-year-olds galloping slowly but eagerly in sets; the older, fitter horses on the bridle, their exercise riders with strong holds; the bad actors, crow-hopping sideways, riders cussing into their ears; the workers flying smooth and rapid on the rail.

Nate would be jogging Wampum, going the wrong way on the outside fence, to the wire over on the front side of the track. She didn't try to follow their progress, just observed the horses going by, gazing down towards the turn by the on-gap, trying to recall what Nate had been wearing. He had a navy and red helmet cover, navy jacket, stone-washed jeans. Wampum was a plain bay, and from this angle she wouldn't see the red and white saddle pad, so she looked for a plain bay, red and white helmet, red polo bandages. There they were.

Wampum was still galloping in the middle of the track, relaxed, Nate perched nonchalantly. Then Nate eased him to the rail, his body position changing, and Wampum's ears went up, like he was saying, *oh, really?* His stride quickened, so when they reached the red and white half-mile pole he was taking flight, all business now with his neck stretched in front of him and legs firing as they headed into the turn.

Faye didn't really know if this was fast, or slow, just that it looked like a joyful thing, and Nate wasn't doing much, which meant Wampum was going the way he should.

She didn't wait to watch them gallop out, stepping carefully down the bleachers, looking both ways on the horse path to make sure she didn't spook anyone. She glanced over at the Triple Stripe shed just across the road – a horse grazed on the lawn, and there was activity apparent on the shed – but she didn't see Liv or Em. Then she hurried along the road so she was there by the time Dean, back at Wampum's head, emerged from the tunnel. She heard him ask for the colt's time, saw Nate nodding, and Dean's satisfied smile. That's all she needed to know. They were happy. She followed them back to the barn.

"Where do you have to go next, Nate?" Faye asked, making it sound like she was trying to be polite.

His eyebrow twitched, like he'd caught himself before it got too high, and he dunked the bit in the water bucket. "Trixie Bigsby's."

She nodded. Not Triple Stripe. Good.

"Listen," he said, and Faye froze. He set the tack on the rail. "I'm having a...thing, next week."

"A thing?" Dean looked perplexed, and Faye exhaled. She'd thought he was going to say something about Will.

"Like a get-together. At the farm. Because we couldn't really do anything after the Prince of Wales. I hope you'll both come."

Faye's lips tightened.

"Thanks for the invite," Dean said. "But I'm off to Saratoga for a couple of days."

"Seriously?" Nate said. "Now I'm jealous. If you're running something and didn't ask me to come, especially."

"No. Just getting a couple of days away."

"Jiro said he'd come. To the thing." Nate was gauging Faye's response, like it was a test, but that carrot wasn't as enticing as it would have been a few days ago. Had Liv told him? Unlikely. Will? Would he do that?

I'll have to check my schedule. I think I have plans. Like oral surgery or something more pleasant than your little get-together. But she forced a smile, without answering at all.

"Have fun at the Spa, Dean. Bye, Faye." And then he was, thankfully, gone.

"I'm going to see Liv," she said to her brother. "I should be back before you go, but don't leave without me unless you hear differently."

Liv wasn't in the tack room, so Faye headed straight to Chique's stall, right beside the office. Because where else would Liv be, if she wasn't on a horse?

"Hey." She was cleaning out the filly's feet, the little metal pick clinking against the aluminum shoe as she cleared edges, then scraped out the deeper parts. Faye knew what the frog was, but that was about it. Liv gave the foot a quick brush so there was probably not a speck of dirt left in there, painted it with oil, then placed it down gently in the straw before reaching under to slide her fingers down the right leg. Chique lifted, Liv picked and brushed and painted. She straightened, then moved closer to the door, to Faye, and Chique's hindquarters. "What are you doing in this morning?"

"Dean worked Wampum. First time since the accident. Felt like I should be here, for some reason."

"Oh yeah. Nate mentioned he was working him. How'd he go?"

"They were all happy. One day at a time I guess, right?"

It always was, with every horse. The horse who was going great one day could pull up sore the next. Or blow apart into a million tiny pieces.

Faye's phone buzzed with a generic tone, and by the time she glanced at the screen, the notification had faded. Some spam text probably. While Liv finished Chique's hind feet, Faye opened the phone, and found it in the unknown senders file. It was an address in Toronto. So very random.

She was going to delete it, when a second text came through from the same number.

This is Will, BTW. Come down Monday if you can make it. 2pm.

A silly, happy, warm feeling flowed through her as a smile spread over her face. She seriously needed an antidote for that, because she was not...repeat, NOT, going to fall for this guy.

CHAPTER ELEVEN

The big black tom twirled between her legs, hopping into her lap when she sat down outside on the deck with a cup of coffee, his motor running at steady RPMs. Faye stroked his sleek coat. He popped by every so often, making like he was homeless when he was clearly well-fed. This is how she liked her cats – just like she liked her men. Short uncomplicated visits, enjoy each others' company, no commitment or expectations. No hard feelings when the visits stopped.

Which is why she probably shouldn't be going down to Will's this afternoon. She was going off-script. She could call him, now that she actually had his number, and tell him she couldn't make it. Stop this thing before it went any further into dangerous territory.

Her phone rang and she grabbed for it, sending the tom scrambling to the deck. Local number. *You were hoping it was Will, weren't you?*

"Hello?"

"Hi Faye. It's Lucy. Is your offer to talk still open?"

Faye stood abruptly and rushed for the door. "It is, definitely. Would you like me to come over?"

After they talked, Lucy sent her off with a fresh half-dozen butter tarts, and the rare feeling that for once, things were going her way.

"How do you get away with a place like this in downtown Toronto? It's fabulous!"

Faye looked up, and around, mouth gaping at the old hardwood floors and brick walls. It was one big room, with a curtained-off section where she assumed the bed, and probably bathroom, were; a simple kitchen; a sitting area; and the music studio. He had everything: guitars, a keyboard, a drum set, and it didn't end there. Inspiration and creativity filled the place. *I could live here,* she almost said, but caught herself. That might sound like she was thinking this was more than it was.

"Thanks," Will said, his expression invitingly uncomplicated.

She found her eyes drifting towards the curtain, and snapped her head back to him. "I come bearing gifts." Faye held out the butter tarts, and grinned.

Will swept them away. "Do I have to share?"

A cat pushed out from the curtain, a pretty little tabby with a white chest, and it piqued her curiosity further. *Music, Faye. He invited you here for music.* Not the things she could think of doing with him behind that curtain.

"I never would have pegged you for a cat person." She crouched down to distract herself again, finding a spot behind the kitty's ear that made her purr. Maybe she wasn't exactly a cat person, but this one seemed sweet. It shouldn't have surprised her that Will had a nice cat.

"I'm not."

"Then why do you have a cat?"

"I don't."

Faye laughed at him, watching as not-his-cat drifted directly to him, rubbing against his leg. "Are you sure about that?"

"It's my neighbour's cat. I feed the cat when she's away for work. She's away so often, this time I asked if the cat could come here instead of me going to her apartment. I'm usually getting in so late, it's just more convenient."

"Looks like you've been adopted. What's her name?"

He picked the cat up, and ruffled her head fondly "Lemon. It's really Clementine, but that's what I call her."

"You renamed her cat?"

"Just extrapolated."

"So you have a part-time cat, and a part-time band...how do you have time for a full-time job?"

"You ask a lot of questions for a guest, you know."

"Just making conversation."

"Do you want something to drink?"

"What are you offering?"

Not alcohol, as it turned out. Restaurant worker, it wouldn't be responsible to serve her when she'd driven here, would it? He brewed tea, set two butter tarts on mismatched plates, and offered her a seat at his little, wooden, kitchen table. He really was too nice.

"This is all very civilized," she said, sipping.

"I'm glad you came."

She could only hold his gaze for a moment before hers dropped to her cup, fingers curled around it. "I want to be clear about this, right from the start." She squared her shoulders, pressing them against the back of the chair, and lifted her eyes again. "I don't do long term. Perhaps you've already heard that.

What happened with Nate was an unexplained blip in the space-time continuum, and I don't intend to let anything like it happen again. I like you. We've spent several hours in a car together and not killed each other. The other night was amazing, but can we agree not to ruin things with feelings?"

His eyes lit with amusement. "Sure. I'm good with that. I'm not looking for some happily ever after here, Faye. I'll leave that to guys like Nate."

Faye tilted her head, the corner of her lips curving up. "It might be too bad though, because I think you could be my soulmate." She grinned right back at him, and almost broke into laughter, except the door opened, and two of his musical friends shuffled in.

"Better make quick work of that butter tart, or things might get ugly in here." Will popped his into his mouth whole, and got to his feet.

He introduced her to the others as a friend. She recognized them from the Plate Party, and wondered if they knew how he knew her; knew about Nate. They didn't seem to care, though. Balancing her cup of tea in one hand, and stroking Lemon with the other, she settled into a battered leather love seat to listen. She could think of worse ways to kill a couple of hours.

After thirty minutes, Will stilled the strings on his guitar. Faye hadn't missed the keyboard one bit.

"What'll it take to get you to sing with us, Faye?"

She set the empty cup carefully to the side, and continued to attend to Lemon. "I'm occupied here, so nothing, I'm sorry." She smiled her best fake-sweet smile.

"Pick a song. Any song." He strummed a chord, then paused, his mouth twisting up as he thought. Then he started playing *Brown Eyed Girl*.

So not fair. She loved that song, but it's not like he could know. It was just an obvious choice.

Sha-la-la, la-la...she couldn't help joining in on that bit. And she hoped he didn't notice her blush when he sang the bit about...

"And on that note...thanks," she said, waving her fingers airily and pushing out of the cushions when the song was over. "I'm going to go before I wear out my welcome."

"We're just getting warmed up!" Will protested, still smiling a somewhat victorious smile.

"It was so nice meeting you all, though!" She sashayed towards the door, when she really wanted to stay. She felt so light and floaty. It was ridiculous, and wonderful. They sounded amazing. Especially because Nate wasn't there.

So why was he approaching her on the sidewalk outside the building? There was no way she could duck him, even though she'd seen him first. He looked up, and slowed, stopping the same time she did – a distance away from each other; slightly offset instead of exactly opposite.

Anger was really just a way of keeping harder to accept emotions at bay. Disappointment. Sadness. Shame. She'd thought sleeping with someone else would remove those feelings, let her shove them aside, and maybe it had, for a while, but seeing him, like this, brought them back. Will had known her three weeks, and he'd asked her to come down. *You never once brought me. You sang for her. You never sang for me.*

He didn't ask what she was doing down here. And he wasn't blocking her way, so she could just step aside and move on, not say anything; leave before he spoke. What was there really to say anymore, outside of social situations? She had no obligation here.

It became a weird little face-off, and she'd missed the window where walking on past would have been acceptable. Or less childish, because, really, it wasn't a very mature plan of attack at all.

"Hey," he said hesitantly, and she read his feelings like she was analyzing a wine. A little bit guarded, a touch uncomfortable with a hint of apprehension and what's that last bit? Oooh, irritation.

"Will said you didn't come down on Mondays."

"I usually don't."

She could tell he was going to say something else, explain it, but that it probably had something to do with Liv, so he stopped.

"Well. I'm leaving now. Perfect timing."

"What are you doing, Faye?"

"What are you talking about?" It was more fun to pretend she had no idea what he meant, when she knew exactly. So much more satisfying to make him spit it out than to second-guess.

"With Will."

She shrugged. "Getting to know him. Is that wrong? He's attractive, he's nice, he's interesting." *He doesn't work at the racetrack, his job doesn't involve him risking his neck, he's not in love with my best friend.* "Why can't you just stay out of it?"

"Because he's my friend. And you're..."

"What?" she challenged. But maybe she wanted to know herself, because she wasn't sure what she was right now.

"Hurting," he said.

It was unexpected, the compassion on his face. He wasn't supposed to make her cry. She was supposed to hate him.

"Goodbye, Nate," she said, and pushed past, feeling a jolt of pain as she brushed his arm. She could feel him still watching her, but didn't look back, rubbing a tear off her cheek and looking up at the sky hoping to quell any more.

Where did Nate get off suggesting she didn't have any business getting involved with Will because she was...a mess? She didn't want to marry the guy, she just wanted a change of pace.

He didn't think she was doing with Will what he'd done with her, did he? Gotten invested, involved, when his heart wasn't right. She didn't intend to let her heart play a part in this at all.

There was a stupid saying, *love is not enough*. But lust was. It was spicy and salty; sharp edges and hard surfaces; bites and bruises, motel rooms and kitchen tables. Nate had said sex was easy, like that was a bad thing. What was wrong with easy? What was wrong with just sex? Not everyone wanted to find the love of their life. She wouldn't be fooled again by thinking she might.

She relied on an insecure world to give her security – the racehorse business, a family farm that needed just one bad season to go under, one year of more losses than gains – more injuries than runners, more owners leaving than staying on. Lost layups, lost foals. The ways it could fall apart were endless.

She needed to be proactive. Personally, and professionally. And that meant constantly adjusting to what life threw at her.

CHAPTER TWELVE

EMILIE AND LUCY stood elbow to elbow, the two of them patting unbaked pastry into tins. It still amazed Faye how the woman had softened since she'd officially stepped in to help. Dragging Em with her had been a good move – not that Em had complained. She was in her happy place. The whole shop smelled heavenly.

The bell on the door rattled, announcing a customer's arrival. Faye swept up a tray of fresh tarts, because who could resist them, fresh out of the oven?

"Oh, it's just you," she said, a slight delay to her smile, a tinge of the disquiet she'd been feeling since yesterday afternoon returning.

Liv grinned. "I feel so welcomed."

"You want one of these, I suppose." She shielded the tray with mock protectiveness.

Lucy appeared behind her and scowled before selecting a tart, setting it on a plate, and presenting it to Liv. Then she turned to Faye. "Are you all right if I leave now? You know how to work the cash?"

"Yes, and I have Em for backup."

Lucy nodded. "I'll be back in an hour."

It was like Faye was a puppy Lucy was leaving out of her crate for the first time. If she couldn't handle an hour, she deserved to be fired.

"Come back here, Liv. It's where the magic happens." Faye ushered Liv into the kitchen and set her up with a stool.

Liv snapped a photo of the tart on its plate, then of Faye and Em, the latter dusted with flour.

"Are you going to manage our Instagram account?" Faye asked.

Liv rolled her eyes. "You set up an Instagram account?"

"Of course I set up an Instagram account."

Liv had started keeping one for her riding when she'd been laid up with a broken arm, and surprisingly, it had taken off. She would never admit that she liked doing it. Now of course, it was mostly about Chique and the filly's journey.

"Maybe that could be my contribution. You two seem to be in your element. How are things coming?"

"Lucy is teaching me how to make the tarts," Em said.

"You look as happy – and as messy – as you did when you were six, helping *Maman* with the baking. I think you were about eight when you started to take over."

"Clearly this is what you should have gone to school for, Em," Faye said. "Not all that science stuff."

"Baking is science," Em insisted.

"That's my kind of science," Faye said. "Science you can eat."

"Everything going smoothly with Lucy?" Liv asked.

"So far, so good." Faye nodded.

"You're coming over this afternoon, right?" Liv took another bite of her tart. Faye didn't know how she could make it last that long.

"Oh...I don't know about that. If Dean were here, it might be okay." Faye turned away from her, and fussed with some dirty utensils.

"I get it. But I don't want to be hanging off Nate all afternoon, so I really hope you do come."

Faye sighed. Liv would not easily fall into the role of hostess for this little to-do, and Nate wouldn't expect it of her. Her anxiety over it wasn't reason enough for Faye to voluntarily put herself in Nate's company after yesterday's encounter. Surely Nate had told Liv about it, and Liv would understand that she was asking a lot, requesting Faye's presence for support. Shouldn't this be a loophole in the "do better" pact? Surely Liv could ghost if it became unbearable for her.

"No promises," Faye said.

Liv nodded, excused herself and disappeared, muttering about getting in a run.

When Lucy returned, she shooed Faye and Emilie away, assuring them she'd be fine for the afternoon – because apparently Em had thought it helpful to tell her about this thing. Having the excuse of Lucy needing her would have done quite nicely to get Faye out of it. She didn't want to explain why to Lucy, though.

Just because she was leaving didn't mean she'd go. When she got home, she might not want to leave. This seemed like a great time to binge-watch something on Netflix. The truth was, she didn't want to be alone.

Gus's boisterous welcome at the farmhouse didn't make Dean's absence any less obvious. Why did Nate have to have this thing while Dean was away? If Dean had been here, they could have gone together, made an appearance, and got out, because Dean wouldn't want to stay long. And why hadn't she heard from Dean? He should have made it to Saratoga by now; he'd left early enough.

She'd worry until he remembered she'd worry and finally send her a text saying he'd gotten there okay. She kept herself from texting him to check in; never mentioned to anyone how much it affected her, those long drives her friends took – like Nate and Liv to Florida every winter – all the things that could go wrong and leave her even more alone in this world. Saratoga was only six hours, and it was summer, but anything could happen on the road.

"Come on, Gus. Let's go for a walk." She didn't want to be in the house right now.

At times like this she wished she ran, but she'd never been athletic. If only they could bottle those endorphins Liv lived on. Liv probably created enough of them she could share.

Before the accident, she hadn't really known Dean. With eight years between them, he'd always been in a different stratosphere from her. He'd been away at university before she was even in high school. He might as well have been a cousin – she'd see him on holidays, mostly. He rarely came home for weekends. He was fully invested in his studies, always got good grades, made their mother proud, and their father content he would not end up a slave to the racetrack. Ironic, that.

Their middle brother, Shawn, she'd been close to. Shawn was funny. Shawn made her playlists of great music. He looked out for her when she started high school. Vetted her potential first boyfriends. He was the quintessential big brother. When he'd decided to go to Queen's for his undergrad, she'd felt abandoned.

He kept in touch, sending her texts of funny things, sharing new music, writing her emails, sometimes even sending snail mail. And unlike Dean, Shawn always came home whenever he could, even though he was three hours away. He'd take a bus, or a train, or catch a ride with one of his school friends who came from the area. But Faye was still harbouring anger towards him for going so far away, so she hadn't joined her parents that February weekend, when they'd picked him up and gone on to visit cousins in Ottawa.

They didn't make it there.

They should have stayed overnight in Kingston and left in the morning, waited for the snowstorm to pass.

Faye should have been with them. But then Dean would have been alone. She felt guilty for not being with them, and guilty for wishing she had.

Gus bounded past the barns – he knew their route – and Faye called him every so often so she didn't lose him. She was pretty sure he'd return, but wasn't about to risk finding out. She couldn't bear the thought of anything happening to him, either.

Dean could easily have shipped her off to the cousins in Ottawa, her rightful guardians, but while he'd presented that option, he'd offered to move back. Faye was sure both affection and responsibility had contributed to that, but she was willing to bet the horses had been a big part. It was his chance to train; what he'd wanted to do all along.

In the bigger pasture out back, the foals, sleek with their new grown-up coats, galloped up and raced Gus along the fenceline. He barked once and Faye called him away – fun and games with young horses quickly turned to vet bills, and possibly, permanent damage, if one of them slipped, or ran into a fence. Those foals were the farm's future. Whether Dean decided to sell them as yearlings, or kept them to race and sold pieces of them to partners...they were commodities. It was the only way Faye could let herself think of them. They were beautiful, but they were fragile, and one freak accident could break your heart and kill the hopes you'd piled upon them.

Faye kept it all as numbers. She would let the others lose their souls to it. She didn't know how they stayed sane. That was just it, though – were they?

She had Bermuda shorts on – leaving not nearly enough of those gorgeous legs bare for his eyes – and a loose, long-sleeved shirt tied over a tank top. Hair blowing around her face, sunglasses giving her an air of mystery, until one side of her mouth curved, pushing her cheek up, creating a dimple. How had he not noticed that before?

"Hello," she said. "You might be trespassing, you know."

The big Golden Retriever gambolled over, ears flopping with each stride, and landed in a sit at Will's feet. He held the paper bag he was carrying to the side, and reached down with his other hand to stroke the dog's head. "He seems happy I'm here."

"He's not the best judge of character. Gus would welcome an intruder and make him tea." She crossed her arms, one hip jutting out, the dimple disappearing and a hint of aloofness creeping in. "To what do I owe the honour?"

"I was in the area."

"Right."

She obviously wasn't buying it, even though it was true.

"I'm headed over to Nate's."

"Oh. His thing." Disdain dripped off her words.

"Aren't you coming?"

"No, I think not."

"Why not?"

"You are not that dense. I got blindsided yesterday when I left your place, and ran right smack into him. You said he wasn't coming."

She was simmering, looking as if she was yearning for a fight, and Will felt a little blindsided himself. Nate hadn't told him that.

"I didn't know he was coming, Faye. He just showed up. I

guess because we couldn't get together this afternoon. I'm sorry, all right? You have to believe I wouldn't set you up like that." He wished she wasn't wearing those sunglasses so he had some hope of reading her, because right now she was a wall; her voice, her face, her stance, everything.

He sighed. "So you would send me on my own. Among those weirdos without my interpreter."

An eyebrow crimped, but there was no smile accompanying it. He wanted that dimple back. "I don't work for free, you know. The Prince of Wales was just a sample of my talents."

"Do you accept payment in pastry?" He held out the bag.

She rushed up to take it, tucking the hair on one side behind an ear as best she could in the breeze, the dog bouncing out of the way. *So, that's all it took.* First she peeked in, then she peered over her sunglasses at him through her dark lashes.

"I'll have to sample the currency." Her voice was like honey on toast, smooth and sweet on the surface, crisp underneath.

"I have cappuccino in the car."

Finally the corner of her lips pulled up on one side, but not quite enough to create the dimple. "Let's have the cappuccino, then I'll make my decision."

She wasn't following him closely, but he could feel the heat coming from her, sense her eyes on him as he leaned into the Chevy and lifted the tray. After closing the door he rested against it. Let her come to him if she wanted it.

Her lips were playing a game, but her eyes were hidden again, not visible to give any clues. She stepped in, resting a hand on the tray as she worked the cup free. She lifted the lid open a crack, as if she didn't believe it was what he'd promised, and followed her visual inspection with a deep whiff. Finally satisfied he was telling the truth, she turned on her heel and marched up the steps to the deck.

ALL THE LITTLE THINGS

"I don't really want to go to this thing either," he said.

She paused, glancing over her shoulder. "So why are you going?"

He wasn't going to tell her that. Because while Nate hadn't mentioned running into Faye, he had asked, before leaving, if Will would come, and if he might see if Faye would come with him and that had been enough. A chance to see her again, and with what might be construed as Nate's blessing? He'd started making the pastry as soon as the guys had left.

He watched her drift to a chair and plop into it, crossing her legs. She opened the bag and reached in, then lifted out one of his little creations, fingers pressing into the creamy mousse as she put her lips around it and closed down. Her eyes closed, and she went still.

"If you keep me in these, I'll do just about anything." She slid him a loaded glance over the shades, sipped the cappuccino, then finished the other bite. "Though I'm not sure I'd call that pastry."

"It's just easier to say than *petit fours,*" he explained.

"Liv or Em could help you with that. Details, though. I'll have to save the others as my reward for after."

She rolled the top of the bag, gave him a smirk, and ducked into the house, but didn't invite him in. He thought about following anyway, because really, neither of them wanted to go, and they could have considerable fun right here.

When she returned, the bag was gone and she'd done something with her hair. Because he'd missed his chance to get his hands on her, he'd just have to enjoy the visual as she closed the door – the way her lines smoothly curved from the hint of her ribcage under her shirt, in to her waist, and back out to her hip. She locked the door and turned, the outer screen door shutting with a click behind her.

For a beat he was pretty sure she was doing her own examination, the sunglasses propped on her head, eyes roving from the top of him to his toes and back again, as if she were mentally mapping his body. When her gaze returned to his, she held it for another beat, then dropped the shades.

"So?"

He shook off the involuntary tremor that fired through him like some kind of energetic residue from her perusal. "Are you coming in my car?"

"Sure," she said, and started walking towards it. "If you decide to ditch me for one of the cute farm girls, I'll understand. It's not that far of a walk."

"So you don't think Nate invited me to distract me from you?" He grinned at her, catching up.

"Hmm, it's like that, is it? Interesting."

He wasn't sure it was, anymore.

"He's been very much an enabler with Jiro, now that I think of it," Faye continued. "Which means we should totally go together. And be all over each other. Just to drive him crazy."

Will laughed. He wasn't going to have a problem with that plan, except the part where it was supposed to be an act.

———

It was a modest gathering. While Nate put on a good show, he didn't really like people much more than Liv did; he just had a higher tolerance. Reason number three-hundred and ninety-nine why they were so suited to each other. At least they'd finally admitted it.

Faye really, really hadn't wanted to come. She was blaming the pastry. The way to her heart, apparently. No, not her heart, exactly. But she needed to be on her guard, keep that heart in check, just in case all that sugar was weakening it. Stick to the script. No ad-libbing.

Nate lived in an apartment over the smaller barn that also housed Triple Stripe's office. While Faye had been to the farm many times over the duration of her friendship with Liv, she'd never spent time with Nate here when they were together; he'd always come to Northwest. Which was understandable, because while the farm wasn't the track, there was overlap, and it still felt like being on display, when he was high enough profile to want a break from that. Now Faye wondered it had just been him keeping a sanctuary, never quite letting her in.

She'd always thought Triple Stripe a strange name for a farm and racing stable, not that there was any shortage of strange names in the business. Liv had explained it to Faye once – it had something to do with Acadian heritage on her father's side, the Acadian flag based on the French flag of blue, white, and red. Their silks didn't exactly copy the flag, just the colours, and the idea, to an extent. They weren't as boring as the Northwest silks. So many things she could do with those silks, given the okay.

It wasn't as fancy as some of the big farms in Ontario, but it was definitely less rustic than Northwest, and larger. Outside money, that's what it took. Liv's father was an investment banker – which Faye probably should have leveraged into some kind of internship that would have provided her with a more substantial income. Given that, the farm was modest – the house was big, a custom design– but the barns were practical instead of showy. It was all well kept though. Things seemed to get fixed a lot faster than Dean managed at Northwest.

But Faye wasn't looking for sympathy. It was that whole, be careful what you wish for thing. Bigger farm meant bigger responsibility. She had a hard enough time with the idea of leaving their little farm. Part of why Liv had dropped out of school was because she was trying to get away from the expectations associated with being part of that family. Her mother had wanted her to be a vet, and control freak that she was, Liv would have taken on the farm's work, and the track work, and made herself miserable, because track work was more about injecting joints and jugulars than problem-solving.

Faye fully expected Liv to take over the farm one day; she was already so involved with the management of it. She wasn't about to oust the Lachance's trainer out of his job, so if she didn't go back to riding, short of going back to school and finishing that veterinary degree, what was she going to do with herself? She didn't suffer from the whole underachiever thing Faye did. She'd get restless. The girl needed to learn how to relax and enjoy life.

And maybe Faye could use a touch of her seriousness and drive. Whatever.

Will pulled up next to Nate's Mustang, and waited for Faye to climb out before locking it. She gave him a look.

He shrugged. "Habit from living in the city."

He fell into stride beside her, and she toyed with the idea of taking his hand. Too much? She'd decided not to change her clothes for that reason. All she'd done was brush the tangles out of her hair and sweep it up off her neck.

A couple of picnic tables that weren't usually there had been set near the paddock fences; a spread of food just inside the open end of the barn, a clean muck bucket filled with ice and loaded with soft drinks. Horses were everywhere at this place, and Faye even recognized Claire, the mare who, as a two-year-old, had taken Liv to New York promising to jumpstart her riding career. Reality hadn't been as smooth as that. It rarely was.

No alcohol. Interesting. A small crowd. The Triple Stripe crew from the track stood in one group, the farm staff in another, and as promised, Jiro, off to the side with Em. Then, of

166

course, Nate and Liv. Nate was dressed not unlike Will, jeans and a neat polo shirt. Liv had donned a skirt and white blouse, her default simple, pretty, always elegant, though she never looked entirely comfortable out of jeans and a t-shirt.

"Dean sends his regrets," Faye said. She'd finally had a text from him on the drive over. There was a faint odour of horses and manure wafting through the air. It barely registered for her, but she wondered if it bothered Will.

"We're not feeling sorry for him, getting to go to Saratoga." Nate grinned.

"Saratoga?" Will asked.

It was so cute when he got that mystified look. He was so wonderfully out of place with these people. Faye had gotten used to being the black sheep – in both her own family, and the greater racing community. It was nice to have someone more displaced around.

"Saratoga Springs, New York," Faye said, falling into the expected role, earning her sweets. She glanced up at him, and caught his eye, part of a smile, their little shared joke. *Oh no, now they were sharing jokes.* "For about six weeks in the middle of the summer, the racing meet in New York State shifts there. Everyone who knows anything about horse racing in North America wants to go. It's a big thing."

"Are you included in that? Or..."

"On the fringes, perhaps. It's not just about the horses. It's about what happens to the town when they're there. I'd go for sure."

"You've never been?"

"No. Somehow I've never pulled it off."

"Have you guys?" Will looked at Liv and Nate.

Faye did too, finding Liv's eyes appraising her. Faye tried to give her an *it's not what you think* look back.

"Twice, very briefly, myself," Nate said.

"I rode there the last three summers," Liv said.

"Like doing the jockey thing?" Will asked.

Liv nodded. "Seems like a long time ago now."

"Chique, next summer," Nate insisted, capturing Liv's attention with that grin of his.

Liv laughed. "Maybe we can focus on trying to win the Triple Crown first?"

They did balance each other. Liv so cautious, Nate gung-ho for the next great accomplishment. They seemed to manage to meet in the middle and make the best of it, professionally. Maybe, in time, Nate would draw Liv out more. Faye hadn't been able to get too far, but guys always seemed to get women to change in ways they'd never thought possible. He'd already managed to do that, without scaring Liv off. That was an achievement, with Liv.

"So, does that mean we could go?" Will was still stuck on Saratoga. "I don't need a horse passport or card or something?"

It's we now? She caught herself. She'd forgotten for a minute this was a performance "Sure. No horse card needed. And I hear there's an amazing French bakery there."

"Mmmm, yes." Liv nodded. "It's worth the trip just for Mrs. London's."

"What are we waiting for?" Will asked.

The idea was so tempting. *I would go, in a heartbeat. If this were only real.* Would she? "We'll have to figure that out. Now all that talk of a French bakery has me hungry, and no pastry in sight." She gave him another sideways look, then felt the beginnings of a flush tingeing her flesh, thinking of him in her kitchen last week, and the *petit fours* she'd left there not long ago, and how both those things held so much potential deliciousness. Later, perhaps. She glanced from Nate to Liv. "Where's the food?"

"This way." Liv swept an arm to the side, dropping a sweet but subtle look to Nate before stepping past him towards the barn. Faye didn't have any trouble picking up on the signal.

"You're safe with Nate, I trust? He can interpret in my absence." Faye leaned in, touching Will's arm, then murmured, "I bet he'll do it for free." She caught up with Liv, and scanned the table in the barn.

"Couldn't wait for the Breeders'?" Liv said, looking at Faye pointedly as she stuck a carrot stick in her mouth and chomped off the end.

"He showed up at my house with pastry. What can I say."

"I don't know, Miss Taylor of Northwest. I think you're being courted." A teasing smile tickled her lips.

Faye looked at her skeptically. "What have you been reading? That sounds so Regency."

"I had a lot of time when I was in Fort Erie."

"I bet you did. If you're looking for an instruction manual, I'm not sure that's the way to go. I could make suggestions. Though I bet that's about the right speed for you two."

"Ha ha." Liv handed Faye a plate before taking one for herself and selecting more veggies and some dip – like she was calculating calories as she went. Old habits died hard. "I'm glad you came."

"Thank Will."

"You seem to like each other."

"We've spent quality time stuck in a car together. We bonded." So there had been sex. So there might be more.

"And you get on me for being cautious. You're one to talk."

Faye glanced at her, then focused on the food. With no alcohol, she'd better go right for the sweets. "Em's been baking again, I see." Better take two of those brownies. "I'm not being cautious. I'm simply remembering to keep men for what I most need them for. My amusement." She'd better take Will one of the brownies, in case they disappeared. Liv scooped up a couple, and restored Faye's faith in her ability to take care of herself.

They walked back into the sunshine, both of them seeking out Nate and Will. Faye hated the pinch left in her heart for Nate, but the squeeze that followed when her eyes rested on Will took her pulse up a notch for a few beats. Fondness, that was all it was. She was allowed to feel that. He was nice. He was cute. He was funny. Attractive, of course. He was good in bed. There would be time for Jiro. He was a project for another day.

Though Em was still chatting with Jiro. She'd have to quiz Em about that later. They looked cosy, but Em had that effect on people, made them feel comfortable with her cheery, relaxed demeanor. Oh-so-opposite to her sister. The physical resemblance was strong between the two; the emotional, not so much.

Faye re-established herself next to Will, making sure their arms touched, and held up her plate. "The brownies are amazing. Em made them. You have to try." Before he could reach for it, in an inspired moment, she broke off a piece, holding it up to his mouth. He grinned before opening it, and she popped it in, then made sure she carefully licked her fingers.

Neither Nate nor Liv looked terribly upset, much to her disappointment. Oh well. It was still fun. And she did like Will. And Liv. And she'd liked Nate well enough to spend nine months with him. She'd like him well enough again. It might be good, the four or them. Liv and Em were the closest things to sisters she had, so this could be nice. Maybe not if Em was interested in Jiro. That might be a little awkward at the moment. She wasn't into two guys starting to throw around testosterone over her. Em had to find herself a man that would fit.

Em seemed to be introducing Jiro to the farm girls, leaving them to gush with him. She flashed a grin at Faye, then sidled up to Will. Emilie was definitely on Team Will when it came to Faye's future prospects, keeping Jiro away like that.

"Great brownies, Em," Will said, the two of them falling into conversation about baking, which Faye kept one ear to, so no one tried to talk to her about horses. Liv had drifted over to visit Claire, and been cornered by Jiro, who had escaped from the farm girls. Liv made introductions to the horse better than she would a person, and was obviously telling Jiro more about the mare, because it was one thing she could converse happily about. He was a captive audience, looking more comfortable himself.

"Do you really like him?"

Faye's head snapped to Nate, finding his eyes on her. Why did the question make her feel defensive, scrape up her irritation like petting a cat against the hair? His words had been soft, a genuine question –that might have been why. That was the Nate she'd fallen for. He felt stuff – maybe too much sometimes, maybe for the wrong reasons.

"Would that be a problem?" she asked, her lips locked in a line, her own eyes thankfully behind her sunglasses once again, so she didn't give too much away.

"Not if you really like him."

She took a bite of a cookie – more aggressively than she should have. "I get why you don't want him to get involved with me. I don't do relationships. It might not end so well for him. I don't get attached."

"But that's not true, is it?"

It's not like she could deny it, standing across from him, because he knew, first hand. He'd been there. They'd been there.

"You're not my keeper. Or his. But it doesn't matter. I'm not interested. It was just a game, to get on your nerves. But I don't even want to do that. I am so over this feeling."

"You know I understand that, right?"

"How could I know? You never told me anything."

"I'm sorry about that, I really am. And I don't really want to tell you that whole sordid history right now. And maybe never, because it would kind of still feel like I'm hanging onto part of it. And maybe I am, and should acknowledge that. I don't want to rehash us, either. I mean, if you do end up being serious about Will, it would be kind of nice if we could sort of get along."

"For Liv's sake, I assume."

"No. For your sake. For my sake. For our sake. I don't want to hate what we had. And I don't feel bad for breaking your pattern."

"You only interrupted it."

"In that case, that's too bad."

"It's so much more satisfying to be snarky. I'm not serious about Will. This *is* just a game."

"You might want to believe that, but I don't. That's one of the things I liked – like – about you. You're totally authentic. I didn't have to guess. I still have to guess with Liv."

"Oh, this is early days with Liv yet. No fast moves, and you'll be fine."

He laughed, and it was a good sound, a healing sound.

"I am tired of hating you," she admitted. "It's exhausting. You're hard to hate."

"Thanks. I think." His smile looked a little tired of it all too. "We were pretty good together, Faye. But maybe we needed each other to be ready for what was to come."

"You're not suggesting Will is my Liv, are you?"

"Could be. If you let yourself believe it."

"Sounds so easy when you put it that way, doesn't it?"

"But it's not."

She didn't know if it was weakness or impulse or cleansing, but she put her arms around him and squeezed. "Thank you. I didn't know how much I needed this."

Finally, instead of the pain of a hot poker, she felt a little closer to whole.

"This looks serious. Should we be worried?"

Will had snuck up on the conversation, Liv with him. Liv didn't look worried about anything. It was nice to see her looking happy and secure. She wasn't threatened. That's how it should be.

And Will seemed to be adapting to his role readily. Nate was full of shit, saying he didn't believe she and Will were simply performing. He thought he saw through it. He thought she was incapable of playing this game; that she was ready for something deeper, but she might never want more than entertainment from the opposite sex.

She should probably go talk to Jiro. But seeing as she almost hadn't come at all, and the unexpected conversation with Nate had worn out what benevolence she had, it felt about time for her to excuse herself. She was even willing to let Will off the hook. It was a nice day for a walk.

"You look tired," he said. "Want me to drive you home?"

Was he actually paying close enough attention to her, that he noticed? She could like this guy, if she let herself.

"Yes, if you don't mind." She glanced from Nate to Liv. "Sorry for ducking out early. It seems wrong to complain about being tired to two people who get up at an ungodly hour every day. Thanks for the invite. We'll get together soon, okay sweetie?"

She saw the look Liv gave Nate before stepping in for a hug. "Are you okay?" she said quietly.

"Just too sober," Faye answered, conjuring up her sense of humour. "I'll be fine."

Will was silent during the short drive to Northwest. When he pulled up next to her Corolla, he met her questioning gaze.

"I need a drink," Faye said. "You in?"

He nodded. "Sounds good to me."

He followed her to the door, waiting while she fumbled for keys. Gus was on the other side, slipping past them and around them before bounding out to the lawn. He lifted his leg on a tree, then bounced back and ushered them into the kitchen.

"What did Nate say to you?"

Faye glanced over her shoulder, kicking off her shoes and shuffling across the old hardwood to the cupboard where she kept the glasses. "I guess, just, things that needed to be said. Nothing unkind, don't worry. I'm good."

She reached in for a couple of tumblers, setting them side by side on the counter, then felt his arms go around her, his face in her hair. He held her against him, his heartbeat steady behind the firmness of his chest, the rising and falling of it grounding her. It was a foreign sensation, that sense of comfort, free of judgment. A small part of her wanted to stay there, let herself feel it. But it was easier, more natural, to pivot to face him, slide her hands to his shoulders, to his neck, and pull his head lower, catching his bottom lip between hers, feeling him respond. She went deeper, making his mouth hers, fingers running down his ribcage to yank his shirt free, breaking apart just long enough to grab a breath and drag the shirt over his head. He dipped back in to reconnect, deftly unknotting her shirt, his calloused fingertips smooth on her bare shoulders as he pushed it off, sending a shiver through her. And now she couldn't wait to feel skin to skin, peeling her tank top off as his fingers tickled her back, undoing the clasp of her bra – which was not a sexy bra, because she really hadn't anticipated her afternoon going this way. She shrugged out of it and arched into him while his hands traced down her back, along her hips, tucking into the back of her jeans. Why were they even still on?

"I know you bribed me with pastry," she murmured, "But I'm the one who should be thanking you. Here, or upstairs?"

CHAPTER THIRTEEN

THIS TIME, when she woke up, he was gone.

It was daylight. She'd slept right past her usual four AM wake up, so she didn't know if Will had left before, or after that. It didn't matter. It meant they were on the same page. So why was she disappointed?

More importantly, where was Gus? He was supposed to be her alarm clock, one who tended to go off much too early. She rolled out of the rumpled sheets and wrapped herself in her robe. When she reached the first step, she was greeted with smells that made her stomach growl. And made her stop in her tracks, skitter back to the bathroom, and brush her teeth.

Downstairs, there he was, his bare back to her, nothing but boxers under what looked to be a long lost apron, standing in front of the stove with Gus flopped at his feet. So much for loyalty. *Can you blame the dog, though?* Gus scuttled up as Will tossed him a piece of something, snapping it from the air. *Nope. Can't blame him one bit.*

She wanted to drop the robe, walk up behind Will and encircle his exposed torso with her arms, then dive her hands into those shorts. They'd made it to the bedroom last night; they could do the kitchen this morning. He'd picked up his jeans from where he'd discarded them last night and folded them, and his wallet rested on the kitchen table. She'd bet he kept the necessary accessories in there, just in case, like she maintained a supply in the end table next to her bed. A hot frying pan, though. And a persistent unwillingness to jump into the fire.

"Make yourself at home," she said, standing in the doorway and leaning against the jamb. A little part of her brain lit up that liked that idea. Of him, in her home, and part of it.

He glanced over his shoulder and gave her such a buoyant smile, he made the thought of that fire seem oh-so-tempting, but she managed to control herself, stuffing her hands in the robe's pockets and sauntering over. Gus thumped his tail a couple of times; that was all she got from the Golden. She wasn't much competition for the bacon collected on a plate.

Will reached for a glass of orange juice on the counter beside the stove, and handed it to her. "'Morning."

Nice, cute, funny, good in bed, and he could cook. Someone needed to give her a slap. Couldn't she make good use of all those things?

"I see someone's been shopping." He turned back to the stove.

"Dean very kindly got groceries before he went to Saratoga. I'm not sure he believes I'm capable of doing it myself. And I'm not about to tell him I am." She sipped the juice, half expecting it to be freshly-squeezed. It wasn't. So the guy couldn't magically transform concentrate. "Can I do anything?"

"Just have a seat and relax." He poured coffee from her French press, and brought it over. Honestly, the man got major points for not just defaulting to Dean's calcium-encrusted coffee machine.

Bacon, eggs, toast with butter melting into it. No one she

wasn't related to had ever made her breakfast, not even Nate. If she hadn't come down, would he have brought it to her in bed? Feelings threatened again. She tightened an imaginary lid on them to keep them safely stashed, and tucked into her spot at the table.

"So much nicer than Lucy's," she purred.

"No butter tarts, though."

"We could still go for butter tarts." The words were out like reflex. She should be chasing him away, but instead she was prolonging contact.

Lucy's face almost brightened when they showed up. It was still so unexpected, it took Faye a second to smile back. Will was close enough behind her she had an impulse to reach back and grab his hand and play along like they were all shiny happy people in a shiny alternate universe.

"What can I get for you? And are you going to introduce me to your boyfriend this time?"

Faye caught herself before she said *he's not my boyfriend.* He wasn't, and she didn't know what to call him, but no need to find a label for it right now. "Of course. This is Will." She glanced up at him conspiratorially. "I've got him addicted to your butter tarts now too."

Will nodded solemnly. "True story."

"We'll take half a dozen," Faye said, seeing a loaded styrofoam tray in the display. When they were available, it would be silly not to grab them. "We had coffee at home, so we're caffeinated for now."

Will had a funny little look on his face. *Yeah, yeah. We? Home?* It was becoming too easy to play this game.

Lucy took the bills Faye offered, and gave her change. "I'll see you tomorrow?"

"Yes, absolutely." Faye nodded. "I'm meeting with a friend of Emilie's who's an artist to see her work. Hopefully we'll come to an agreement about hanging some of it. And I have a couple of other ideas to run past you."

Will was staring at her, but not like she'd lost her mind. That's exactly how he should have been looking at her. Not like...that. Like something she'd said had started up a ferris wheel in his head.

"Bye Lucy!" she called, and herded him back outside. She had work to do, and imagined he did, too.

"Are you going to tell me what that's about?" he asked.

"It's nothing. I just offered to help her out a bit, so maybe she doesn't have to give up her business."

"I saw the place is up for lease."

"I hope she'll change her mind about that. The sign makes me nervous, like someone will come along and grab it before I convince her it doesn't have to happen."

There was that look on his face again, but he didn't say anything, didn't give her any clues as to what it was about.

"I'd better get going," he said. "But I will call you."

"Don't leave without your butter tarts."

She stacked three of them in his hands, and thought he might kiss her, but he didn't. That was fine. He wasn't *really* her boyfriend.

Something in his chest had swelled, when he'd heard Faye talking to Lucy. It was like fate had a finger on each of their shoulders, nudging them closer together because of their shared interest in that plain little café.

He wished he hadn't had to leave, but maybe it was for the best. It would have been too much, everything he wanted to talk to her about. The way they seemed so easy together made him brave, and that might not be a good thing.

He would call her...but some things he didn't want to say on the phone.

Lemon was waiting for him, on an extended stay. Really, the cat might as well be his. He attended to her, feeding and cuddling her as his job as her loyal liege demanded. Once she was satisfied, she went slinking away. That's probably what it would be like with Faye, too.

He needed to shower and get ready for work, but he picked up the phone and dialed her.

"Miss me already?"

Even miles away on the other end of the phone, that voice of hers did things to him. He cleared his throat. "So, are you going to tell me more about this arrangement with Lucy?"

There was a beat of silence before she drew out her response. "Why?"

"I don't know. I just thought you could possibly use my expertise. Given my restaurant experience and all."

"Does that mean you're offering to help?"

"I guess I am."

"Hmm. Does it involve pastry?"

He laughed. "It could."

"Well then. Perhaps this requires a meeting."

"I think that could be mutually beneficial."

There was a long pause. Okay, that comment did leave a lot up to interpretation, but he'd leave the direction it went up to her, entirely.

"Fine. As you heard, I'm at Lucy's tomorrow at eleven. If you think you can pop by, we'll chat."

So he had been hoping it might go another way, but hey, that was good too.

CHAPTER FOURTEEN

IT HAD TAKEN SELF-CONTROL. She did have some.

Three times made a habit, isn't that what they said? Maybe it was three weeks. Either way, she was going to have to do something about him. Usually her relationships were good for a couple of months or so, but she couldn't let it go that long with Will. Because he was breaking the rules.

So, yes, best that he met her here. She could see what he was thinking, and what he could offer by way of his restaurant experience. Those baking skills of his were clearly valuable. She had ideas, but they'd been fed by his ideas, so why not put their heads together?

Lucy looked extra stressed, and relieved to see her. It would have been a good feeling, if it hadn't been so concerning, and it put seeing Will right out of her mind.

"Busy morning?" Faye asked, fearing it was something more.

"My mother had a bad night. My neighbour was able to stay with her for a few hours, but I'm worried."

"Go," Faye insisted. "I've got this."

"Thank you, Faye. Call me if you need me."

It was a good feeling, that Lucy trusted her enough to go. She really was serving a purpose. She could adjust her schedule to be here all day. If Lucy needed her to be here more often – if her mom was on a steady decline – Faye would step up, do more food prep. Get Em to help when she could. It was just a matter of re-prioritizing. Faye was winding things down with the MacIntosh Stables account, so it was time to shift her focus to this place.

Lucy must have been up as early as any racetracker to get all the baking done. There was a healthy supply of tarts (butter tarts were healthy, and no one could tell Faye differently; mental health, right?). Not that there were ever enough; they sold out each day. There were little quiches that made perfect, quick, lunches. A few uninspired breakfast wraps remained. Those were things Faye could easily make, with a little help from Lucy to get her started, because the quantity required would be more than Faye was used to preparing. She poured herself a coffee, managed to resist the butter tarts – she didn't want to eat all the product, after all – and opened up her laptop to take advantage of the window of time where it was typically quiet, between the morning madness and lunchtime.

The coffee was harder to take when there was no butter tart sweetness to help it out, and it was even worse when it got cold. Maybe just one tart? Then voices outside distracted her, and she shut the laptop, rising to see Emilie entering, Liv behind her with a box in her arms.

Faye arched an eyebrow and crossed her arms. "This looks suspicious."

"My friend who does the artwork should be coming by shortly," Em said. "That's the real reason Liv's here. My friend also wants a job on the farm, so it made sense to have her meet both of you here. You can talk to her first, before Liv kills her dreams." Em grinned.

Faye laughed, and Liv said, "I'll try to be nice."

"I don't suppose you stopped for cappuccinos on the way home from the track?" Faye asked hopefully.

"Sorry," Liv said. "I was at the farm before Em let me know about the plan."

"Somehow I don't think an espresso machine is in the cards here." Faye sighed. "Lucy can't both take me on and have an income and also buy that. One day, maybe."

"Where can I put this?" Liv asked, her chin indicating the box.

It looked heavy. "What is it?"

"Book donations. For your burgeoning library."

"Oh! Perfect. Right over here." Faye ushered her to the corner where she'd set the bookcase Dean had found, a shelf already stacked with paperbacks.

The bell on the door jangled, and a tiny, young, blonde woman stopped just inside with a thin, black case.

"Now I really feel old," Faye whispered. "That must be Em's friend."

Liv nodded. "I've met her. Em's had her to the farm before. She looks like a young Julie Krone, don't you think? Cuter, even."

Faye hadn't missed learning who Julie Krone was growing up. Her father liked to tell the story of how she'd come to Woodbine in the 80s to ride in the Queen's Plate, when he'd been just starting out working on the backstretch.

"Hi Cory," Liv called, her tone impressively welcoming.

Cory was even tinier than Liv. Her hair was cut in a practical bob but not styled, the ends flipping every which way, a ready smile on her lips. Rubbing one palm on her black jeans, she tugged nervously on the corner of a bright blue t-shirt. Em scampered from the kitchen and hugged her, directing her to one of the tables to spread out her work.

"You've had Lucy's butter tarts before, right?" Em said. "Want one?"

"Yes, please!" Polite, too. Her voice was as bright as her smile.

"Go ahead and pull out your work, and I'll grab it. This is Faye, by the way. Faye, meet Cory."

First Cory laid the portfolio flat on the table, then her hand jutted out in front of her. Faye closed her fingers around it, getting a firm squeeze back.

"Nice to meet you, Cory. Let's see what you've got."

Cory spread out a series of painted panels. "I have some photos of my larger work on my phone."

Liv looked over Faye's shoulder. "These are good, Cory."

Cory flushed at the praise, her grin widening. The kid was good, Faye had to agree. The subject matter was heavy on the horses, of course, but given the area, that was okay. An equine theme seemed like an appropriate place to start with this art initiative.

"What are they?" Faye asked, trying to sound like she knew something about art when all she really knew was what she did and didn't like.

"Acrylic," Cory said. "I'd have to frame these panels. The larger ones are on stretched canvas, so they can hang as they are."

Faye nodded, scanning. "Why don't we start with three months. We don't want anything – no commission. We'll just pass anyone interested on to you. Em can rep you when she's around."

Em grinned, Cory's champion of the moment.

"Thank you, Faye!" Cory said, and set about putting the work away.

Faye didn't know how the kid's smile could get any broader, but it did. "Just let me know when you're ready to hang some stuff. Em, can you give her my cell? She's all yours, Liv."

"Why don't you start on that butter tart first?" Liv suggested. "Em can grab you a coffee, or whatever you'd like to drink."

Cory was excited and chatty as she sat with Liv. Faye imagined working at Triple Stripe, helping start yearlings, would be any horse girl's dream job. What better mentor for a girl with riding aspirations – because that was no doubt, with her stature, what Cory was dreaming of – than someone like Liv, who had lived and breathed the struggle of a female apprentice jockey.

Faye served a few customers as Liv and Cory talked, Emilie working away in the back. Her phone buzzed with a notification, and considering the two people most likely to text her were with her at Lucy's, she was guessing it was either Dean, still in Saratoga, or...

Will: *Still at Lucy's? If so, will be there shortly. - Will.*

As if she hadn't set him up as a contact after the first time he'd messaged her. She responded: *Still here. I hope you brought real coffee.*

He didn't answer, so she set the phone back down, looking up to see Liv was finished with Cory and coming over.

"Hey Em," Liv called. "Cory's all yours again."

Em popped out from the kitchen. "Did you hire her?"

"She earned herself a working interview." Liv gave her sister a sly smile, then turned to Faye. "I haven't worked with the yearlings since Chique."

Faye tilted her head, her mind going back. "You were such a mess then."

Liv didn't deny it, but neither of them took the topic further. So many emotions were tied up in those days now. For Liv, because she'd been trapped in the wilderness after losing her mentor, Triple Stripe's old farm manager, who had died suddenly while she'd been away in New York. And for Faye? On the one hand, Faye had wanted to strangle Liv for her behaviour at the time, but that had been just a tiny bit hypocritical, because Faye had been there once herself, wallowing in her own loss a few years earlier. That was also when she'd finally met Nate, and she very clearly recalled the day, one afternoon as he and Liv were working with the yearlings. Not that they'd gotten together until the following summer, because Faye hadn't been convinced Liv didn't like him then. *Hindsight.*

Liv's phone started a tune now, and even Faye knew who it was, because it was a clip of a Switchfoot song. *Speak of the devil.* Of course she had a ringtone for him. She had to stop herself from sending a text of her own to see if Liv had a custom ringtone for her, too.

Emile was saying her goodbyes to Cory, and Liv still had traces of a mischievous smile on her lips as she put away her phone. Faye didn't want to know.

"So I'm assuming Nate told you about our little conversation?"

Liv raised her head and nodded, meeting Faye's eyes. "So very grown up of you both."

"At this rate, we're going to be old and in rocking chairs in no time."

"I said grown up, not growing old, Faye." Liv smirked.

———————

"You're sure in a chipper mood. Please don't tell me this is to do with Faye again."

Will didn't think Nate was being completely serious with that comment; it was actually starting to feel as if he'd softened to the idea of Will and Faye getting together. If that's what was happening. "Yes, and no."

"Just tell me."

"You know Faye is helping out Lucy."

"Yessssss?" Nate drew out the word, an eyebrow raised.

"So that's something you could see?"

"What do you mean? I'm pretty sure she's capable of figuring out a cash register and taking people's money."

"I mean, what about, if Lucy decided to give it up? Could she take over?"

Nate squinted at him, questions collecting behind those eyes. "For sure. She's smart, she's got a great business brain, and her degree is along those lines. And she can cook. I've always thought Faye's undersold herself. It would be great for her to sink her teeth into something like that. Give her a bit of space from Dean, too, and maybe Dean would get off his ass and find himself a girlfriend." He laughed at the last bit.

"Okay. I need a hand with something."

"With, what, exactly?"

"Physical labour. You can still do that, right? It's not below you?"

"You think my job isn't physical?"

"Not what I meant. I just need half an hour. Follow me. Maybe drive your own car."

Will made sure Nate was in his rear view mirror as he drove out the maple-shaded lane of Triple Stripe, turning up the music. This plan was falling together so easily, he felt guilty.

He pulled up behind the plaza, to the back of Lucy's. Nate climbed out of the Mustang, looking even more distrustful.

"What are we doing?" he asked.

"Nothing nefarious, I promise." Will grinned. "Text Liv or Em and let them know we're here."

"So they're in on this? But I'm not? What's with that?"

"Don't take it personally, it's just the way it worked out."

With only a little more side-eye, Nate pulled out his phone. It wasn't long before the back door popped open and Emilie's head peeked out.

"Now help me with this." Will waved Nate over.

"Ahhhh," Nate said, a smile taking over his face. "Why didn't you tell me in the first place? I can totally get behind this. Might be a little overkill though, y'think?"

"Just grab an end, all right?"

Emilie held the door for them, and they set it in the space she'd cleared.

"Hey, Faye!" Emilie called. "Can you come here for a second?"

Liv grinned over Faye's shoulder as they came through the door. Faye's eyes landed on Will, a solid gaze, but as much as she was trying to control it, she couldn't hide that she was happy to see him. At least that's what he was going to tell himself.

"Is there a party you forgot to invite me to? What are we celebrating this time?" she asked.

"I brought you something," Will said, motioning to the gleaming machine resting on the kitchen floor.

Faye's mouth fell open, then the corners of her lips curled upwards, the lift reaching to her eyes, then brows. "An espresso machine! That's amazing! But –" Her face fell slightly. "I really should run this past Lucy."

"Already cleared it with her." Will smiled.

But there were complicated gears churning behind the look he got back, and he wondered if he'd overstepped.

"How soon can you set it up? It looks complicated, like I might need a degree to operate it, too."

"It just so happens I have such a degree. Or the equivalent experience, at least. I've got it covered."

There was the slightest tilt to her head, and no one was speaking, until Emilie saved the day and spoke up. "I can't wait till you get it fired up. This is going to be the best!"

Nate pulled his car keys from his pocket and tossed them in the air. "I'm guessing that's going to take more than a few minutes, and not something I'd be much help with, so I'm going back to doing what I was planning to do before I was shanghaied into this mission. Sleeping. Wednesday night racing, yay."

"I'll see you later too, Faye. Call me when it's up and running." Liv smiled and gave Faye a hug. She went out the front, while Nate slipped out the back. The timing of their departure, just after Nate said *sleeping*, was that a coincidence?

"I'm guessing this is part of the grand plan," Faye said finally, holding her hands out to the espresso machine. "Thank you. It's amazing. The coffee we'll be drinking while we talk is going to seem even more horrible than usual, knowing we have that to look forward to."

"I'll make you guys some fresh, at least," Emilie said. "You two go ahead with your meeting."

She didn't wink, but she might as well have, with the look she gave Faye. *No, it really is just that...but I'm hoping too, Em.*

"Really Will. This is...amazing," Faye said again as they sat at a table out front. "It must have cost a fortune."

"I got it from a buddy who was upgrading, so he gave me a good deal. It'll pay for itself in no time. I told Lucy not to worry about it until it does."

"I can't believe she didn't flip out."

"Are you mad I didn't tell you about it?"

She leaned back, pressing her lips together as Emilie set

cups in front of them. "A little. But the prospect of being able to get cappuccino right here in town makes up for it."

"So this was my big idea. What have you been working on?"

Faye wrapped her fingers around the hot ceramic cup. "Emilie's friend Cory came by with her artwork, and she's going to get some of it ready to hang. We've started our little library..." She nodded toward a bookshelf. "And there are a couple of things you could definitely help with. I'd like to think about a few new menu items. Nothing too extravagant. And..." She took a careful sip of the coffee. "I want to do a little music night."

"I see."

"I hope you know what that means."

"I do. I'll talk to Nate."

"Tell him Em asked. It'll improve the chances of him saying yes."

"And I'll do some thinking about the menu."

"You're being very helpful."

"I might have an ulterior motive. For all this, and rescuing you the other day."

"You rescued me? You came, you bribed, I went with."

"Fine. I'll just go with the espresso machine, then."

"That is pretty huge." Finally, a slight lift to the corner of her mouth. "Okay. Spill."

"I saw my dad last week. He's in town...with his brand new fiancé."

There was mild surprise on her face. "So your parents are divorced, obviously."

"They're getting married Friday night. Here. Like, in the city. And well, he wants me to be there."

"Oh." She shifted in her chair, eyes darting to the side.

"Yeah. You know what I'm going to ask."

"I don't know about that, Will. That's like family."

Will snorted. "Barely. Trust me on that. Here's the deal. He's invited Nate, and whoever he wants to bring which means Liv."

"You don't know her that well, do you? She's not big on social things."

"That's why you'll talk her into it. It works both ways. It'll make Nate happy so he doesn't hold this over me forever for making him come, and if Liv comes, you won't feel like you're there with me, exactly. Then I can be present at this thing, when I'm not even sure I should be, and not feel like a fool."

"United we stand?"

"That's what I'm hoping. I have to give my father credit for thinking allowing my own little team there might convince me to actually come. Plus he didn't ask me to be his best man or something ridiculous like that, thank goodness."

"Team, huh?" She hesitated, bringing the cup to her lips again.

"Please? I don't want to go to this thing alone."

"All right. If I can get Liv to go, Nate will go, or if you get Nate to go, he'll find a way to talk her into it, probably. So we go at it from both sides. But we're a team, not a couple. Got it?"

Will sighed, and nodded. "Got it."

"And, you have to talk Nate into the music night."

"Deal."

CHAPTER FIFTEEN

THE WEDDING WOULD BE FINE. It would be a way of thanking him, for being such a nice guy. And she could be nice, for five minutes, and let him down there, instead of on the phone, or in a text, because that was just wrong.

It was time.

She was on the verge, she could feel it. The verge of falling again. She recognized it, this time. Him standing in her kitchen, half naked, making her breakfast, had almost pushed her over. The espresso machine was her wake-up call. It jolted her back to her senses as much as the first cup of coffee in the morning brought clarity.

Even beyond her history, it was a logical decision. He lives in Toronto, and she was out here, so it wasn't exactly convenient for them to get together. He had his own life; she wasn't going to drag him into hers. If he wanted to continue as a consultant for Lucy's, that was up to him.

She poured over the numbers, analyzing. Lucy made a modest income from the business. Faye wasn't in a position to do a complete overhaul – it's not like she had financial resources to draw on – so she'd have to make changes slowly. Being able to offer espresso was a big deal, so she hoped Will came through getting the machine set up before the wedding, in case, well, things went south and he took it personally. She'd talk to Em about helping with the website. Faye was fine with maintenance, but the design part was not her thing, and smarty-pants Em did them for fun in her spare time. She'd probably take payment in butter tarts. In time, they could add e-commerce, start to sell online. Butter tarts for all!

It kept resurfacing, over and over, that a café like this was Will's dream. All the things she was doing, he'd talked about. She shook off the thoughts invading her headspace about how nice it would be to have him work side-by-side with her on this. He wouldn't want to leave the city anyway. And it would be too complicated, because they were definitely headed into something, if she didn't put a stop to it right now.

Look what she'd achieved. She'd never felt so...alive, dammit, as much of a cliché as that was. She'd grown up wanting to get away from the farm, and landed herself right smack in the middle of it. With this project, she could keep her commitment to Dean and her parents' memory, and have some-thing that was hers. Something not based on the unpredictable world of horse racing. Except for its tie to something very reli-able: this area was populated with horse people, and horse people ran on coffee.

The tone repeated in Will's ear, and finally Nate picked up.

"Everything okay?" he grumbled.

"Sorry, I know," Will said. "You weren't actually asleep yet, were you?"

"Close enough."

"Just want to bring you up to speed."

"And it couldn't wait till say, five o'clock?"

"You're here now." Will grinned into the phone, but was met with silence. "So. Faye agreed to come to the wedding, if you guys go. It's up to the two of you to convince Liv to come, because I'm guessing it would be awkward if it was just you, me and Faye?"

"If it came to that, I'm pretty sure Faye wouldn't come, no matter how much ground we've made up. But I'd be your Plus One, dude."

"Good to know. Next favour."

"Here we go." Nate's sigh was audible. "What?"

"This one's for Em."

"I don't even need to know what it is, then. I'm in."

"That easy?" Faye had been right.

"For Em? Absolutely. She's always there for everyone. She's social convenor and team therapist. She should be a mental health coach instead of studying to be a physiotherapist. It's what she does anyway."

"Great. This one will be fun. She wants us – you and me – to do a little duo thing at the cafe. They're going to do an evening event. Her friend Cory is hanging some art; we'll do the music, they'll serve cappuccinos and dessert."

"Sounds great. Acoustic?"

"Yep."

"Count me in."

He couldn't wait to tell Faye. Maybe he was trying too hard, when he hadn't intended to try at all.

Faye left Emilie in her happy place, fists kneading flour into pastry dough. Liv unpacked a second box of books, slotting them neatly into the shelving unit. Probably alphabetically.

Yep.

Liv scowled at her when she started pulling out titles. "Here you go, Liv. Em knows good romance. Read this one!" She waved a Kari Lynn Dell paperback.

"Cowboys?"

"It might help you figure out what to do with your own cowboy. Better than this, for sure." Faye peered at one of Liv's thick contributions. "Was this even written in this millennium?"

"Not sure he'd appreciate being called a cowboy, even if he is from Calgary. Or maybe because he's from Calgary."

"Well no one's saying you have to call him that to his face."

Em emerged from the kitchen, pushing a loose strand of hair away from her face with her little finger. "We need to convince the world that gallop boys and jocks are the new cowboys of romance."

"Is that going to be your next thing, Em?" Faye teased. "Romance writer?" Faye unloaded more of Liv's box, which was dramatically lacking in romance in any way, shape or form. Suspense and thrillers and big, fat historical fiction. No wonder the poor girl was so lost.

Faye's phone buzzed. It was Will. All it said was, *Nate's in,* with musical notes.

Awesome, she fired back. This would not shake her decision about breaking things off with him. She'd been up front with him from the start. She was not responsible for his reaction. He'd probably be relieved, and wonder why more women couldn't be like her.

"Em! Let's start getting the word out. The boys are going to play."

"Yes!" Em shot a fist into the air. "What if we make it a fundraiser for New Chapter?"

"That's a great idea. I know we won't have a lot of lead time, but let's make the best of it."

Faye's phone buzzed again. Will. *I'm sending someone to get the espresso machine running for you. I gave him your number to set up a time, hope that's okay.*

A clench of disappointment squeezed her stomach. But she couldn't tell him she'd been hoping he'd come, when on Friday night she was going to push him away.

196

"WELL, THIS IS QUAINT." Faye's lips curved with her trademark sarcasm as her eyes roved around their table.

Will reached for one of the bottles by the centrepiece. A drink was long overdue. "Red or white?" he asked Faye first.

"Red," she replied coolly.

Will looked to Liv next, and she nodded. "Same."

As he poured their glasses, Nate nudged his forward. Red all round it was, then.

Will settled back into his chair, raised his glass, then drank, giving Faye a sideways glance. There would be enough toasts; he wasn't going to make them wait for one of his own. "All the same, I'm grateful for you guys coming. I mean, Nate I could guilt into it, being my oldest friend and all, but you two are going above and beyond." Will's gaze went from Liv's careful smile to Faye, whose expression had been behind a curtain since he'd first laid eyes on her this evening.

He was still awestruck she was actually here, and then there was that dress. It had made him forget everyone else in the room. He didn't know any of those fashion terms about

197

necklines and waistlines and hems. All he knew was it was distracting, and she was beautiful. If she intended that veneer to put him off of something, it wasn't working. No, it was having the opposite effect.

She'd come down with Nate and Liv, and seemed to be making sure she wasn't alone with him. Will had no idea what that was about. He'd endured the service, complimented the bride on how lovely she looked, introduced his troupe to her and his beaming, fake-as-hell, father. It wasn't a big wedding, but there were enough people around that after that formality, dear old Dad was kept busy enough with people he wanted to be around that he left their group to themselves.

"At least he picked a good spot," Will continued, leaving his sentimental thoughts and moving on to something less awkward. "They put on a good spread here. I'd hate to have to miss a night at work for bad food."

Faye stuck close to Liv when they went to the buffet. Maybe he should have just had Nate come solo, because this was almost as awkward as coming alone would have been. He decided against asking Nate if he knew what might be going on. It might be bad form, given the history between them. He didn't want to push things when Nate had really done him a solid by being here; bonus points for getting the two women to cooperate. Things seemed smoother between Nate and Faye since the afternoon of Nate's thing at the farm, but that might not include Nate being willing to provide frank insight on her state of mind, if he even had any.

None of them moved when the dancing began, the formal ones not something Will wanted any part of joining in on. Nate seemed to feel the same. Will was happy just to scowl openly at the bride and groom's first dance, and blocked out the father of the bride one as soon as he noticed the bride's father was probably the same age as her new husband, her mother looking more appropriately matched with Will's dad than his own, new wife. It had to be ridiculously uncomfortable for all of them, but that wasn't Will's problem.

When they got those out of the way and the DJ started something more upbeat, Faye popped to her feet and stretched out her hand.

"You're up, Miller," she said.

Once Nate got over the shock, he grinned and scrambled up, shedding his jacket and going with her. Will stared after them feeling like he'd been socked in the gut.

"What just happened?" he said to Liv. "Are you okay with that?"

"Relieved, actually. Better her than me." She smirked, reached for her wine, and sipped. "I'm happy they've come far enough that they're okay with that."

"So we don't have to be worried?"

Liv laughed quietly. "I don't think so. And if there were something to worry about, what would be the point in worrying?"

"I'm not sure I know what that means, but it sounds wise." He took a slug from his own glass.

"I don't know what exactly is going on with you and Faye, but I didn't think you were yet in a position to merit feeling that way."

Well. That was direct. This one didn't pull punches. "Maybe I'm not." So, he didn't feel right about asking Nate for his thoughts, but Liv might be up for sharing intel. Considering her own position, she seemed remarkably neutral. And she was Faye's best friend, so she might know better than anyone but Faye herself. "But with that outlook, you're either very secure in your relationship, or...indifferent."

"I'm not sure I'm either of those things. Sure I care, but if that –" She inclined her head toward the dance floor where

Nate and Faye were working up what Will had to admit looked like a very innocent sweat, "is actually the rekindling of something between them, and they're both convinced it's real, it's not going to do me any good to fight back, is it? Seems to make more sense to cut my losses and go back to what was working just fine for me before."

"Is that what Faye's doing, then?"

"She's trying."

"I guess that'll make Nate happy then. He wasn't impressed with the whole idea of the two of us anyway."

"I do get that, though. You know what happened to him. You two are close, right? From what I understand, you're practically the fourth brother in that family."

"Yeah? So?"

"So his brother went and married his first girlfriend after she broke up with him. Now his next girlfriend breaks up with him, and starts seeing you. Maybe it's not exactly the same, but there's enough similarity that on some level he might not even be aware of, it triggered him."

"There's a big difference. He was still in love with Cindy when she married his brother. I don't know how deep his feelings went with Faye, but either way, he's not in love with her. He's in love with you."

"No such declarations have been made," she said, glancing down at the wine glass with one of her small smiles. There was a fresh pinkness to her cheeks.

"Only because you are how you are, and he's going to be extra-careful this time. It's going to be excruciating for the rest of us to watch." He grinned.

She laughed quietly. "It might be just as excruciating watching you and Faye trying to sort yourselves out, so, touché."

He chuckled, and contemplated pouring himself another

glass. The wait staff had replaced the empty bottle with a new one. He wasn't sure he'd figured anything out talking to Liv, except that Nate was in good hands with her.

Faye returned laughing and breathless, the energy that surrounded her a contrast to the quiet calm of the discussion at the table. Will's chest tightened with jealousy he, as Liv had pointed out, probably didn't have the right to feel.

Nate gulped down half a glass of water, fit enough he'd hardly turned a hair, then nudged Liv. "C'mon. I let you off the hook for the fast stuff, but you're not getting away with sitting at the table the whole night." He lifted her to her feet and slipped his arms around her, taking the time to kiss her before sweeping her away.

"Would you dance with me?" Will's voice was wobbly. He hadn't intoned it like he'd thought in his head, had he? Would you dance with *me*? Like he was suddenly second rate.

Faye turned her head swiftly like she'd forgotten he was there, her dark hair swinging from her shoulder in waves and layers. Their eyes met for a moment, hers still frustratingly cloaked. She set the water glass she clutched back on the table.

"Of course."

She couldn't say no, but his arms just made what she had to do harder. They transmitted that unicorn feeling that had fallen on her when she'd stood in front of him at the Plate party, looking into those magical eyes as she swayed, and he sang. But there was no destiny between them; that had just been the cheap champagne in her blood that night, amplifying misdirected feelings.

She'd put it off for a moment, and just rest her head against his chest, pretending this was everything it wasn't. The music was all oldies, classic rock. Which had been fine when she'd been out here with Nate, bopping to Crocodile Rock. That had been cathartic, like the history between them was finally documented and archived. Unlike this, a full-fledged war raging inside her as she tried to resist the feelings that assaulted her when he held her against him. And he was *singing*. She didn't even like the Eagles, so why was it getting to her? She needed a new rule. No guys who sang.

Okay now, Faye. Do it now.

She lifted her head and looked up at him, and her neck kinked. See? Again. That was why she didn't date tall guys. Not that it had mattered when they'd been horizontal.

Stop it.

She rested a hand on his chest and tried a wry smile. "So after tonight, we're even, right?"

His eyes fell to hers, a slight furrow to his brown. "Yeah. Tonight carried a lot of weight."

"The espresso machine is a big deal, of course, and I'll always be grateful for your part in the recovery of my sense of self. That one was priceless to be honest." She fingered his tie, letting her smile persist. How did she do this again?

She'd never found it hard, before Nate. Her script had fallen apart with him, but she'd been fed by her desperation and dismay. There was none of that here. All there was, was...senselessness.

Oh, please, Faye. This was the deal, all along.

"And dragging me to Nate's thing, even if it was to our mutual benefit. If you hadn't talked me into going, I never would have talked things out like that with him. I feel like I've got a clear head now. Being part of Lucy's is...I mean, I'm sad for her, but I'm happy I can help. And maybe this is going to be my thing. Like today is the first day of the rest of my life, and all that."

She felt his chest rise and fall against her hand.

"I have to tell you, though." His tone was too serious, and it was robbing her of the vibe she'd been trying to create. "I like you, Faye. For real. I think we could have something."

He'd figured her out. Her rambling little speech had been too obvious a set up. And fine, she liked him too, more than the passing amusement she'd intended him to be. Because he made her think of Shawn, and what it was like to have fun. The music. The silly songs they would do for their parents on special days. Her voice had died with him, and she'd traded passion and adventure for duty. With Nate she'd felt a glimmer of its return, but as a sidekick, future trophy wife. Will made her think of combining their talents to make something bigger and better. He'd made her sing again. But that didn't change what needed to be done.

"If there's one thing I learned from my time with Nate, it's that it's best to get out while things are still good, instead of waiting till it all goes bad. And Nate is probably right about you and me anyway. It's a bad idea."

"Did he say that to you?"

"It's not exactly a secret, is it?" This wasn't the time for honesty, for the revelation that Nate had backed down on that stance, *if you really like him.* "Besides, I was up front about this. I don't want a serious relationship. I had one of those. Except it wasn't serious. I just let myself believe it was, for a heartbeat. And I never want to have that feeling again. So let's quit while we're ahead, all right? If you still want to help with Lucy's, that would be great, of course. We may have hit our personal expiry date, but that's something we could have."

"Like a consolation prize?"

The lines around his eyes and mouth were tight, and she had to look away.

She glanced across the room to where the bride and groom

stood, chatting with their guests at one of the tables. "Your father's a good-looking man," she said. "You have good genes. It's kind of a shame; we'd have beautiful children." Not that she'd ever imagined it.

She closed her fingers around the tie and pulled his lips to hers, hoping the kiss sealed it. So long, and thanks for the pastry.

He didn't say anything. Because what could he say? She'd been honest with him from day one. No more means no more, right?

When she stepped away, the space between them generated a strange emptiness in her chest, and she quickened her pace, hoping more distance would make it go away. It didn't, and Will caught up anyway.

Nate and Liv looked wilted, and Faye put on a bright smile to chase away the melancholy and doubt invading her mind. "It's late for you two. We should probably go."

Liv straightened hopefully, and Nate looked past Faye to Will. "Is that okay with you?"

Faye didn't turn, because she didn't want to see his face. She just wanted to leave before she rushed back to him and started babbling silliness like I *think I've just made a big mistake.*

"Of course." His voice, even speaking, still struck that chord deep inside of her. "I totally understand. I could get out of here myself. I don't think I'll be missed."

The four of them walked out, Faye and Will deflated bookends to Liv and Nate. Faye stood back next to Liv as the boys embraced and nodded about needing to talk about their plans for Monday night. Faye had totally forgotten about Tuesday night, thanks to her chaotic brain. Their music night at Lucy's. Em had been doing all the legwork.

It would be all right. As long as Will didn't back out, now that she'd said her piece.

"Do you want me to drive, Nate?" she asked hopefully. None of them had had more than that early glass of wine, but she hoped he'd appreciate the chance to doze. "If you trust me with your cherished rust bucket, that is."

He surprised her by agreeing. That just proved how tired he really was. He climbed into the back seat, letting Liv ride shotgun.

"What happened," Liv said, her voice hushed. "Are you okay?"

It wasn't all that surprising Liv had picked up on it; she could read animals, and in Liv's mind humans were just another animal, albeit predators.

Faye nodded firmly, as much to convince herself as Liv. "Yeah. It was time. He's a nice guy. He needs to move on and find himself a nice girl."

"You are a nice girl," Liv said, quietly. "One of these days you're just going to have to admit it."

Faye wouldn't look at her. Eyes on the road only. She liked herself the way she was. She would never call herself nice. She could be civil enough in social and business situations to give people that impression, but no, she wasn't nice, below the surface. But Will had made her question that, too. Not because he'd suggested there was anything wrong with her; in fact, he seemed to appreciate her outlook on life. But because he'd made her think there could be more. And there could be, to herself, at least.

CHAPTER SEVENTEEN

"WHAT'S ALL THIS?"

Nate peered around Will's elbow, watching him mash butter and flour together, fingers buried in a bowl.

"Pastry. French pastry."

"You should have warned me you were stress-baking. I'm not sure I can be in the same room as that stuff." He leaned over a rack of cooling croissants and inhaled. "I'm sure even the smell of them has calories."

"I thought some stuff was worth it," Will said, looking at him sideways.

"I know what kind of volume you can create when you get on a roll. I have to be sensible."

"Sometimes sensible interferes with your ability to be supportive."

"My job interferes with my ability to be supportive, not to mention a bunch of other things. What are you stress-baking over, anyway?" Comprehension overtook his face. "Hannah. I'm sorry, man. I forgot."

Will stepped back from the counter before he abused the

delicate mixture. Hearing the name stopped him, even if the thought had been in his head all day. "That's okay. It's been a long time. I should be over it."

"No one gets to tell you how long it should take."

"So does that mean you're still holding onto old stuff?"

"Well – if by stuff you mean a certain amount of anger, and a sense of betrayal...yeah. I know I am. But isn't admitting that a step? And I'm not letting it hold me back from believing there can be something different anymore."

"But not better."

Nate grabbed an apple from a bowl on the counter with obvious frustration – and probably not just because he'd rather have had one of the beautiful buttery pastries.

"It's not that simple, is it? If I said it was better, I'd be admitting that things with Cindy were a mistake. And I'm not ready to do that."

"Does it have to be a mistake to just be not the right thing?" Will swung open the fridge.

Nate laughed then. "Funny, that's kind of what I said to Faye." He set down the apple in favour of the bottle Will offered him. "Does beer go with French pastry?"

Will wiped off his fingers, encrusted with flour and butter, before twisting the cap off his own. "It is hard to believe it's been nine years."

Nate held the bottle out. "To Hannah."

Will tapped it, and they drank, then he leaned back against the counter. "My mom called this morning."

"Ooh."

"My dad said he'd tell her he was getting remarried. Which I guess he did, after the fact. He's lucky I didn't talk to her sooner, assuming he'd done it already. If I had, and I'd said something about it..." He shook his head slightly, and set the bottle to the side, returning to the counter. "It's not like I can do anything for my mom except agree my father is a jerk. And I'm not going to hop on a plane for that."

"She wasn't asking you to, was she?"

"No. But I still feel as if I should." Even though he knew if he did, he'd get to Calgary and find his mother submerged in her job like she'd always been. That was how she dealt with unwanted emotions.

"There's more though, isn't there?"

"More? More what?" *More poking around in my head?*

"To this." Nate waved his hand over the accumulating baked goods.

Will filled the tart shells he'd formed and slid them into the oven. "What's up with the psychoanalysis?"

"The sooner we get it over with, the sooner we can focus on tomorrow night. You haven't cared this much about anyone since Hannah, have you?"

"I don't know what you're talking about."

"You can't lie to save your life. You never could."

"Fine, all right? It's true. You warned me though, so I'm gonna be graceful in defeat and just accept it."

"Nah, nah. This ain't over. Just sit chilly and let her think she knows what she's doing. We'll go there tomorrow night and you'll take piles of pastry, obviously..." Nate looked at the counter again, a bit longingly, Will thought. "Then you'll melt her some more with the music. You'll act like you're cool and not say anything to her about it, and in a few days, she'll make the right choice."

"You're funny. Where did you get all that from? She seemed pretty confident about her decision last night."

"Hardly. You forget I know her. She'll come around."

"Promise?"

"Well that would just be stupid, wouldn't it?" Nate slapped him on the back and walked over to the piano.

He probably shouldn't be taking advice from Nate when it came to Faye. The guy's overall track record with relationships was, technically, better than Will's, however. Even if the first two hadn't ended successfully, at least they'd had some length to them. It wasn't a bad plan, really. Pastry and music? It could work.

————————

"Em, you're a genius. You seriously should go into event planning. It's such a shame you want to do that physio stuff. Helping people," Faye scoffed light-heartedly.

"This is helping people. And by people, I mean horses," Liv pointed out.

Em nodded. "Every donation of $10 to New Chapter gets a ticket for the draw for that painting Cory donated; 10 for $50. Song requests for the guys – $20. And we have a little silent auction. Next time we do this it'll be way better. There just wasn't enough time."

Volunteering for New Chapter Thoroughbred Retirement was another of Emilie's side projects. While Faye would gladly support the group, aligning with them could be valuable PR for the café.

"We should auction off a private show with the boys, with coffee and dessert here at the cafe. A live auction, of course," Faye suggested.

Emilie laughed. "That would be great, but we'd better run it past them first. And have very strict conditions."

"Probably wise," Liv agreed, her gaze landing on Faye. "For people like you who might have unwholesome ideas."

"The fact that you mention that gives me hope for you, sweetie."

"The guys should be here any time to set up," Emilie said.

Faye was not going to think about seeing Will for the first time since Friday night. "How about Cory? We should have had her paint live."

"Oh, I tried that. No go. She says she could never paint in public. In fact, she's too terrified to even be here."

"That's a shame," Faye said.

"Not that I don't understand," Liv said, "but she's going to have to get over performance anxiety if she wants to be a jockey."

"See, you really are the best mentor for her." Emilie nudged her sister with an elbow, then pressed her hands together. "All right, let's go. We have half an hour."

Em had outdone herself, decorating the little room. Strings of fairy lights surrounded them, little flameless candles on all the tables – Faye had really wanted real ones, but Liv had pointed out it was an unnecessary fire hazard and Faye agreed it wouldn't do to burn the place down. Dean and the guys had gotten together and sent them flowers, and Em had plucked some from the generous arrangement to put in vases on the tables. The lighting might not be best for Cory's artwork, but the paintings had been placed in such a way that they caught the available illumination.

"It looks fabulous, Em. You really are the best." Faye captured her in a hug, then released her to continue her scurrying.

She needed something to do herself – Emilie was far too efficient. Was it going to be weird with Will? He hadn't called her, begging her to reconsider, telling her they were meant to be. That was a relief, not a disappointment, contrary to what a very stubborn part of her brain kept suggesting. The important thing was he hadn't backed out of tonight.

It wasn't like she could hide anywhere to avoid him here. She busied herself lining up cups for the hot drinks. Maybe, after all, Will agreed it was for the best. He had sent someone else to set up the espresso machine, so he'd probably been feeling it too, even before the wedding. She helped Em place the last few butter tarts on plates, and Liv joined them to set them on tables. Emilie had sold tickets because they had limited seats – each guest would get a tart and the espresso drink of their choice – and they'd sold out.

The guys came in the back, with just a couple of guitars, no speakers, because they'd decided the room was small enough the sound would be fine. Em planted water bottles by their stools as they unpacked the instruments, and Faye stayed out of the way until everything was ready. They all gathered in the kitchen.

"This is great," Nate said, stealing a butter tart from a nearby tray.

Em scowled at him, then just shook her head with an eye roll. "Go ahead, Will. Consider it part of your payment."

They weren't getting paid, even though Em had offered. They hadn't asked for anything, of course. All of it was very sweet. Very *nice*.

Liv glanced out the swinging door to the front. "There are already people waiting outside."

"It's only ten to. Should we let them in?" Faye asked.

"No!" Emilie gasped. "Make 'em wait."

Emilie gave a short nod to Liv, and Liv nodded back. She pulled a tray of flutes from under the counter as Em ducked away to the refrigerator, reemerging with a clean white dish towel and bottle of champagne. Real champagne.

"We might not be serving alcohol, but we most definitely must have a toast." She held up the bottle and grinned.

"Here, Em, I'll open it for you," Nate said.

"No! Don't let him!" Liv warned, then their eyes met, like

no one else was in their universe, and they both started laughing.

"This place is clean enough we could eat off the floors, so definitely not going to happen." Emilie angled herself away from Nate and opened it conservatively, a quiet pop followed by a whisper of released pressure.

"Here's to you, Faye," she said once everyone had a glass, "and this new adventure."

"Here's to all of us," Faye replied.

Will's gaze pinned her before the glass made it to her lips. Faye had to look away, quickly tossing back a mouthful.

Everything about the evening was perfect – the gentle music, the soft lighting, the muted hum of voices – but she managed to feel lonely in the midst of it. This new adventure, as Emilie had called it, was supposed to fill her up more than this. That's what she got for stealing Will's dream, and only letting him be a tiny part of it.

An hour had passed when Dean slipped in – late, but Faye was more grateful than ever to see her brother. He stood just inside the door, eyebrows up and eyes wide as he scanned the packed room. His gaze finally rested on Faye, and he weaved through the tables and pulled her into a hug.

"This is extraordinary, little sister. You have done an incredible thing here."

"Couldn't have done it without these two." She tilted her head at Emilie and Liv with a smile. *And those two.* She didn't say it out loud, but cast a gaze at the Calgary boys.

Dean gave Liv and Em a squeeze in turn, and Em rushed away, presenting him with a cappuccino and a golden butter tart when she returned.

"Want to make a request, Dean?" Emile said, turning on her fundraising charm. "I have to warn you, though. There are bidding wars over them. This one went for $100 on the secondary market."

"Secondary market?" Liv choked back a laugh. "You'd definitely better plan to do this again."

"What's it going to cost me then, Em?" Dean asked. He finished off the tart, balanced his cup on the empty plate, and pulled out his wallet. Faye was awed by Emilie's ability to draw out that behaviour in people. Dean handed her cash, and she gave him a slip of paper and a pen, on which he scribbled something Faye couldn't see. Emilie took her fistful of slips to the front and waited till they finished the current song to present the fresh requests.

"They really are amazing, aren't they?" Faye said, swaying slightly to the next tune. All the requests so far had been pretty generic, things it seemed they hadn't had to think twice about to play.

"Do I detect a note of regret there?" Liv leaned closer, so Faye heard her words despite how softly she'd uttered them.

"It never would have worked. He lives in the city. He works evenings and weekends."

"He seems to have found ways to see you despite that. Maybe it's not such a bad thing to have to work at finding time."

Faye's eyebrows raised. "Everything all right with you and Nate, sweetie?"

"Yes, totally. Can it be too perfect?"

"No, it cannot, so shut up. You're just so used to being dark and twisty, I realize accepting happiness must be a challenge." Faye hadn't meant for it to sound caustic, but Liv didn't seem offended. She just sighed.

"It's hard to keep my own identity, when our lives are so intertwined."

"You were someone before he was, remember."

"But how quickly do people forget that?"

"Um, hello. You train a filly who's just one win away from the Canadian Triple Crown. If you pull that off, you'll be the first woman to do it. You are still someone. You are remarkable."

Liv's sideways glance was part grateful, but part dubious. "Sometimes I just wonder where work ends and we begin."

"Has anyone told you that you think too much?"

Liv laughed, quietly. "Oh yes. I don't seem to be able to stop, though." She was silent a moment, listening. "We should request a song."

"How much do you think that will cost us?" Faye asked.

"Shouldn't we get special consideration?"

"Em's a hardass when it comes to raising money for a cause."

Liv laughed. "True. What would you request?"

What would she give to hear Will play *Brown Eyed Girl* again? But that would send the wrong message. "Let's see. It has to be a little obscure. Something no one else would think of, but the two of them will know."

"Like, *The Sand and the Foam*," Liv offered.

"That's obscure enough I don't know it."

"It's Dan Fogelberg. Don't ask me how I know."

"But now I must."

"Emilie!" Liv called, blatantly ignoring Faye. She grabbed the pen in Em's hand and scribbled the song's name on one of the blank tickets. "I'm pulling strings."

Em grinned, plucking the ticket from Liv's fingers and reclaiming her pen. "It's only right."

The next song Faye knew well, from the first note Will picked with the guitar. Dean nodded in time, so it must have been his request, but Will was looking directly at her as he started singing, *Where Are You Going?*

Had he and Dean plotted this somehow? *It was just a song.* But oh, that damn hum, made worse by all the emotion that came with the memories the music conjured up. She shut down the feelings, opening the camera on her phone. Lifted it, hitting record, forcing her thoughts to content for social media. They would pass, those feelings, fading with the melody as it ended. The next song, and the one after, would free her of them, except the intoxicating resonance of his voice kept stirring it all back up.

Faye glanced at the time as Em passed Liv's ticket to Nate, Em leaning over, her lips moving close to his ear. He looked at it, looked up...found Liv, and smiled. Faye gave her a little squeeze. Liv would master this happiness. And Faye would not envy her for it. She'd figure out her own.

"Last one." Nate spoke into the crowd and was met with a restless rustle that indicated they all would have stayed long into the night for more. Faye would have.

Nate passed the slip to Will, who nodded, his gaze travelling over and around heads till he found them, again settling uncomfortably on Faye. Faye had long ago perfected a benign smile for moments such as this. But as they began, she couldn't keep herself from studying every motion, every nuance in his expression, hopelessly entranced.

"That is a beautiful song," she said softly, head tilted towards Liv, and she tried not to assign personal meaning to the words. They were nostalgic, a little sad, a place to which she didn't want to return.

The guests were slow to leave at the end, the boys flooded with compliments and back-slaps. Liv had disappeared, probably hiding out in the kitchen to avoid any unnecessary conversation with strangers and vague acquaintances. Faye and Emilie cleared cups and plates from the emptying tables. Liv assumed dishwasher loading duties in the kitchen, and they disappeared into the machine as quickly as Faye and Em brought them.

Emilie shooed the stragglers out and locked the door, and they gathered again in the kitchen. Nate set down his guitar case and slipped an arm around Liv, kissing her cheek then resting his head on her shoulder, looking beat. Liv barely even squirmed.

"That was incredible," Faye said, trying to keep the tremor of emotion from her voice. She wanted to say, *I hope we can do it again,* but needed to let it all sit right now. She couldn't shake that it felt so natural for Will to be part of this, but she wasn't ready to figure out how to make that so. Every time she invited the thought, fear roiled back to the surface.

CHAPTER EIGHTEEN

THE CAFÉ's Facebook page was alive. She'd shared photos and the video clip from last night, and the post was going wild with comments and reactions. Half the video plays were probably hers, though. She kept listening to it again, and again. She'd thought she'd known where she was going. She'd been happy to go there alone, while occasionally enjoying company along the way. It was probably time to revive Operation Jiro.

She sent Em a text to try and dislodge the heavy lump in behind her ribcage. *Races tonight? I need a fix.*

It was a frustrating few minutes before Em's response. *Sorry, I can't. We've got a horse in, though, so try Liv.*

Being a Wednesday night, Liv wouldn't necessarily be there, but Faye could hope. *Are you going tonight?*

The little reply bubble popped up immediately. *Good girl, Liv, replying so fast.* The text whooshed in. *Yes, saddling the horse in the second. Roger's in Saratoga. Why did I not go to Saratoga this year?*

Faye: *I can think of one very good reason, about five-six, blond, killer grin and hot as hell.*

Liv: *I don't think it would be hard to convince him to come along. Don't think it's going to happen this year though. See you tonight?*

Faye: *You know where to find me.*

The excitement she should be feeling was missing, though. Of course Liv wasn't as fun to hang out with at the races as Em, and having saddling duties would make her even less so. It was Will. She'd only known the guy for five weeks, and she was miserable. It was almost as bad as after she'd split up with Nate, only this time, the only one she could be mad at was herself.

She let the aroma wafting gloriously from the kitchen distract her. Lucy must've pulled a fresh batch of butter tarts from the oven. Time for a break. These days, Lucy offered a tart without Faye having to ask. She hadn't gotten Lucy on to drinking cappuccinos yet though. Faye set up the machine to make one. Will had taught her. It wasn't as difficult as she'd thought it might be, and last night she'd had lots of practice.

"I have to tell you something, Faye."

Uh-oh. Lucy's tone caught her attention. Faye poured the espresso into a cup, and topped it off with the steamed milk. She took a sip, telling herself the sense of foreboding she had was ridiculous. Lucy would have told her as soon as she'd arrived if her mother's condition had changed.

"What's up?"

Lucy rubbed her hands together, then slid them down the front of her apron. "I have a buyer for the business."

Faye's mouth dropped open, and she quickly took another drink to hide her dismay. "Wow!"

"It's not a done deal yet, but it's just a matter of details, really. Everything you've done in the last while clinched it for him."

So, she'd shot herself in the foot. Perfect. Faye couldn't even fight back the way she wanted to, couldn't beg for a chance to see if she could buy it instead.

Lucy continued. "Would you be willing to help with the transition?"

A small sigh escaped Faye's lips before she could stop it. "Of course. That's great for you, Lucy. You've been stretching yourself thin trying to keep it going and take care of your mom, even with me around."

"Thank you for all your help. This wouldn't be happening without you." While Lucy looked sad, the tension that had riddled her features had softened a little. "It will be strange, not coming here, but it's time to let it go."

"Just let me know whatever you need. You can give the new owner my number. I'm happy to meet with them." Maybe she could still finagle a job out of it.

Gus was the only one to greet her when she got home. As much as she loved the silly dog, she could have used Dean's ear right now. She didn't know where he was. It didn't look as if he'd been there since he'd left before dawn. Something was going on with him; he'd been away more than usual lately. Maybe he had found a girlfriend. Maybe he was going to leave her. So much for her life plan. Sexy spinster was turning into lonely old maid.

Faye had gone to the races alone many times in her life, and never felt uncomfortable, but as she leaned on the rail across from where Liv saddled a horse named Just Jay, she found herself glancing from side to side, wishing someone were here next to her. At least with the Triple Stripe horse in the race, she didn't feel conspicuous, but what was that? She never felt conspicuous. She was Faye Taylor, damn it. She'd been scouting short men in this paddock for a decade. She was a fixture here as much as any of the horseplaying regulars.

Nate joined Liv in the stall as the groom led the horse away to start walking him. He greeted Liv professionally, the affection he'd shown last night put on the shelf here, probably because Liv would kill him if he tried anything. Liv said something in his ear, and he looked out at the crowd. He gave Faye a quick wave and a smile, which was nothing like the smile he would have given her a year ago. Faye smiled and waved back, and realized, finally, she was fine with that. If she admitted it, it was because someone else had taken up the space that had been left. But that didn't change reality, that she'd pushed that someone away, and found herself with a new trench to fill.

Liv threw Nate up on the horse after the riders up call, and instead of following the horses and keeping her eyes peeled for Jiro, Faye waited by the gate. Liv wasn't as keyed up as she would have been with Chique, but her mind was still solidly on the horse. It was comfortingly normal, when Faye's own life had stopped being so.

"This is his first race back?" Faye asked, falling on the little bits of knowledge she'd retained about this horse. Last spring, Just Jay had been one of the most promising two-year-olds in the Triple Stripe barn. He was a half-brother to the nicest horse they'd ever had, Just Lucky – now on his way to being a successful stallion, Chique the most notable of the offspring from his first crop – but, in one of those promise versus reality stories, injury had kept Just Jay from actually making it to the races until now.

Liv nodded as the escalator took them to the next level of the grandstand. "Now we get to see if he might still be everything he's supposed to be."

They navigated through the spotty Wednesday night crowd on the second floor to the outside seating. Liv was good at silence, and if she found Faye's unusual, she didn't question it. Faye sat back and followed the post parade and warm-ups, something she only ever half-watched – a contrast to Liv's binocular-aided scrutiny.

Faye was happy when the horse won, even though it had been expected – as much as one could ever expect a horse to win a race. It was encouragement for everyone with horses whose careers hadn't gone the way they were supposed to, and it renewed Faye's hope that Ride The Wave might get there one day; that not getting to the races as a two-year-old wasn't the worst thing that could happen.

"Coming down for the picture?" Liv asked, her mouth lightened from the serious line of moments earlier now that Just Jay was galloping out, still far ahead of his foes.

"Sure," she said. "And congratulations."

Liv shrugged, far too restrained as usual, and headed for the stairs down to the apron. "I'm just the stand-in."

"But this was Jay." Because Faye remembered that part about the colt, too; that he was named for Geai Doucet, and it always meant a little more when a horse you named for someone special turned out to be special too.

Liv didn't comment, focusing harder than she needed on the steps, and fingering the pendant at her neck.

Faye almost ran into Jiro as they walked against the traffic of jockeys headed for the scales; the also-rans who had finished behind Nate and Jay. He lit up in recognition, and it should have thrilled her, because that's why she'd come, right? But all she mustered back to his cheery hello was a lukewarm *hey, Jiro.* Those aspirations were vexingly dead in the water. The heart wants what the heart wants. *Stupid heart.*

After the photo, when Nate dismounted, Liv released some of her professional guard and hugged him, and let him kiss her. Faye stood out of the way, keeping well clear of the horse, who seemed a sensible type, but exuded enough triumphant energy to rattle her.

"I have to go back and check on him. Do you want to come?" Liv asked once Nate had gone to weigh in, the groom and horse test barn-bound.

Faye didn't blame Liv for sounding so unsure – not that the offer wasn't genuine. It was more that she was bewildered she felt it was necessary. Where was strong, *laissez-faire* Faye?

"Sure," Faye said. She had officially begun to resort to monosyllabic responses.

"I think mad-at-Nate Faye was better than sad-without-Will Faye," Liv said quietly, eying her carefully.

"I'm not sad without Will." Faye scowled, which was a sure sign it was, at least partly, a lie. She did agree that post-Nate Faye was better than post-Will Faye, though she didn't particularly like either of them.

They reached the test barn just after the horse, in time for a *so far, so good* response from the groom to Liv's "how is he?" Liv watched as they bathed Jay, and waited while the hotwalker took him a few turns.

"Want a ride back to the barn with us, Michel?" she asked the groom once they were both satisfied everything was under control. The hotwalker would bring Jay once he was cooled out and the necessary samples had been acquired.

The Triple Stripe barn was deserted when they got there, nothing but the rustling of haynets and snoring of horses. Liv went straight to Chique's stall. Considering how close the big race was, Liv was remarkably calm right now; either that or she was hiding it well.

Faye stared outside the front of the barn at the bank across from it. The glow of the main track lights rimmed its top, the announcer's voice coming eerily from the distance. She heard a deep rumble.

"Was that thunder?" she asked. She hadn't looked at the forecast all day. Not like the people around here, who followed it obsessively because it had such an impact on racing and training.

"Probably," Liv said from behind her. "I think the turf is going to be soft for Sunday. A storm rolling in tonight, and rain predicted for the next couple of days."

"Is that good, or bad?"

"For Chique? Who knows. First time on the grass for her, so it's anyone's guess."

That phrase was used a lot with Chique. *It's anyone's guess.*

Faye glanced at her phone to check the time, and saw she'd missed a text. Dean: *I'm staying down here tonight.*

There he was. So maybe this time his absence was about a horse, and not a woman.

She Brews was a little colicky earlier, and with this weird weather, I'm worried about the others.

And by the others, he meant Wampum, four days out from his return to racing.

All racetrackers were superstitious. Even the one who insisted they weren't. For all she knew Dean was sleeping in a stall next to the horse. You'd think he was running in the Breeders' Cup, not the Breeders' Stakes. She probably wouldn't see him again until the day of the race.

Faye responded. *Have you been here all day?*

Dean: *Yeah.*

Faye: *I came for Just Jay's race. Liv was saddling him.* That wasn't why she'd come, just how it had worked out. *I'll get Liv to stop by on our way out.*

Once Jay returned to the barn, Liv was content to leave him under Michel's care. They checked in with Dean, then Liv drove Faye back to her car on the front side.

"Are you waiting for Nate?" Faye asked.

Liv shook her head. "I'll see him in the morning."

"Should I be worried about you two?"

"We're fine, Faye. Sunday's kind of a big deal. We'll get a breath of normal after that."

Until the next big race drew near. A relationship made up of breaths.

CHAPTER NINETEEN

WHAT A MISERABLE NIGHT.

The rain had started as she'd driven home, a wind-whipping, driving kind of downpour that forced her to go slowly so she could keep the car between the lines. The low-slung clouds left everything under the cloak of premature darkness.

It suited her. She was happy Dean was staying close to the track tonight because he was worried about his Breeders' horse. Happy for her brother's weirdness. Happy to be alone. Misery loves a rainy, stormy night.

She'd made herself this person. The woman who saw men as something to be used. It made her just as bad, just as sexist, as any man who treated women that way, didn't it? *I deserve to grow old and die alone.*

If one was ever really alone with a bottle of wine. And a Golden Retriever.

"C'mon Gus. This definitely calls for a bottle of red."

She didn't care about the weather. She didn't care how Wampum ran. Win or lose, as long as no one was hurt, it really didn't matter to her. The money took the pressure off, then got used up, and something else broke, and it was like it had never been there. Wampum wasn't connected to her fresh start, because there was no fresh start.

A brilliant flash lit up all the windows, stopping her short. The crack that followed – within seconds – almost made her drop to the floor, it was so loud. Everything went dark before the windows had even stopped rattling.

That was close. Really close. But there was no way she was going out to have a look around. The way that gale was gusting, she and Gus would end up in Oz. She preferred to get her ruby red slippers the traditional way, with a good, old-fashioned shopping spree downtown. Not that her credit card would appreciate such a thing. Now where were the candles? *Kitchen counter, I think.*

The next flare of lightning was gentler, the interval between light show and rumble farther apart. It gave her a glimpse, and she saw her phone on the kitchen counter. There was already a text from Liv. *You get home okay? Power just went out here.*

She sent Dean a message before answering. *If that horse wins on Sunday, first thing you're doing Monday morning is calling the electrician and getting that damn generator wired into the panel.* She'd watched Dean hook it up before, but it had never really stuck in her mind. She should have paid more attention.

Dean: *Hydro out, I presume.*

Faye: *Good guess, genius.*

Dean: *Have you heard from Stacy? If it's out for long, you'll have to get it running. The horses will need water.*

With any luck Stacy, the barn manager, had done night check early, anticipating the possibility of this happening. But Faye kept that comment to herself. *I'll text her.*

First Liv. *Yeah, home and okay. At least nothing a bottle of wine won't fix. Power just went out here too. Do you know how to start a generator?*

Liv: *You need help? I'm sure someone on the farm could do it. I'll ask Nate. He just texted saying they cancelled the last two races, so he's on his way.*

Faye: *Because that's just what I need, Nate coming to my rescue.*

Liv: *Really? You want to be picky like that now?*

Faye: *Why is there not a tongue-sticking-out emoji? Because I could use one right now.*

She got a rolling ROTFL one for that.

Now, Stacy. *Do you need help with anything? I'm at the house. Horses have water?*

Stacy: *Good for now. I'll let you know if that changes. I'm just going to make sure everyone outside is okay.*

Thank goodness for small mercies. Faye opened up the bottle of wine, counted to ten – long enough for her to breathe, if not the wine. Glass filled and in hand, she padded into the living room. Dean always made sure there was kindling and wood for a fire, even in the summer *because August can get cold, you know.* And so it could. And tonight it was.

She felt a hundred times better once it caught, flames spreading from the paper and cardboard to the pile of dry branches, and she sat in front of it, staring, until she was convinced it was ready for a larger log. Then she waited until the fire was committed to its consumption, and pushed herself up, grabbing the wine again – because it would not be far from her side tonight – and began the search for candles.

They were never all in one place. A couple in the kitchen cupboards, a couple in the rarely – as in, almost never – used dining room. Striking a match, the wick on the first one hissed to life, settling into a steady, comforting flame. She lit the others, until little flickering lights dotted the kitchen and living room.

What now?

Well, she would drink wine and feel pathetic so that tomorrow she could put it all behind her and figure out how to move forward from here.

The rain was pelting against his windshield like it was personal. Like he shouldn't be driving up the 400 at this time of night, on an evening when there were wind warnings, maybe even tornado warnings, going to see a girl who didn't want to see him. At least the weight of his old domestic car kept him on the road; kept it from hydroplaning over the glassy sheet of water that covered the asphalt.

A headwind fought him when he left the highway, pushing back as he drove along King Sideroad. If it had been words, it would have been saying, *don't you see, any rational person would not have left the city on a night like this?* And why were there no lights? Anywhere.

He turned up on the sideroad Faye's farm was on, creeping. Everything was so dark. But he was almost there now. No turning back. She couldn't turn him away, could she?

Thunk.

He braked, hard, pressing into the headrest, back braced against the seat. His knuckles were so tight on the wheel his hands hurt. What the hell was that? The windshield wipers tried to beat back the rain as he peered through the glass, trying to figure it out. He climbed into the soaking downpour, and stepped towards the front of the car. A tree! And not a small one. Right across the road. A matter of seconds had been the difference between it landing on his Camaro, and where it had ended up. Except now he was stuck here.

There had to be a way around. Or maybe this was a sign from God. *Hello, idiot, you should have stayed home. She doesn't want to see you. You're too tall, or nice, or...something.* Cripes.

So...now what? Faye's house was literally a hundred feet away. He could text Nate, and see if Nate could help with the tree. Or, it wasn't much of a walk to the apartment. Maybe back up the car and get it on the side of the road before he abandoned it. And pray another tree didn't fall on it.

Were things ever dark. Had he told himself that already? He climbed back in the car, and punched a message out to Nate. *Hey man, crazy question, but do you have a chainsaw?*

Sending it into cyberspace felt a little like setting a message in a bottle to sea. Who knows when Nate would see it; it was nine PM on a Wednesday night. The guy was probably asleep in bed, and would be pissed off at Will for waking him up. This wasn't exactly an emergency, was it?

The logical thing would have been to text Faye. But that would ruin the surprise. Ha. That element might not work in his favour right now. Showing up at her door on a night like this? He wouldn't put it past her to own a gun. Farms had shotguns, didn't they? He'd bet Faye knew how to handle one.

But, he was committed now. And that tree wasn't going anywhere. So, if he was doing this, he was doing it on foot. He retrieved his backpack from behind the front seat, slung it over his shoulder, and pulled up his hood, which really didn't do much to protect him from the angry elements.

It would probably be smarter to ask to sleep on Nate's couch. Instead he climbed through the downed branches, snagging his jacket on something and hearing the tear as he pulled it free. Sheets of rain stung his eyes. A southeast wind never brought good things. But he was fighting it, pushing into it, come what may.

A light outside the window – was she seeing things? Faye sat bolt upright, clutching the glass, heart hammering against her chest. Gus slept like the dead at her feet. *Great, Gus. You'll be lying there passed out as some ax murderer is slashing my throat and leaving me to bleed out.*

The rain still beat against the window pane. She set the wine glass on the coffee table, stepped over Gus – that dog was unbelievable – and crept into the kitchen, like her footsteps might, what, alert whoever was out there to her presence? She should probably be hiding in the basement, instead of investigating. Except the basement of this old Victorian was scarier than whatever might be out there.

It was times like this she wished they had a shotgun – but Dean was too nice a guy to shoot coyotes like most farmers. She had nothing with which to defend herself. Except – yes. That's what she'd grab.

The light flashed around the back door. Then the ax murderer knocked. Did they do that? Wouldn't they just barge in? She closed her grip around the wooden handle, and opened the door a crack.

"Will!" He was soaked, hair plastered to his face, his jacket clearly not waterproof. "What the hell are you doing here?"

"If you put down the rolling pin and let me in, I'll tell you. I do love your weapon of choice, though."

She backed away from the door, leaving the wooden pin on the kitchen table. Then she grabbed him with both hands, pulling him against her, his clothes so wet they made hers damp as she clutched his waist. Her heart finally started to temper.

"You need some dry clothes." She reluctantly peeled herself from him. "Take off your shoes."

He did as he was told as she lifted the backpack from his shoulder, holding it, dripping, out to the side. It took him so long to get his coat off she thought it must've been adhered to his skin.

Will reached for the backpack and glanced around before setting it on the floor. Gus lumbered sleepily between them, sticking his nose into it and wagging his tail.

"Sure, Gus. Now you decide to make an appearance. Lucky for you, there's no blood to clean up." Faye rubbed the Golden's ribcage.

Will looked at her strangely, then reached into the bag and withdrew a paper bag.

"What is that?" she asked suspiciously.

He handed it to her. "I brought dessert?"

"I didn't know you were coming for dinner."

Accepting, she placed it on the counter. The paper bag was so wet it tore, so she just ripped it the rest of the way off to reveal a white paperboard box. She eased open the sodden lid. Four small, perfect pastries. They looked part chocolate, and part tart, and totally melt-in-your-mouth.

"They're prototypes. For the shop. Your shop."

She'd let herself forget when she'd seen him. She looked at the perfect little confections with a sad smile. "I don't have a shop."

"Sure seems like your shop."

"Lucy's selling it. I'll help with the transition, then, I guess I'm done. These look delicious, though." She pushed them back from the edge, because Gus was known to counter surf on occasion. "Come on. About those dry clothes. You're about the same size as Dean."

It was just plain human decency to bring him back from

the verge of hypothermia. She'd decide if she was going to jump his bones after he'd had a chance to warm up by the fire. Nothing had changed, but she certainly wasn't sending him back out into that horrible night.

Will could hear his phone buzzing, he just had no idea where it was. He was warmer, sure, but the effort his body had put into reheating had left him exhausted, and his head hadn't caught up.

Then there was another ringing, and it wasn't until Faye went dashing toward the next room saying, "If the landline rings, it has to be serious," that he realized that's what it was.

He found his phone on the counter, and glanced at the screen. *A chainsaw? I don't understand.*

He chuckled at Nate's text. *Go back to sleep. I'll tell you about it tomorrow.*

Wednesday night racing, dude. I just got home. Where are you? Are you okay?

NVM. I'm fine now.

Nate seemed convinced enough to leave him alone. He disconnected in time to hear the tail end of Faye's conversation.

"Okay. We'll be there in a few minutes."

We? "What's up?" he asked when he reentered the living room.

"That was Stacy, the farm manager. One of the outdoor horses managed to slice her leg. She saw it when she was doing one last check before going to bed. Can you start a generator? I'm totally hopeless at remembering how to do it."

"Where is it?"

He followed her to a laundry room off of the kitchen. "It's outside. Dean got as far as building it a little shed. I know you have to take this long cord and attach it - unplug the dryer and use that outlet, then the other end goes in the generator."

Will walked to the electrical panel and flipped off the circuit breakers and the main switch. "So we don't blow the place up."

"See, this is why it petrifies me. Here, take one of Dean's jackets." She pulled on a proper Gore Tex raincoat and led the way out.

The generator had gas, thank goodness, and was soon chugging away with ear-piercing determination.

"So what do you want power for?" he asked, back in the house where they could hear again.

"Water. Lights in the barn might be helpful too. Barn one on the panel. Then we'd better go see if she needs any help. Not that I'm much good as far as horses are concerned."

"Well I don't know much about them, but they don't terrify me, so I'll do what I can. My grandfather had cows. Now they're terrifying." He flipped on individual breakers for the barn and the pump, hearing the pump run immediately. "There you go."

Faye keyed in a text to update Stacy, then started blowing out candles. "Do they bite?"

"Cows? I don't know, but they sure can kick."

Faye didn't run – except sometimes, through the rain, when it was gushing down like this. Nervous whinnies travelled through the barn as they ducked inside. Simple bulbs illuminated the aisle – and Stacy filling a bucket with warm, soapy water.

"Thank you! Of all the nights. Horses!" she said, but with a laugh in her voice that carried more affection than Faye felt for the species at the moment. Love is patient, love is kind, love is stupid, love is blind. It should be the horse girl mantra.

"They know how to pick 'em," Faye agreed. "This is Will. If you need help, he says he's your man." She stopped short of saying, *he's actually my man*, because he wasn't, and wouldn't be. No amount of pastry and heroics was going to change that, not even on a night like this.

"Perfect." Stacy was too engrossed in preparing to doctor the horse to give Will more than a quick glance. "I've almost got stuff ready, then I'll bring her into the aisle – if you can hold her for me? She's a sweetheart, she won't give you a hard time. One of the barren mares."

Will held the leather lead awkwardly as Stacy tapped bubbles out of a small syringe. She put pressure on the mare's jugular and deftly slipped it in, pulling back the plunger so the colourless medication was quickly turned a deep red before easing it into the vein. Faye had watched it enough times she could probably do it herself, if she could ever get over her fear enough to be that close. Even as the shot took effect, the mare blinking before her eyes began to droop, Faye was glad Will was here to hold that shank so it hadn't been up to her.

"I don't think she'll need stitches," Stacy said, standing with hands on hips as she waited for the injection to kick in further "But I want to clean it up and put a bandage on it. I'm sure the vet would love to come out on a night like this."

"He's probably dealing with a bunch of colics," Faye said. "Dean had one at the track today, Mild, thank goodness, but it put him on edge."

"Oh – there's a tree down on the road," Will said, breaking out of what seemed to be intense concentration on the job he'd been given. It was cute.

"Really? Where?" Faye asked.

"Right before your driveway. Between here and Triple Stripe."

"So that's why you were soaking wet? You left your car and walked?" She hadn't even not-seen his car.

"Do you have a chainsaw?"

Faye looked at Stacy. "We do, right? I am feeling very much like a useless woman tonight."

"We do. But I think it's best you call the township and have them remove it. It's kind of dangerous."

"I can do that," Faye said. "Just not in a steel barn. You two okay?"

"Yep," Stacey said, grabbing a little stainless steel pail and carefully dousing soapy water over the wound with gauze sponges, the scent of the air tinged with iodine.

Faye left them. The horse was really quiet, her eyes droopy. Every now and then her head would twitch, and Will would jump, but the horse didn't move.

"You can relax," Stacy said. "She's got good drugs on board, and this won't take that long."

The suds pooled on the mat under the horse's hooves. Once Stacy seemed satisfied she'd cleaned the gash enough, she ripped open a small packet and placed a pad over it, then wound a gauze roll over that, then a longer roll of something that covered the lower leg.

"That's quite a production," he said. How she managed to do it so that it wouldn't fall off, he didn't know.

"Done it so many times I don't even think about it. Horses like to hurt themselves. It's like every day is a fresh chance for them to find a new way to die."

"That's a morbid way to look at things."

Stacy grinned, and glanced up at him. "True horse people are in a constant love/hate relationship with these animals. There's a fine line between how they help us stay sane, and how they drive us completely *in*sane."

"So why do you do it?"

She paused, like it was justifiable to question it. "Because they're everything, wrapped majestically together. Power and fragility, strength and vulnerability. Honesty and bravery. They can literally kick your head in if you let your guard down, but they can lift a peppermint from your palm with such gentleness. Once they're in your blood, there's no getting out." She was applying another, thicker, pillow-looking layer, then held it all in place with a red bandage like the white ones Jo and Nate had put on Chique after the Prince of Wales.

Stacy's soliloquy was just more proof the whole horse world was beyond his comprehension. "She's not looking so majestic at the moment," he said, convinced now she wasn't going to cause any trouble. He stroked her long face, and the mare's lids slid over her glassy eyes.

Stacy laughed, securing the end of the bandage and smoothing the whole thing with both hands.

"Does Dean know about this, Stacy?"

Will glanced over his shoulder. Faye stood at a safe distance, snapping.

"No, I didn't want to contact him till I knew how bad it was. And it's not that bad, so it can wait till I'm done."

A few flicks of her fingers later, Faye said, "I just sent him a text."

"Thanks. One less thing for me to do." Stacy stood, reaching for the lead. "She's done. Here, I'll take her."

Will stepped back, and Faye inched up to his elbow. "Good job, cowboy."

He laughed, and resisted a very strong urge to put an arm around her. "I had the easy job."

"You know, there is one thing about you Calgary boys that disappoints me. Like, where are the white cowboy hats? Isn't that part of the uniform?"

"Right." Will laughed. "For the Winter Olympics, maybe."

"You'd look good in one," she said, sliding him a wry grin and turning away. "I don't know about you, but I need wine."

Gus scrambled to his feet in a clatter of nails when Faye pushed open the door, behind which he'd been right behind, worrying. Somehow he wasn't afraid of thunder or fireworks, but the noise of the generator outside unsettled him enough to temper his usual enthusiasm.

She dragged off her rubber boots and shuffled to the wine bottle, gauging its contents. "Do you want some? Would you prefer beer? Or I can make coffee or hot chocolate." He was looking chilled again, after standing still holding the mare.

"Wine is fine, if you have enough."

"I always have enough," she assured him. She divided what remained between two glasses, handed him one, and wandered into the living room, settling on a cushion in front of the fire. Will dropped into a nearby chair.

"How do you know when the power comes back on?" he asked.

"Stacy will tell me, if she's still awake. She said she's okay with her electric lantern if it's just short term. Her apartment is wired separately. If it were winter and she needed heat, I'd have invited her to the house."

She'd invited Stacy anyway, but Stacy had shot a look at Will and declined. Having Stacy there would have provided assurance Faye would not stray from her resolve with him. Now, she'd have to just rely on self-control, which was an unpredictable thing. She kept her eyes on the fire, because watching the way the light moved over his strong features would tempt her too much.

"I have to tell you something, Faye. It's major.'

Well that was scary.

"I'm the one who's buying Lucy's."

All she could do was stare at him while she tried to process his revelation. Because how should she react? She was angry, like he'd kept an affair from her. She was happy for him, because that had been his dream, right? She was relieved, that someone was buying it who would do right by Lucy's legacy. She wanted to be hopeful, but that was a precarious emotion at the best of times.

"Congratulations," she said, trying to keep all of it out of her voice, waiting for him to fill in more details. "You could have told me."

"I am telling you."

She rolled her eyes. "You could have told me sooner."

"It honestly just came together this week. Okay yes, I've been communicating with her. And you ending things between us should have ended that, too, but it seemed to have the oppo-site effect. So I might have just taken a way bigger risk than I'm entirely comfortable with."

"Why didn't Lucy tell me?" Faye was just wondering out loud with that one.

"To be honest, she never made the connection. And I didn't help her make it. So to her I'm still some random guy. We've never met in person to discuss anything. It was always over the phone."

"How are you even affording this? You work in a restaurant."

His smile was elusive. "A little help from my mother. A little help from my friends."

The pieces started to slot together, one by one. "Liv."

"Nate too. Not a huge investment, because Lucy's letting me pay for it over time. So she gets a decent lump sum, then a monthly income for a while. Liv's dad is helping her set the money up in investments so she can focus on her mom and not worry about trying to pay the bills."

"All of you. All of you kept this from me. I can't believe it." She pushed up from the cushion with one hand, turning away and taking a slug of wine to try to calm herself.

"Please don't be mad. Listen, Faye. The last five days have been hell. I know you don't do this. I think there's more to the why than you let on. But I do know one thing. I want you in my life, and not just as a guy on the periphery, the friend of your friends."

She dared a glance over her shoulder. His expression was so...earnest. The hair on the back of her neck had risen, little bumps manifesting on the skin of her forearms. Will set his glass on the end table next to the chair, coming over, hovering behind her for a moment before turning her gently. She relinquished her glass against her better judgement, letting him set it aside. Then he grasped both her hands in his, and she wanted to drink in whatever coloured his golden hazel eyes. She was in trouble.

"Faye...will you..."

Oh, no way. No. Way. He was going to ruin everything, wreck any chance she had of reconsidering him and a future. But she couldn't speak, needed to hear it anyway; like maybe that would convince her that it truly was not meant to be.

"...help me run Lucy's?"

She blinked, then felt a warmth spread through her like that first, glorious sip of a steaming cappuccino. Her lips spread so wide she was sure the corners were in her ears, and she threw herself at him, laughing with a ridiculous sob as she attached herself to his shoulders.

"I will."

She reluctantly detached herself, pushing him away with a smirk. "Smart ass."

He caught her arm, and pulled her back in. "This probably isn't the best way to start a working relationship, but..." Keeping one hand on the small of her back, he pressed her into him, brushing her hair away from her face. Then, curling his fingers to the back of her long neck, he met her lips, carefully, until he was convinced she wanted to find out what this thing between them was as much as he did.

He finally made himself pull away, and she very nearly fell into the small space he'd created between them. "Could this be considered sexual harassment?"

Her head tilted slightly as she answered. "You haven't actually bought the place yet, so if this happens before you do..."

"This being?"

"Us," she said, her voice a low tremor.

"Do you want to try that? Us?"

"I do." She looked up at him with a very impish grin.

"I will. I do. Those words carry some serious intent. Are you sure?"

"As long as right now they only mean I will help you, and I do want to try something that doesn't have an expiry date, then, yes."

"I'm happy to hear that."

He started kissing her again, but she ducked out of his hold. "We need a toast. We have all night for the rest of it. I'm not letting you go back out into that." The room lit up with a flash for emphasis, followed by a crack of thunder that made them both jump.

After throwing a log on the fire, Faye parked him there before going to the kitchen, returning with another bottle of wine. He sat cross-legged, resting his refilled glass on one knee, staring into the flames. When she joined him, he tucked her under one arm. Truth be told, it was physically uncomfortable, but cosy and right.

She sipped, nestling closer. "Part of why I was attracted to Nate was because he was so obviously wounded. I probably should have pushed, to find out why. Hindsight and all that. I just never expected to be with him long enough for it to matter. And as it went along, I think I just didn't want to know. Maybe he never opened up to me, but I never asked. So I have to know, with you. Something happened to you, too, to make you leave. Something deeper, submerged. His was right there, only barely contained. If I'd been brave enough to uncover it, I would have known far sooner that I had no chance with him."

"Nate was blameless in what happened to him, unless you can blame him for being naïve. He fell in love with the wrong person."

Just like she had. "I'm not asking what happened to Nate. What happened to Nate doesn't matter to me anymore. I'm asking about you. Because if I really am going to do this, I need to know if I have a better chance with you."

He sighed, letting the wine and her hand, reaching over to touch his chest, draw it out of him. "It wasn't really one thing. More a combination." He filled his lungs with air; released it slowly. "There was a girl on our street named Hannah, growing up. She was a tomboy, one of the guys. She used to play street hockey with us, could climb trees better than anyone else, ride her bike just as hard. She'd come out to my grandfather's farm and hop on horses bareback and ride around with Nate. We'd go climbing in the summer, skiing in the winter. We were best friends. Then things changed in high school, of course. For me, anyway. But she didn't change, she still played just as hard, so I never told her how I felt. Which is all fun and games until someone gets hurt. Or dies."

"Oh Will – no..."

"Climbing accident. So I think she's forever suspended in my memory, as the ideal, because we were so close. I just wanted to be closer. She didn't though, and then she was gone, so it didn't matter."

"How old were you?"

There was so much dark tension in Faye's voice he glanced down and tightened his arm around her, but she wriggled slightly, and he eased off. "Fifteen. It was around the same time my dad decided to leave my mom and move to BC with his then-girlfriend. Father of the year. So he was gone, and my mom was so upset she threw herself into her work twice as hard. It didn't leave a lot of time for me. Sure she did all the things she thought was right, getting me counselling, and the Millers were amazing. But none of it set me up for success when it came to relationships. Then when I met you, and you were so open and life goes on about losing your parents, it made me think I should be able to get over it, too."

She laughed. "Ironic, though, that maybe life goes on, but mine has been totally dysfunctional."

"Do you try and figure out why?"

"The therapy thing never worked for me, probably because I didn't care why. I figured I deserved it. You know the weekend my parents went to visit Shawn, I was supposed to go? But I was mad at him, and I had a new boyfriend. He'd always vetted the guys who were interested in me because we had a one year overlap in high school – his last year was my first.

When he was around, none of them were good enough, in my eyes, even if he'd think they were okay. Because I was always comparing them to him. When he left, I started dating a guy who was totally the opposite, who he never would have liked. And that weekend, I stayed home, because I could have the boyfriend over, and they would never know. And then they were all killed. And I've never been able to shake the thought that it was somehow my fault."

"You know that's crazy, right?"

Her shoulder lifted and fell under her arm. "Hasn't stopped the feeling, though. I don't think I really realized, till Nate, that my pattern might be a little game I've played since then. Getting involved with these men with high-risk jobs, to feel something – anything – and getting out before it got serious enough that I cared. None of them have died, thank goodness... but that day at Keeneland, when Nate went down with our colt, Wampum, was like a trigger. It was a reminder that the relationship had gone far beyond its best before date. Beyond safe."

"So it was more complicated than just Liv, and Nate falling for Liv."

"It was, wasn't it? But it's all turned out okay. Nate was fine. Wampum is ready to run again. Liv and Nate got together. And I'm happy they're happy, even if it's hard to tell with Liv sometimes, she keeps her feelings so close."

Will nodded against the top of her head, and kissed it. "I think of Nate, and Liv, and how much of a risk their life holds. How they have to live with that every day. I don't want to be completely sheltered, but I'm done with needing that level of adrenaline to feel alive. That kind of physical challenge, where the threat of death is always looming...it's not worth it. Hannah was like that. She and Nate were always egging each other on. Neither of us were there when she died, though. Nate was spending more time with horses by then. And some of the crazy climbing shit she did, I just stopped going. I don't want to be with someone like that again. This right here is risk enough for me."

"Seeing if you can break my pattern of dysfunction?" She tipped her head back, hair falling from her face as her eyes met his.

He leaned in and kissed her. "You read books and cook. You play with numbers. You run a café. I think the biggest danger will be that you won't have time for me. If I can get you to sing more than the vocables in a song, you're my perfect woman."

"Well, you're going to have to work on that." A smile twisted her lips, and she brushed a still-damp lock of hair from his forehead, stretching up to kiss him back.

CHAPTER TWENTY

DEAN HAD VENTURED home the next afternoon, Faye luring him with a proper meal after he'd consumed more takeout than she deemed good for him. He was out in the barn, getting the rundown on the horses from Stacy. The mare was fine, and thankfully no one else had found trouble during the storm. At the track, She Brews seemed to be back to her old self, though Dean was still playing it safe with her. Wampum was fine too. This had been entry day for the Breeders', so Dean was worked up, though he would never admit it.

She yawned, peering into a fridge that was looking too sparse this soon after grocery day. She had to pull dinner out of it, somehow. Time to use up bits and pieces before they went bad. She set out the wok, tipped in some oil, and when it was hot, threw in all the veggies she found, sliced and fried up the last bit of chicken breast, cooked some rice noodles. Simple, but it smelled delicious.

"Mmmm, looks great," Dean peeked over her shoulder, inhaling happily. He pulled a bottle from the fridge, one of those nice honey-brown craft beers she'd found for him last week. "Want one?"

"No thanks." While she wasn't hungover after last night's wine, she was tired enough alcohol would just make her drag more.

She hadn't been able to sleep with the generator running. Will, on the other hand, had passed out in front of the fire, back to back with Gus. The noise hadn't bothered him, used to constant sound in Toronto, whereas anything more than country silence kept Faye awake. The power had come back on sometime in the middle of the night, at which point she'd roused Will and Gus out of their slumber long enough to shepherd them to her bed.

Dean parked at the kitchen table and unfolded the *Form*, spreading it out and immersing himself; studying of a different sort from what he'd done during his formal education. He took it as seriously as he had his degrees: poring over pages of past performances, filing away names and numbers and combinations. Trainers had to be handicappers too, even if they never bet.

Dean stopped reading, his head at an angle. "What's that?"

Faye could hear something out of place too, beyond the sizzle as the stir-fried veggies became tender. She pushed them around, added more soya sauce, and stirred. "Someone having a party? Sounds like music."

"On a Thursday?" Dean pushed himself to his feet and went to the screen door. He grinned, then looked over his shoulder at Faye. "Come here."

She turned off the heat, wiped her hands on a towel, and padded over, peeking around him. Then she grinned too.

Will. He stood on the deck with a guitar, picking and strumming and tapping...and singing, in that voice. Her hand went to her mouth, because her lips didn't know what to do.

Smile, wail, because she had to smear away a tear. The guy was singing to her.

"I don't know, Faye," Dean said, "but I think you'd better ask him to stay for dinner."

He moved out of the way, pushing her forward gently with a hand on her back, and turned back to the table, his *Form*, and his beer.

Faye swung open the door, holding it so it wouldn't slam shut, and stood in silence listening to the sweet words and melody...more than words...and watching the champagne eyes, the curve of his lips as he sang, the movement of his hands. Part of her wanted the song to go on forever. Part of her wanted it to be done so she could kiss him silly.

She crept closer, until she was a few feet from him. He was winding down, the notes fading into the summer breeze.

"Dean says I have to ask you for dinner."

"I like Dean."

"Now what are you going to do with that guitar? Because I don't want to hurt it."

His lazy smile turned the warm fuzzies she was feeling into something red-hot, but she stood her ground while he lifted the strap over his head, and, grasping the guitar by its neck, leaned it carefully against the deck's railing. Just in the nick of time, because she was on him, coming short of jumping up and wrapping her legs around him...but only just.

"You are a glutton for punishment," she breathed into his ear.

"Don't flatter yourself."

"I could rip off your clothes right here."

"Dean's probably hungry."

"Who's Dean again?"

He pried her arms from his neck, but it took longer for

them to pull apart. Faye straightened her shirt, smoothing the front, but there was no calming the bounce of her heart.

"The serenade was nice," she said, trying to compose herself. "But I hope you brought dessert."

The closer the Breeders' Stakes came, the more stressed Liv got. Pressure building on pressure. Faye had to intervene.

"You're not going to sleep, so just come over. We'll get a little bit drunk, eat junk food, and talk about boys. Like normal girls do as teenagers. You missed out on that, so we'll do it now. Bring Em."

Dean came out of the office and eyed them with raised brows, the three women camped out on the floor of the farmhouse's living room. The fire roared, a bottle of wine soon empty. They each had their own cartons of Haagen-Dazs. Faye guarded a plate of Will's decadent creations from the nose of Gus.

"Ice cream and wine? Does that work?" Dean asked.

"Go away, Dean. Girls only," Faye scolded, scraping her spoon around the edges of her carton to collect the softest ice cream.

"Fine." He tried to grumble, couldn't keep the smirk off his lips. "I'm going to get some sleep."

"No chance of that here, so get some for all of us!" Emile called.

He turned for the stairs. "See you in the paddock, Liv."

"Shut up, Dean," Liv growled. "I'm trying to forget about that right now."

Faye laughed, and topped up the wine glasses. "You know he adores you."

Em shot her a look, but Faye just threw her irises up into her eyelids.

"Don't even joke about that. He's like the brother I never had, Faye." Liv sipped a bit too much wine, and it caught in her throat, making her cough. "Like you're the sister I never had."

Faye laughed. It didn't take much to get Liv a little drunk.

"Um, hello?" Em said.

"The older sister I never had," Liv corrected.

"I don't know, I think Em fills that role quite well. For both of us."

"True." Liv had her wine glass in one hand, and ice cream in the other, and seemed to be weighing the relative benefits of each.

"How's Jiro, Em?" Faye asked, reaching for one of Will's perfect confections and popping it into her mouth, whole.

"Jiro and I are just friends. Letting people think otherwise keeps us both from the wolves."

"Wolves like me. Or what used to be me."

"I'm so proud of you, Faye. I'm so proud of both of my girls." Emilie grinned, looking from Faye to Liv.

"One day, Mom, it will be your turn," Faye said. "Your perfect man is out there."

"Is he, though?"

"There's a brother," Liv said.

"That's right," Faye said. "Nate has a younger brother."

"I'll need a picture."

"I have seen one," Liv mused. "He's taller, with dark hair. Just as good-looking. But still in Calgary."

"Calgary boys do seem to be the way to go, though, Em," Faye said. "We'll just have to figure out how to entice him here. Unless you want us to set you up with Dean. Because it may come to that."

"Poor Dean," Em said.

"Why poor Dean?" Liv asked. "He could be perfectly happy alone. I was perfectly happy."

Faye snorted. "You were not."

"Well if Nate had never existed, I would have been."

"Ah, but he does." Faye grinned. "And your life will never be the same."

"When does it stop being scary?" Liv asked.

Faye held out the plate, because Liv clearly needed chocolate to amplify the wine and ice cream. "I don't know. I'm not there yet. Fun, isn't it?"

"There is something that's even more terrifying."

"Which is?"

"Tomorrow," Liv said solemnly. "Tomorrow, I have to saddle a potential Canadian Triple Crown winner."

"If Chique wins, you'll be the first female trainer to pull it off." Like she likely hadn't heard that how many times since the Prince of Wales?

"Shut up, Faye."

"Snappish."

They laughed at each other.

"Either way," Emilie interjected, "I need to raise my glass to both of you. Liv, turning things around to get your trainer's license, and have a relationship with something other than a horse –"

Faye snorted again.

"– And you, Faye, to chance another relationship, and to take on a new business, making yourself a pillar of the community..."

"I'm blushing now, Em."

"Cheers to both of you. You're inspiring. No matter what happens tomorrow."

"Gah, tomorrow," Liv moaned. "Pour me some more wine."

Liv stared into the fire, fixated on the flames, having set her ice cream aside to wrap an arm around Gus. Em sampled a chocolate mousse bite, closing her eyes as the ecstasy of it hit her taste buds. Faye leaned back against an armchair, legs tucked underneath her, grateful for the warmth of the fire, and friends.

"This is how I imagine the night before your wedding," she said.

Liv sputtered out her most recent mouthful of wine. "My wedding?"

"I'd better be your maid of honour," Faye said.

"Fine," Em said. "As long as you have at least one brides-maid. Me."

"My wedding?" Liv repeated.

"So that means no eloping!" Faye warned.

"Unless you take both of us along," Emilie said.

"And Will," Faye added. "And the brother. A destination wedding might be nice."

"When do I get to meet the brother?" Emilie asked, looking at Liv.

"My wedding?"

"Yes, he'd come, wouldn't he?" Faye said.

"That's not what I meant!" Liv groaned.

"Well that took your mind off the race, didn't it? Yes, your wedding. Don't worry, we'll help you plan it."

"Of course we will," Emilie agreed.

"Will's restaurant can cater it. I mean, he'll be too busy to do it himself, as Nate's best man, but his in with Chef Gerry will come in handy. I'm sure he's got a favour or two to call in with that monster."

Now Liv was laughing, like the idea was totally absurd to her. "You'll definitely be married before me."

"Wanna bet?"

"Careful now, you're looking a little lovestruck," Liv whispered, leaning into her ear.

Faye batted her away. She needed to stop looking so obvious. "It's happening again, isn't it?"

"Who would have thought, eh?"

"So lightning can strike twice?"

"Statistically improbable, but not impossible." Liv grinned.

"You know, I really wish you had become a vet, or gone and got a PhD or something, because it just feels like we should call you Dr. Lachance."

They weren't new, these feelings, but this time, she hadn't been caught off guard. If she was careful, she'd see them through. Make something tangible from them....like a future.

CHAPTER TWENTY-ONE

DEAN HELD Wampum as Nikki gave him a bath, steam rising and blending with the cool grey sky. The colt had just walked, casually touring the shedrow. Chique had trained.

Faye had walked out to the track to watch, following Liv on the Triple Stripe stable pony, Paz. More evidence of her fresh start, a continuation of their promise to do better: she'd risen with Dean to come in, not to set up a not-so-chance meeting with a hot bug, but to stand by her friend in the anxious morning hours before the race. Her friend – the trainer of the horse Dean was trying to beat with Wampum.

She could cheer for them both, couldn't she? It would be amazing if Liv's filly won. It would be great for Northwest if Wampum won. Then again, this was horse racing, so maybe neither of them would win. All that mattered in the end was that they both came through safe and sound. Losing a race was disappointing. Losing a life was devastating.

Chique had galloped an easy mile – easy relating only to the speed of her effort. It hadn't looked anything close to easy for Nate up there as he held her, his weight balanced against

253

her fire, the puffs of vapour from her nostrils like smoke from a dragon. Liv had escorted her protectively off the oval, Chique vibrating in the uncharacteristically chill August air. *Filly weather,* Faye's father would have called it – though it was supposed to show up in October, conjuring up talk of Florida departures and the speedily approaching end of the Ontario season.

A groom called for Dean from a stall, and Dean glanced around as Nikki began the rinse, clearing the layer of suds with alcohol-laced water. Wampum gave a little shudder, when a horse like Chique would have likely erupted from the tiny sparks the brace sent over sensitive skin.

"Here Faye. Hold him." Dean waved her over.

Faye blinked. "Uh..." She glanced around, sure there must be someone else who could step in. Dean knew better. Dean knew why.

"He's quiet as a pony, Faye. He won't hurt you. I promise. You don't have to walk him, just stand here until Nikki's done his bath."

She inched forward timidly, taking the long length of leather with both hands, but standing back. Wampum's ears flipped closer together, his big, soft eyes penetrating skin and bone to see inside her. Her trembling didn't seem to bother him.

She still had the scar, and the misshapen nail on the middle finger of her left hand – the one a broodmare had taken the tip of. She'd been five, feeding the huge animal a carrot. Her father had likely only blinked – things like that happened so quickly. Wailing in the back seat of the car in her mother's arms, he'd driven to the emergency room. When she'd been older, she'd learned from her mother that her father had struggled to forgive himself for that incident. To Faye, it was just an indication she lacked the horse gene. He'd stopped trying to foster a love of horses in her after that. She'd kept a safe distance from the animals since.

Wampum lipped the shank, his neck telescoping, somehow getting closer without moving his feet. Faye stood her ground, though her heart was racing. She held out her other hand, palm flat, and grinned as he licked it like a huge dog. A big, kind, gentle giant. Her fear eased just a little with the tiny connection she felt. She wasn't in any danger of becoming a horse girl, but it felt somehow like moving forward.

The colt's comeback, his second chance to show who he was, matched her own, didn't it? They'd both gone down that day at Keeneland. They'd both been broken. And now they were both healed, and stronger than before. If she could do this – stand here, this close to a horse, and not get bitten – maybe lightning could strike twice, and set her on fire again. Fire wasn't always bad – especially when it came with pastry.

THE END

NEXT UP

"Auggghhh! Who wins the race?"

That was the exact response from my first early reader of *All The Little Things*. If you're dying to know, keep flipping for a teaser from *All Good Things*, the next book in the series.

The Canadian Triple Crown is on the line, and Chique's back to her old tricks, leaving her trainer, Liv Lachance, and jockey, Nate Miller, scratching their heads in frustration.

Figuring her out — for now, anyway — earns Nate the chance to ride in California for the winter. It means being apart from Liv and Chique. Is he sacrificing his tenuous relationship with Liv for his career? Ambition isn't sitting easy when it means risking everything he's ever really wanted.

While Nate struggles to get a foothold at Santa Anita, Liv throws her focus into Feste, Chique's full brother and heir apparent to the scrappy filly. But when Chique draws Liv and Nate back together unexpectedly, they're left questioning who they are apart from her.

Career, Chique, relationship — which comes first, or are they just intertwined?

EXCERPT FROM ALL GOOD THINGS

EXCERPT FROM ALL GOOD THINGS

Voices, nervous laughter, peripheral movement; on the fringes of her consciousness, none of it important. All that was worthy of her focus was skin sliding over muscle, muscle extending and contracting. Liv analyzed every stride down to each footfall, and tried to gauge the ever-unknown unpredictability factor in the sleek filly before her.

Chique was light years away from the unraced two-year-old she'd been a year ago. There was a swagger to her step now, the glint in her eyes behind the blinkers self-important, if you could say that about a horse. With eight races under her belt, at five different tracks — five of them wins — the professionalism she displayed here in Woodbine's walking ring, willow branches whispering overhead, wasn't unexpected. Liv just didn't trust it.

A touch broke her concentration, her head snapping to the side like the wind whipping from the northwest had picked it up in a gust. She didn't bother to fix the dark hair flying around her face. She should have put it up. She was usually practical about such things, like the "turf shoes" on her feet — flats, when heels would have punched through the rain-soaked carpet of grass. Not that she ever wore heels.

She extracted a hand from the depths of her trench coat pocket, and Nate returned the firmness of her grasp, the amusement playing on his features a contrast to the seriousness of her own. She could tell what he was thinking. *No, Miller, it wouldn't be appropriate for the rider to kiss the trainer in the walking ring.*

"So?" He crossed his arms, stick tucked under his elbow.

"Stay off the inside," she responded, though she wasn't saying anything he didn't already know. They'd discussed strategy ad nauseam, walked the full mile-and-a-half of the rain-sodden E.P. Taylor turf course that morning, and he'd ridden over it in an earlier race. The course was soft, but safe.

"Breathe," he said. He squeezed the elbow of the arm that was now folded over her chest in a less-assured reflection of his posture.

"Sure, Miller. It's only the Canadian Triple Crown on the line. But if you're cool, that's what matters."

This was the first possible first in her fledgling training career. A woman trainer had won the Queen's Plate before her. A woman trainer had won the Prince of Wales, the second jewel of the crown. A woman trainer had won this, the Breeders' Stakes, third and final jewel. But no woman had won all three.

The paddock judge gave the riders up call. Liv glanced at Nate.

"Let's do this," he said with a nod, trying to be serious before he let go the grin that was the only thing with any hope of distracting her from the stormy sky, the very un-August-like cool, and everything that was on the line.

"Bonne chance. Don't screw up. Come home safe." She threw him up onto the moving filly, and felt the too-familiar helplessness seep in.

He was so sure about Chique. Like he was so sure about them. Liv envied his confidence in both — but now wasn't the time to think about it.

All Good Things is available now from your favourite book retailer.

ACKNOWLEDGMENTS

First of all, I'd like to thank Michelle Lopez, author and business accountability partner, for keeping me on task with this. I honestly do not think I would have managed it without her support!

A big thank-you to my beta readers on this one: Allison Litfin, Kristen Frederick, Sheri Keith and Bev Harvey. Be sure to check out Bev's butter tart recipe!

MORE BY LINDA SHANTZ

I hope you enjoyed *All The Little Things*, the second book in the *Good Things Come* series. Reviews on your favourite retailer and GoodReads are always appreciated!

If you'd like to keep in touch, sign up for my newsletter at lindashantz.com/writes for sample chapters (including more from the first chapter of *All Good Things*), updates, and more! You can also follow me on BookBub.

Good Things Come Series:

Book 1: Good Things Come

Book 2: All The Little Things

Book 3: All Good Things

BEV'S BUTTER TARTS

Butter tarts are a Canadian staple, the earliest documentation of their existence in eastern Canada dating back to 1901, according to Chatelaine magazine. They're a really big thing up here – we have whole festivals dedicated to them, with vendors creating a variety of flavours and claiming they have the best ones. I have yet to discover where to get the best butter tarts in my new area, but if you're ever in Moffat, Ontario, where I used to live, be sure to check out Dar's Delights on the corner of First Line and Fifteen Sideroad! You'll need to put "Nassagaweya" in your Google Maps search to find it.

The recipe on the following pages comes courtesy of one of my beta readers, Bev Harvey. I've added a couple of my own notes, as well as following it with a recipe for Butter Tart Bars. They're not the same, but do nicely in a pinch!

BEV'S BUTTER TARTS

PASTRY

2 cups cake and pastry flour
Sprinkle of salt
⅓ cup of lard
(Linda's note: you can substitute vegetable shortening for lard; the pastry just won't get as flaky.)

EGG MIXTURE

1 egg
1 tablespoon white vinegar
Whisk egg and vinegar and add cold water to bring to 1 cup.

Blend flour well. Add the egg mixture slowly to blend to desired workability.

Roll out dough and cut with 4" cutter.

Gently drop into muffin tin.

FILLING

½ cup brown sugar
¼ cup butter
½ cup golden corn syrup
1 egg
1 teaspoon vanilla
¾ cup raisins

Cream the butter and sugar. Add egg, corn syrup and vanilla and mix thoroughly.

Add raisins (a must in this house, but can be optional) to the shells.

(Linda's note: chocolate chips and/or pecans are common substitutions.)

Spoon in the filling.

Bake at 375° F for approximately 15 minutes, or until brown. Undercooking will result in runny tarts...it's personal preference at this point.

BUTTER TART BARS

If making pastry seems like too much work, these are a good approximation.

Lightly grease a 9 x 9 pan. Preheat oven to 350° F

CRUST:
    1 ½ cups all-purpose flour
    ½ cup brown sugar
    2/3 cup butter

Press into the baking pan and bake for 12 minutes.

Mix filling as above from the butter tart recipe. Return to the oven and bake for 25 minutes. Cool, and cut into squares. They always taste better the next day, so do your best not to eat them all right away!

ABOUT THE AUTHOR

It was an eight-year-old me, frustrated that all the horse racing novels I read were about the Derby, not the Plate, who first put pencil to three-ring paper and started what would become this story. Needless to say, we've both grown up a bit since then.

I began working at the track before I finished high school, and after graduating the following January, took a hotwalking job at Payson Park in Florida. Once back at Woodbine, I started grooming and galloping. While the backstretch is exciting, I found I was more at home on the farm — prepping and breaking yearlings, nightwatching and foaling mares. Eventually I started my own small layup/broodmare facility, and in the last few years I've transitioned into retraining and rehoming. Somewhere along the way I did go back to school and get a degree. I should probably dust it off and frame it one day.

I live on a small farm in Ontario, Canada, with my off-track Thoroughbreds and a Border Collie who thinks we should add sheep to the mix. I'm probably better known for painting horses than writing about them — if you like my covers, you can see more of my work at www.lindashantz.com

Author Photo courtesy of Ellen Schoeman Photography

CPSIA information can be obtained
at www.ICGtesting.com
Printed in the USA
LVHW040825070222
710434LV00003B/29

9 781990 436031